AMYL ION 1

DESCENDANTS OF BLOOD

CARROLL HOLST

AMYL ION 1
DESCENDANTS OF BLOOD

iUniverse books may be ordered through booksellers or by contacting:

iUniverse
1663 Liberty Drive
Bloomington, IN 47403
www.iuniverse.com
844-349-9409

Because of the dynamic nature of the Internet, any web addresses or links contained in this book may have changed since publication and may no longer be valid. The views expressed in this work are solely those of the author and do not necessarily reflect the views of the publisher, and the publisher hereby disclaims any responsibility for them.

Any people depicted in stock imagery provided by Getty Images are models, and such images are being used for illustrative purposes only. Certain stock imagery © Getty Images.

ISBN: 978-1-6632-2347-0 (sc)
ISBN: 978-1-6632-2348-7 (e)

Library of Congress Control Number: 2021916581

Print information available on the last page.

iUniverse rev. date: 08/25/2021

CHAPTER 1

Medusa's head on the shield of Athena had unexpectedly vanished. The image was gone and what remained was a riddle. A mysterious voice had come from the Heavens and, said.

"[Oh, White crow where have you gone from]?"

A beautiful woman's voice said.

"[From your direct sum]."

What man can solve this is the man that completes the second half of her and, seal's the ring of fire. The ring of fire will be extinguished when the black rose is thrown into it by Maximilian and, Amyl ion together as both their hands will be touching the black rose and, releasing it at the same time.

Medusa's body that had fallen into the steaming hot molten bubbling lava had surely been burned up. But wait, something was brewing, and out of the smoke came a White crow flapping her wings and, crowing as if her very life depended upon it. Everything of the crow was white including her beak, legs, and claws. The eyes of the White crow were black and, green with the outer eye having a ring of fire. The next part of her eye started with black and, faded into green until it too faded and, we look deep into her eye and, Medusa had changed and, no more of the ugliness that came from her soul if she had one. The snakes were gone that once made up her hair and, we get a glimpse of what Amyl ion would appear as. She was directly inside the eye with a maroon outlined background and, in all her glory and, not a monster any more. She is a beautiful woman now and, with that certified smile. She was slowly moving her head around and, that black curly long hair flowing just a little bit as if she was in a breeze. There are dark permanent markings of thick wings that stretch just beyond her eyebrows starting close to the nose on her eyelids and, getting larger at the

1

middle of her eyelids then spreading out wide. She goes from smiling with beautiful white teeth then to a closed lip smile and, back again. We see her full lips that are rose petal red with just a little bit of her teeth showing as she relaxes her smile. A widow's peak brought her lovely coal black shinny hair together that's a gathering of her and, facial features that is complete with a statement. Need we add more?

The Music starts [Rush-Limelight].

Then she cleared the edge from where her body as Medusa had fallen from into the bubbling molten lava and, landed several feet away then looked around and, the memories had come over her for only a few moments. She collected herself with shaking her head and, knew she was on a mission for God that put it there. She squatted and, prepared herself and, was ready to take off. She spread her wings and, leaped into the air and, lifted magnificently up into the cave and, then she saw an opening in the ceiling and, flew towards it. The opening was made just for the shape of her body with wings head, tail and, of course, she flew right threw it. There was a gathering of black crows and, ravens outside that must have numbered in the hundreds perhaps thousands. God must have brought them together from the surrounding land to encourage her on as she flew out of the perfectly outlined exit from the ceiling of the cave. They were on the ground and, trees looking like a sea of black and, surreal with the trees full but, you could still see a little green.

"OORAH!"

That's what was heard as the White crow flew through the exit. She lifted herself up and, mysteriously was starting to get larger and, larger until she was over three times larger than when she first flew out of the cave.

She now had a destiny and, the way she was climbing nothing could stop her. The moment she thought that she was in the clear and, she knew that she was being drawn to the heavens that's when two red tail hawks spotted her and, attached thinking she would be easy prey but they were wrong. The minute the two hawks landed on her that's when Oh White crow drew upon the killer instinct and, cleverness that God had given her from all her previous battles as Medusa went into action. The two hawks were coming in with a one-two punch that's when she turned upside down and, grabbed the first one by the neck with her talons and, with her beak tore the head right off. The second one she flipped back over on its back as it flew by and, stabbed it in the back with her beak and, her talons grabbed its wings and, tore its head off.

"OORAH."

That came from the crows and, ravens back on earth as they watched her dispatch the two red tail hawks. She thought that she was in the clear again but, out of the blue came a beautiful bald eagle that was diving down upon her. She saw the bald eagle at the last second. They collided together and, some feathers flew around and, they tossed around then finally, the bald eagles head came off too. White crow watched the eagle's body and, head fall to the earth then said.

"How dare you ... to wear white like me!!! ... HHUHH."

"OORAH!"

The sound of her buddies again was encouraging her on.

Oh, White crow started to climb again right into some dark clouds that were churning and, rolling with rain, lightning, and thunder. She realized by now that forces were battling against her. The heavy rains were weighing her down, the lightning strikes were getting closer and, she thought that she couldn't dodge them anymore. Then she dug deep inside and, closed her eyes with bowing her head like crows do and, she gave out a mighty yell she said.

"HHHEELLPP MMEEE."

Quickly the dark clouds moved away the rains stopped and, there was no more lightning strikes. The sun appeared and, she knew her cry for help had been answered but, to whom? She was climbing into the heavens and, that the air was becoming lighter and, lighter, then eventually her wings didn't have to lift her that much and, then she was able to tuck them into place. Stunned and, with her all looking down and, up and, all around. Oh, White crow was floating with no clouds or earth beneath her with her talons on an imaginary surface.

The stars appeared and, started to flicker and, some were larger and, some smaller and, that they made her feel comfortable with calmness coming over her. She gave out four squawks' as if to say I'm not afraid.

Then she heard the sound of someone humming a tune that she knew owe so, well. How she knew music I can't really tell ... maybe the parties and, neighbors nearby the cave where Medusa dwelt, she could have over heard them. She began tapping her feet together and, then a voice began to speak.

"I knew you would like that one."

Oh, White crow looked baffled and, blinked her eyes and, said.

"How did you know?"

She was looking around and, thought maybe she could get a glimpse of something that could help her put the voice and, some object or, person together.

"I know everything about you."

"May I ask to whom am I talking too?"

"I am that I am."

The stars at that moment turned to red for a moment as she bowed her head and, closed her eyes. The stars then changed to white again and, she looked up and, her thoughts were. This must be the one true deity, celestial, divine, immortal being and, she began to struggle with the magnitude of this and, just accepted it and, felt at ease and, comfortable.

The voice began to speak when her thoughts were over and, said.

"I have a plan and, a destiny for you to fulfill ... you will be going back to earth and, the wind will guide you were to land."

Oh, White crow said.

"What is the purpose of all of this?"

"When you meet your mate Maximilian your bonding will be instantaneous and, when he notices you, he will say "Hello Gorgeous" then he'll guide you to your next step together and, you will love each other as I have commanded it to be so."

"I will do the best that I can."

"I know that you will for I have created you and, the riddle on Athena's shield Maximilian will solve it. Do you remember everything about your past life as Medusa?"

"Yes, I do and, it is as a nightmare."

"I will cleanse you of that and, even as I have just spoken it is gone from you but, I will leave the cunning and, your crafty ness there and, your husband will teach you necessary fighting abilities ... for me and, your husband also your country and, friends."

"Thank you I feel refreshed and, clean throughout my body already ... and, with as eager ness to learn."

4

"Now it is time for you to descend back to earth and, I will direct the wind to where you are to be and, don't fight it just let go and, Maximilian will be working on an old space ship discarded by the space force you'll see it as you descend. When you land near to him give him a squawk and, he'll turn to you as he's working and, he'll say,

"Hello gorgeous."

Maximilian will say to you. Oh, White crow where have you gone from? and, you will say, from your direct sum and, Maximilian will be sum what surprised but, will realize that his good premonition's and, dreams have started to come true and, I have purposely put those things in his mind and, heart."

"But how can I ... being this beautiful White crow be Maximillian's mate?"

God put on more emphasis and, said.

"I have summoned you up here to purify you and, to tell you things that will be for your future and, Maximillian's. The beautiful White crow that you are now will be transformed into a beautiful woman of my creation and, I will grant you ability's that most people have to learn in a lifetime and, with them coming to you at a moment when you need them."

"Amyl ion shall be your name and, I will tell you the rest as you descend back to earth."

"I love that already and, what is our future together?"

"The people that I have chosen are on the planet earth 2 and, it is similar to this one and, earth 2 is growing and, mixed with development and, they live on a continent of the planet called the 12 valleys of the 99 hills. They have cried unto me for a King and, Queen to rule over them. That is why I chose you and, Maximilian."

"Thank you for choosing me and, I want to be the best that you ask of me."

She was thinking that this is incredible and, almost too much to believe.

God knew her thoughts of doubt and, replaced it with assurance and, belief then said.

"Go now to Maximilian ... he waits for you and, when you go back to earth, I will transform you to be his wife and, Maximilian will be your husband. I will set your desires to be with your husband and, his desires will be for his wife."

CHAPTER 2

It was now approaching the time for Oh, White crow to leave after that last negative thought removed and, God said.

"Go now just spread your wings and, gravity will pull you down and, you'll glide on your wings as you descend on down and, remember that I will be with you and, Maximilian all of your life."

"Oh, one more question before I go. Is there anything wrong with this planet earth 1?"

"No, and, it has developed into a stable world of good people everywhere finding out about the progressives to destruction and, there plans of power over the masses to control them. The devil's children just wanted to live in luxury and, kill innocent men, woman and, the children. One way or, another I gave my children the abilities to discover how to stop their witchcraft.

Oh, White crow spread her wings having been satisfied with that answer. She was passing through the clouds with all kinds of things that were running through her mind like what color hair he would have and, how tall was he and, what color eyes he would have?

She eventually cleared the white puffs of clouds and, about a minute she saw a large billboard sign that said Meramec caverns and, close by was a space ship having a charcoal color with a satin sheen to it and, saucer shaped in a private open valley surrounded by trees of all kinds.

Oh' White crow was dropping to the ground as light as a feather and, never has anyone seen a beautiful White crow coming down from the sky as she did.

She glided alongside of the space ship with its 8 legs supporting it but, close to the ground and, not fully extended so, he could work on it. He was on the starboard side and, it read [27-trips] with a United States

Flag and, stars on the right and, it waves when the ship is in flight. Even though it is a saucer shape space ship it still has to have the name on the starboard side. Recognizable to all men and, women in uniform. There she spotted Maximilian sliding a panel back on with the suction of a sealing sound and, the same time she landed. Then tucked in her wings and, she was just 12 feet away from Maximilian as she watched and, observed then squawked to get his attention and, of course he looked to his left and, couldn't believe his eyes as he finished with the panel and, said.

"[Hello gorgeous]" Pause …

"Oh, White crow where have you gone from?"

She had a new rush of things going through her head plus coming down from the heavens as she did and, she'll never be the same and, said.

"[From your direct sum]."

"Hello My Beloved."

Maximilian looked calm but, inside his mind everything was stirring around. Then he collected his thoughts and, it was like there on cue when they both said.

"We've got work to do."

He got up from underneath the space ship with it automatically rising to its normal landing height as they turned their heads to watch it then whipped his hands and, they looked at one another with her thinking … I know I can trust this man because I feel it and, she said.

"Well Maximilian where do we go from here?"

"In my dreams our God has directed us through to a clearing at a spot where there is an open space and, that's where God will transform you into the woman that will fulfill his purpose."

"Maximilian but, what about you."

"I will be a part of his plan too and, you will see as this all plays out and, lets both ask him now."

"[God let's begin]."

Then there appeared a path in the woods as God opened it up with the sounds of leaves and, limbs with weeds moving and, then they looked at one another and, took a deep breath and, smiled with them exhaling at the same time sort of like a belly laugh and, well here we go. They both started towards the path and, white crow heard the chickadee's sounds with other birds singing. She looks around and, he points to a cardinal and, heading through the path they came to a clearing with a circle of trees about 25 feet across both ways. They stopped in the middle and, were looking around with the leaves falling and, there accumulating on the ground as they do in October and, he said.

"Well, here is where we complete the direct sum that our God will perform your transformation."

"Yes and, I won't be a crow anymore."

"Oh, sure come on your just getting used to it." [Adding a sense of humor].

"Well not on your life." [They both laugh]. She thought for a moment he doesn't even know my new name that our God gave me and, I want to tell him right away and, she said.

"Amyl ion that's the name that god gave me."

"Oh, when was this?"

He was really intrigued and, with a name that he never heard before and, she said.

"When I was in the heavens, we had this great conversation. Well, I can't wait; I'll tell you later."

Then as they stood there the leaves began to move and, swirl around him and, it looked as though he fell asleep but, he was aware of what was going on. The leaves kept accumulating and, rising higher as they swirled on up till you couldn't see him anymore. Then what came out from behind him from the circling leaves was two short ribs taken from his lower rib cage. The two ribs floated through the air and, were placed at her talons. The leaves around him gradually fell back to the ground.

Then God spoke that only she could hear and, said.

"Oh, White crow now step on the bones one for each of your claws."

He stood there and, watched as she began to step on the ribs. When she did the leaves began to move around her that's when he tapped his watch without looking away to record the time it took to create her.

She spread her wings and, went up that touched the tips with the swirling leaves majestically to welcome it. The leaves for her must have been a special selection on the ground because they were enhanced red, yellow and, gold with a glow but, not to take away from Maximilian. It's just that God had to personally select each leaf to give her what ingredients he planned for her. Then you could hear some slight drum roll as the leaves were moving up to a measurement of 5' foot 3" inches tall and, that's where the leaves stopped going up. They stayed there moving around her for quite some time with crackling sounds like from a large fire a few music scales spinning around with many songs all bunched up and, not distinguishable and, he was getting curious but, a smile was beginning to show. The swirling leaves started to slow down and, dropping to the ground and, he went to stand in front of her.

That's when the [James Bond theme 2.54] began and, all the leaves had fallen down.

The transformation was complete and, she was being revealed which God made for him and, the music was perfect and, of course she is his direct sum.

Then as she stood there at 5' foot 3" inches tall and, I guess a little thin but, a striking beautiful looking woman with her clavicles showing just a little and, very shapely arms and, shoulders like she worked out with weight training that you could see the separations of muscle's and, not much body fat. Her coal black shinny hair that was a little wavy at just 10 inches past her shoulders.

He was stunned but, he didn't let on … he held it inside and, thought could this be a new beginning of human species never before seen. She had natural rose-colored full lips with teeth showing just a little bit and, her nose was straight with a widow's peak. Her ribs were showing in an athletic way, just a little and, smooth with a little darker skin than his but, it would be a small comparison. Her breasts stuck out like bullets of 34 D, cups and, that they needed no support with slightly puffy areola's that were a beautiful reddish brown, normal hips for child bearing. Thighs that touched all the way just above the knee caps to the top with small knees and, small ankles with her calves almost touching as she stood there with feet together. She had no pubic hair or, under arm hair [later he would discover] and, there was no belly button because she was created … and, not born from a woman that needed an umbilical cord. Let's not forget her hazel eyes. She would never have a menstrual cycle. Then there's the thick black permanent markings on the side of her eyes like wings that curled up to a point just past her dark black eyebrows and, her black eyelashes were longer than normal and, made a magnificent touch which only God could have done.

God knew what Maximilian would Love because God made them for a long life together as you will hear later on. There was no woman on the 2 earths that would hold a candle to her.

Then God breathed into her his spirit and, gave her a soul that you could actually see the vapor trail go up her nose as she inhaled which made her chest expand with her fingers raising up and, exhaled out her mouth with her lips throwing out what was not used. He tapped his watch again without looking away to record the time it took for her creation and, her time of birth. God's creation stood there and, what would be later his Queen as they rule the 12 valleys of the 99 hills on earth 2.

She drew her long breath and, came to life and, he couldn't believe his eyes but, kept himself under control. He was thinking that this is a female being sent from above and, sealed with her distinguished stance in all her qualities. She looked at him as her eyes checked out her beloved, she went from his hair to his eyes and, the shape of his face and, overall, his hands, arms, legs, and, feet, and, right here we get a chance to see this beautiful smile of hers which she will display for us many times. She didn't have a chance when she was the White crow to really check out her future King but, thinking I shouldn't doubt God, and, oh, yes, our minds will be perfectly matched too.

"God spoke so, they could hear and, said.

"Go now to the house that I have prepared for the both of you. There you'll find uniforms designed for you."

The Music starts. [Eddie money's, two tickets to paradise].

After God spoke those words, a path appeared from the edge of the woods right to an average looking house. God pushed her to him with his index fingers on her upper hips which created dimples as a lasting reminder of there being joined by God and, no one can separate. They both reached out for one another and, their hands joined with big smiles as they walked down the path towards the house.

His physique was of the Olympian type at 6' feet 1" inch tall and, everything she would need to fulfill her needs, wants and, desires. His hair was dark brown and, layered very nicely with it parted in the middle not too short just a little over his ears with a little wave to it and, blue eyes with her thinking … oh, he is so, cute and, handsome and, he said.

"Amyl ion tell me more about this conversation you had with God in heaven?"

"I will be transformed into what I am now and, to be your wife and, later you'll be King and, I will be Queen and, that we both shall rule the 12 valleys of the 99 hills. He said that his chosen people have cried to him for a King and, Queen to rule over them and, God choose you and, I."

He had no reason to doubt her about the future because he believed her 100%.

"That is very fascinating."

She was curious as she looked at his wrist and, said.

"May I ask why you tapped the object on your wrist?"

"Why of course … I was recording the time it took for God to create you and, also mark the time of your birth."

"Oh, well then … how long did it take and, what time was it when I was born?"

He looked at his watch and, he will never forget it from now on and, he said.

"83 seconds … and, your birth time is 9am-14 minutes 19 seconds … in the year of our lord 2227."

She just smiled and, he'll never forget that one.

They walked and, she looked around again and, a couple of blue jays pass by. She looked up and, saw several turkey vultures floating on the air currents. He pointed to a red belly woodpecker and, she stopped then it made its unique sound and, pounding with its beak to draw out the ants. There was plenty of sparrows as they walked on and, they fluttered by her as a sort of welcoming. When they got to the grassy area, she stopped to watch a red breasted robin pulling a large worm out of the ground and, took off. She looked at him as she glowed to this green earth and, finally reached the average house with a porch and, railing along the sides and, front. He was thinking about that she doesn't realize she's naked. They stepped up to the porch and, looked around and, he didn't feel right and, sensed a presence. He opened the door and, to their surprise it was full of furniture and, things that it would take a life time to fill. When they were in, he closed the door and, she did a few spins with her black hair flying around as she felt free. They drew back together and, looked around the first floor. They noticed a picture of his family with the family cat walking around them and, rubbing his coat on their legs and, his dad reaches down to scratch its head and, they all wave at Maximilian and, Amyl ion which they look at one another and, start smiling and, laughing and, his dad in the picture said.

"The family wishes you two the very best and, don't forget were praying for you."

He thought … I got to get her into her uniform so, she doesn't get comfortable in her skin and, with that he leans towards her and, kisses her cheek. She saw that coming and, turned her right cheek up to receive his first kiss and, he said.

"Let's see if we can find those uniforms for you and, I … Amyl ion that's my family."

She smiles and, looked into his eyes that would have ignited the wood in the fireplace and, said.

"I am very happy to meet your family with great pleasure."

Their arms are around each other from side to side as if it was just as natural as could be and, she said.

"I would love to meet them in person."

He noticed the layout of the interior and, said.

"Right down the hallway here maybe there's a bedroom with the uniforms in the closet."

In one of the bedroom's there was a closet with silver flex tight uniforms with a maroon circle insignia on their left upper chest with a green leafy encircling an A for her and, a M for him and, black Y shaped collars to wear. They had a top and, a bottom for each. She spotted a full-length mirror and, looked at herself as she turned from side to side raising her arms and, he noticed she had no hair under her arms or, pubic hair with the belly button nowhere to be found with dimples right at her upper hip level that he noticed too and, there so, cute and, wondering at her nakedness then realized more and, more her physique was very shapely. She saw him gazing at her from the mirror and, turned to look at him and, said.

"My Beloved what do you think of our God's creation of me for you?"

"Well, that is just it. I only think of you because you're the most important being to me or, should I say the most important created human being and, not only physical but, your whole being … mind, soul and, spirit. Please don't misunderstand me when I say something about your physicality … it's just that God created humans to be drawn to one another one way or, another."

"That was the best answer because you're the most important … if I may copy that from you."

"Why of course it's like we think alike."

CHAPTER 3

He took his clothes off and, she paid attention at him as he moved and, as he portrayed himself naturally which she knows now she could not look at another man. He was thinking now she will look me over but, that is okay because I belong to her now. Then she had a few questions but, will ask later.

They put their uniforms on them and, they fit perfectly with a utility belt for accessories. There were some new shoes for them to wear. He wore a size 12.5 and, she wore a size 8.5 and, she said.

"I think these uniforms and, shoes were made to order."

She looked at him and, turned from side to side while looking at her uniform in the mirror and, he was thinking that this is astonishing but, God can do anything as he noticed the fitting of her breasts and, her figure that actually enhanced her appearance on the outside of the uniform. The uniform with its 34 D cup shape that you could barely make out her puffy areolas and, her pants were skin tight [like sprayed on] which stopped right above her ankles. Then it dawned on him she could have been an Olympian at a 100-yard dash or, the 200 and, with some training and, proper nutrition she could do very well and, he said.

"Yes, they were and, thank you God."

"Yes, thank you God and, the uniform on you Maximilian looks so, professional I will have to watch the woman that might be around you."

They draw close and, he looks at her with a serious but, playful face and, said.

"I will hide myself when I'm around people."

He gives her a smile with his hair a little in his eyes and, she smiles back with combing it aside and, back with her fingers from both hands and, they put their arms around each other for the first time with closing their eyes tight and, her right cheek pressing on his chest and, hugged. Then they walked around some more and, they came to the bathroom.

That's when he explained the functions of her body and, when she starts eating food and, drinking liquids the elimination process of what the body doesn't need and, the waste will go here and, he would help her through all the questions she might have. He told her of her menstrual cycle she will have if at all and, that maybe God didn't give her a period every month but, decided to spare her of that since she never fell into sin nor, was she born into sin but, created. He noticed while in the bathroom an old writing devise and, notepad [pen and, paper] and, he was going to pick it up after the shower and, take it to the bedroom to place [pen and, paper] on the edge where he would sleep and, wake up at times to jot down poems, rhymes, lyrics when he was under the inspiration because of her that had jolted him and, he said.

"I think I'm going to take a shower."

"Oh, okay but, what for?"

"I was working a little today and, probably had some perspiration come out with my hands having a little dirt on them and, I don't want to get this new uniform dirty."

"HHMMM, can I watch?"

He thought for a moment that she would see his body again cause after all I got to see hers and, said.

"I wish you would."

They draw their faces together and, laugh.

He started to take his uniform off and, she said.

"I won't join you for now cause I'm already clean as I was just made."

Well, they busted out laughing again and, having a very good time.

They slowly calmed down from laughing and, she was looking at his penis with wonderment and, said.

"Umm, Maximilian what is that between your legs?"

He thought for a while as he was formulating an answer while looking at her and, said.

"Well, it was to consummate our marriage in a Holy Union when we join together and, that it's also for pleasure when we have intercourse and, also for child bearing."

He was thinking that might be a little too much information but, in time everything will be okay. She with a curious look said.

"I Guess you'll have to show me."

She said that with all the maturity a person could call upon oneself on their inner feelings and, he said.

"I want to wash your feet and, ankles first."

"Oh, what for?"

"They've gotten dirty when you walked through the woods."

"Oh, okay I'll sit on the edge of the bed."

"I'll get a pan with warm water and, some soap with a towel don't move."

Pause ... he places her feet in the water and, begins to wash with the rag and, she wants to play with his hair but, holds back. He notices that she wants to do something and, said.

"What are you thinking about."

"I wanted to rub my fingers through your hair."

"Well, what's stopping you?"

"That's right ... I guess it's me all along."

She went ahead and, started to play with his hair and, she thought hhmmm he will let me do what I want and, I like that and, it won't be the last time. He dried her feet off and, said.

"I must say those are some pretty amazing feet ... and, you know what ... what's that ... there's no wear and, tear on them as mine."

They have a good laugh as he dumps the pan of water and, showed her his feet with the calluses then got in the shower but, not before he gave her a kiss on her forehead. He washed and, rinsed off and, the air dryer came on to dry him off and, stepped out and, she was waiting with her arms out a few feet away and, her finger tips were moving up and, down like beckoning her man and, soon to be her husband with a thirsty look and, half smile as her head was turned just a little bit to her right for an alluring look that only a girl or, young woman can give a man. He thought to himself she has hardly any restraint. Then went to her as she looked at him from head to toe and, they meet with her hugging him and, he responded with that first hug they'll never forget as he caressed her shoulders and, moved down her back. Then they released and, she knew he needed a comb because she just got done with combing her hair and, grabbed it for him and, he combed his hair. They were close to each other and, she looked down and, noticed how his penis was growing and, turning upward and, she said.

"Well, what do we do now? I see that your penis is growing and, I see a sack with I think two balls inside am I right?"

He was thinking with a smile of how blunt she is but, he loved it with the acceptance that that's the way she is going to be and, said.

"I'll explain the sack and, the two balls later my love and, if I may pick you up and, carry you to the bed and, we will stand beside it and, I'll will explain what will happen."

She spread her arms like the white crow with total submission and, she said.

"Take me please Maximilian I'm not afraid because I have this peaceful feeling coming over me right now and, being with you is so, natural and, that's the best that I can explain."

While her arms are still out, he puts his left arm around her lower back then his right arm around to the back of her knees and, picks her up and, he asks her to pick up the [pen and, paper]. She did and, he takes her to the bedside with her arms snug around his neck as they gaze at each other and, places her down gently. He wanted her to lay the [pen and, paper] on the side where he would sleep so, she did. She was thinking only of the romance now and, she will ask him later about the [pen and, paper] on the bedside and, she said.

"My Beloved something is happening inside of me I'm getting warm all over."

"That is natural, because I feel it too and, does it feel really good?"

"Yes … it's like I'm aching too … but, in a way I can't explain … I just want to … oh, help me?"

She was thinking, as she looked into eyes how does this all work out? What does it mean to consummate? Her thoughts were deep with what about that Holy Union thing?

His hands are placed at her sides and, her hands are on his front shoulders. He leans into her and, begins to kiss her puffy lips with a touch and, release kind of kissing and, saying to himself I am so, so, so, crazy for her. By now he's at full erection and, she looks down and, said.

"Your penis got bigger and, hard."

She places her hands around it and, feels the warmth of it as she looks back at him with a inquiring face and, he said.

"Amyl ion can I take off your uniform please."

"Why absolutely."

She raises her arms as he slowly takes it off slowly and, places it on the bedside.

"Amyl ion my love please lie on the bed on your back and, open your legs please?"

So, she did as he followed her to the position in which he would inter her.

"This my love, is where I inter between your legs with my penis that you held in your hands."

She looks down towards her legs then takes her hand and, feels down between her legs and, said.

"Oh, I see and, I'm beginning to feel weak."

As she lays her arms to the side of her with palms up and, elbows bent and, resting on the pillows next to her and, he said.

"Amyl ion are you ready?"

"I'm starting to jump and, roll a little inside WHUWWEE."

The music starts [Mary Wells, Strange Love].

She is watching as he is just about to enter her and, as she figures it out very intently about that Holy Union. He is leaning on his hands and, she keeps her eyes open and, she has a look on her face of euphoria and, he starts pressing and, searching and, enters her little by little. He gets more and, more inside her when she begins to take a deep breath and, starts to shake and, convulse. She comes to for a couple of seconds from closing her eyes and, looks at him with her face showing OH, this is what it's about. Then closes her eyes and, goes right back to her shakes and convulsing. While he is enjoying every moment looking down on her and, not aware that she would have her sexual climax upon entering her. She finally comes back from her rolling earthquake and, then she breaths out and, in and, blinks her eyes then starts that particular laughing that only comes from having achieved it. There laughing now and, with hers is sounding like a sexy deep throated woman.

"Oh, Maximilian that was incredible and, our Holy Union together, did we consummate our marriage just then?"

He said with a great big smile.

"Yes, my wife."

She responds by pulling him down to her lips and, starts kissing him the same way he did to her earlier.

"Maximilian but, what about you now that you are my husband?"

"I too will reach the pinnacle of my Orgasm but, only after I pleasure you many times because I just enjoyed yours and, I want you to have more and, more and, I want to learn about your travels to distant lands."

He smiled when saying that as his face was childlike with her pleasure. She caught on fast because she loses the presence and, enjoys the satisfaction in her body and, said.

"HA, HA, HA, HA that was funny. Distant lands."

His life has totally changed because of her and, said.

"I do want to please you more?"

He had a quick thought go through his mind that the research he's done thinks maybe she is multi orgasmic and, he said.

"Tell me more about your conversations with God?"

"Well, when I was descending down here for you My Love, I ask God could you answer a few questions for me please?"

"It was like an instant response with him being beside me at all times and, God said.

"Go ahead."

"Medusa was she created by you?"

"No that was a creation by Satan a monster of his creation to perform and, fulfill his wants and, desires with Medusa designed for killing and, she would go berserk with cunning abilities and, craftiness to hunt the would-be killers that were after her for fame, but Perseus needed her eyes for good. He cut off her head and, successfully completed his mission."

Max knew of the account and, having this new human species as wife his mind was being blown away and, he said.

"Incredible! … how interesting."

He was slowly moving with his strokes that had a variety for her and, sometimes in and, out for pleasure and, he didn't say anything else. There enjoying now their union of husband and, wife. She was slowly closing her eyes and, putting her finger around his ear and, she was fussing with him and, maybe rearranging his hair to what she liked and, she started her climatic voyage again. He knew he didn't have to stroke very much and, said to her.

"I'll watch till you come back."

He was thinking she will be in her ecstasy for a while and, that he was right about her being multi-Orgasmic. She wanted him to have his too together and, experience it and, she said.

"I want you to have yours and, lets time it together."

He was impressed with her catching on and, couldn't agree more and, he said.

"I'll speed up to our hurting pleasure."

CHAPTER 4

Well, they had many conversations during the rest of the night. They fell asleep and, when they were fully rested, they cleaned up and, were fixing breakfast.

They finished their breakfast and, he explained to her that with a couple of more meals she should be having her body's elimination process kicking in.

While still at the table with her left hand on his right arm and, so, close together and, getting acquainted they sipped on their drinks with the quite sounds of sipping and, swallowing. She looked around and, noticed his dad and, mom in a picture hanging on the wall across the living room as there sitting at the kitchen table and, she said.

"Who is that couple on the wall there?"

He turned in the old chair as it squeaked to see that cracked from age and, said.

"Well how about that, that's my dad and, mom. I never noticed that."

She thought I know why with a smile. He was busy watching me.

They noticed that his dad and, mom was walking in the house [they were actually in motion] and, pointing to a spot on the wall.

They looked at each other and, then a bomb blew up and, shook the whole house. It exploded in the second story of the house and, parts of the ceiling were coming down around them with the sounds of pots and, pans with plates crashing all around. The concussion knocked them to the floor and, they immediately crawled to get under what was left of the table. They were dodging pieces of shrapnel and, other material as another bomb went off and, shrapnel hit them in their backs. The table was blown away and, the picture frame of his dad and, mom had landed right in front of them. It must have traveled 20 to 25 feet and, they both picked up the picture to see that their pointing at the spot where that picture of themselves came off the wall. They were desperately shocked and, looked at the spot on the wall where it came from and, there was a button. They got the message and, jumped up and, were stumbling over debris and, pushing away 2 by 4s and, simultaneously touched the button when a sliding door opened and, revealed 2 belts with 2 laser guns for each belt and, those 2 laser guns were in there 2 holsters. She was on his left and, they hustled to put them on and, made them tight with a strong buckle to keep them in place.

When that was done, they heard voices as they stood facing each other and, drew out one laser a piece to see their new weapons taking a second on how to fire them with the laser guns already on stun with options for kill and, there was a safety and, he said.

"Well, my wife we are being attacked and, trying to kill us so, set the lasers to kill and, then just point and, fire."

She released her stun to kill and, looked up and, then behind him when she saw a movement and, put her laser gun between his left arm and, side then fired immediately as sparks flew around going through the enemy's black metal uniform and, putting a hole in him that left a fiery ring. He was stepping through a hole from the outside that was getting ready to fire on them. Max turned his head and, looked for a second and, turned to her with a surprise look and, said.

"Thank you!"

She came back with conviction on her face like this is what must be done and, she said.

"Nothing to it."

He looked at her and, laughed and, said, "YAW, YAW … nothing to it." They were beginning to bond like no other couple.

They heard some rustling in the back. It was obvious that the enemy was planning an attack and, whispered to her and, he said.

"We've got to get to the ship Amyl ion."

They slowly approach the front door that was hanging half off its hinges which is a few feet away and, he sees a weapon coming through the door opening and, he fired immediately through the door killing that soldier with the sound [Ker-plunk] of the soldier falling down on the front porch. He turned to her as he was pulling the other gun from its holster and, said.

"A gun in each hand please and, let's go."

She pulls her other gun out and, placed the stun to kill and, gave him a look and, whispered and, said.

"Okay I'm ready."

They ran out the doorway a gun in each hand and, jumped off the porch. He begins to zig-zag and, she follows in the same way.

The music starts [The Ramones She's the One].

There looking in front and, to their opposite sides while scanning for the nearest trees with their weapons pointing in different directions as they scan the open front yard with a couple of spins to see their back sides. Her beautiful black hair is flying around as the soldiers began to fire and, the shots are getting too close with the white streaks flying by and, they turned around running and, firing back hitting 2 of the soldiers coming out the front door. They finally reached their covering behind a big oak tree. They catch their breath and, looking at each another and, seem to be very happy with this catastrophic surprise. [I must say it looks like they are in their element with nothing … nothing could be better than what is happening right now with each other by their side and, just caught their breath and, he said.

"Do you remember where the ship is?"

"YAW, I do Maximilian! WWHOOEE."

He was concerned for her but, a feeling came over him that never happened before and, trusted his gut and, said.

"Well, we might get separated."

Just then explosives were landing close by and, on the tree that's when she said.

"LET'S GO!"

They were gone in a flash and, ducking behind trees as they went and, still firing at the soldiers as they ran with a few side steps as they see the streams of the laser beams coming at them. They duck and, fire and, jump over bushes and, get a couple more. They look at each other in recognition of each's talent then get separated but, could tell by the direction of each other's return of fire where they were and, eventually, they meet in the path that God had made for them earlier and, there still firing to their left and, right … then behind them. [I can still hear that music]. They both busted out from the bush's and, bumped into each other as they looked at one another and, smiled with her giving out a squeak but still running. The lasers were still flying around them.

That's when he hollered out.

"Samantha lay down some cover fire directly behind us and, lower the ship to 4 feet off the ground lower the hatch put on the reflector shield … Oh, and, set coordinates to a million miles with zig zag evasive action. When we jump inside close the hatch and, set the ship at number 3 thrust out of here!"

"AYE, AYE Captain."

A couple of seconds earlier when the hatch was lowered an enemy scout was creeping about the ship that was sent ahead to spy on it and, jumped on in when it was lowered.

Just then the ship laid down a barrage of laser fire that leveled the playing field. Leaving fire, sparks, and, smoke. The enemy soldiers were flying in the air with some body parts spinning around with blood splattering around and, trees being cut down with bright white flashes.

She was surprised with that outburst he just outlined and, turned a little to see the enormous damage done and, said.

"WHO IS SAMANTHA!!!?"

"Oh, that's my internal voice command."

She turned her quickly to see and, said.

"Thank God for that and, everything behind us has been leveled."

He looked at her like love has come to him and, answered her but, what really, he meant and, said.

"Yaw right! What a sight to see!"

That's when the ship came into view and, there running harder. They didn't bother with taking the steps into the ship they just leaped in and, slid on the floor. The hatch closed and, Samantha said.

"Hold on to something."

The ship took off as they held on to the floor cleats with surrounding trees being sucked in and, uprooted and, the smoke from the fire was pulled into the draft. After the initial thrust of the ship subsided, they were able to get up and, took their belts off with their laser guns in the holsters and, set them on safety and, put them on the counter's edge away from the bridge and, sat in the captain's chairs. Amyl ion looked around at the very illuminating lite aqua ceiling, walls with various gadgets of red, white and, blue. The chairs were black faced with maroon on the back and, the bridge with its colors of dark matte grey and, lighter grey with levers and, buttons. The floor was mixed with maroon and, grey. The viewers were just above head level when standing at the bridge and, many wrapped around the entire circle of where they sat. They weren't held up by anything but, images were put on from behind them and, could swivel in their chairs to watch things.

That's when Samantha notices on the scanner that they were wounded on their back side with shrapnel and, said.

"Captain … your friend there and, you are wounded on your backs with shrapnel so, get to the nurse's station remove your top uniforms and, put your back side to the scanner healer."

They turn to each other as he looked at her backside and, then his and, he said.

"Better do what she said."

She was sort of bewildered at the voice inside the ship and, looked around but, accepted it in only 2 seconds and, she said.

"Well, there goes the nice uniform's God had reserved for us from the closet."

They walk a few steps and, she stops to look at something opens the door and, said.

"What is this … it looks like a shell that's hollow inside with a few screens and, knobs and, a small seat?"

"That my dear wife is the ships time traveling unit."

Her mouth drops open and, turns to him as he smiles and, she placed her hands on his chest then got close to his face and, said.

"I've got to be dreaming … really?"

She looked into his eyes as her face is captivated with this. She grabbed his left arm when he turned as she kept looking at him and, they take a few more steps to get to the nurse's station and, take their tops off and, sit down on the examination bed and, it moved to a location at the wall where it opened up with the small like hands coming out in coordination and, the fingers were pulling the shrapnel out and, cleansing and, closing the wounds up as if they weren't there and, you could hear the pieces of metal drop in the pan and, she said.

"This is quite a ship you've got here … I just love it and, everything is close by … with a future that a person can experience and, only with you Captain."

"Thanks … now it's time for you to get acclimated to the ship that's where you sit in the captain's chair and, I tell Samantha to make you a Captain of the ship as well as I so, let's get some clothes on and, have Samantha fix our uniform's."

"Really!"

Her mouth drops open with a surprise but, with a happy look on her face that said. "YAA … this is very interesting."

Then he reaches under her chin and, lifts her jaw up with 4 fingers and, gives her a kiss on those beautiful lips.

He takes her by the hand to the bedroom closet and, she is not shy about being naked on top. She is loving that he is leading her to the bedroom and, she shines with her smiles with a little twist in her body and, then stopped at the closet. They're getting some clothes on with her deciding on his white dress shirt then looks in a mirror. She has to tie it in the middle that shows her mid-section with no belly button and, rolls up the sleeves but, leaves a couple of buttons at the top unbuttoned to see if he would notice her cleavage because her breasts were close together or, because there 34 D cups. How she knew that I guess it would be a woman's instinct. He grabbed a handkerchief from the shelf and, stuck in his back pocket. He's done and, has his dark blue shirt on and, looks at his Bride in White and, he thinks of how cute she is and, couldn't be happier. There's a hair brush on the counter and, she grabs it. She went to brushing her hair while looking in the mirror and, it went [SWWOOSH, SWWOOSH] almost a dozen times and, sets it down. She turns towards her husband and, smiles that would make the Supreme Court pass a new Law that [HER SMILE IS NOW CERTIFIED] and, required to smile back and, cannot be reversed.

"[UUMMM] were you going to say something my husband?"

"Do you want to know why I want to make you a Captain?"

"Why?"

He comes over to her and, lays his hands on her shoulders with her insides just softening up to his touch and, looked at each of his hands on her shoulders slowly with a smile then looked at his face all over and, him looking in her eyes and, he said.

"Cause you're a warrior!"

After a brief moment he took her by the hands and, he said.

"Come over to the captain's chair with me please."

He walked backwards as he pulled her along as she twisted her body a little to the left and, right with a surrendered look squealing in delight.

She was thinking in the back of her mind I hope he noticed me in this white shirt?

Yes, he did notice her in that white shirt. I personally would have seen her too. He looked her up and, down and, said.

"I think you just created a new fashion statement."

She looks herself over for a minute with the silver flex pants and, the dress shirt with the collar up and, her breast's sticking out and, puffy areola's then she turns with a pose and, she said.

"Well do you like it?"

There facing each other and, he puts his left hand behind her neck and, head then draws her close to kiss her. She was thinking Oh, yes, he has noticed me I caught him looking. Her insides are getting excited and, can't wait for what is coming next. He reaches for her breast and, squeeze's as he kiss's her simultaneously. She just let go and, brought her hand up to squeeze his hand that tells him how much she enjoyed that. Her hand fell back down to her side and, she was about to melt but, had to control her emotions for a while. He releases his kiss and, grip and, there both breathing a little heavy but, try to focus as they sit down in separate chairs and, he said.

"Samantha incorporate Amyl ion as Captain of the [27-Trip's] please."

Samantha said.

"Just relax and, put your head back and, close your eyes."

CHAPTER 5

A couple metal devices came out from her headrest and touched on her temples and, one on her prefrontal cortex. One came out from each of the arm rests and, touched her wrists. He watched her while that was going on, he said.

"Samantha who attached us and, why?"

"Searching captain... and, here you go. Dominic Roku a retired Olympian whom a Gold Metal was lost and, that you won and, is a [unfriendly]. His brigade has been decimated with no replacements and, what remained is 50 or, less solders."

He relaxes in his chair and, watches her as she is incorporated into the ship's memory banks, computer's, with bonding their command codes together for the ship. She stays still as she experiences this tingling sensations through-out her mind and, body and, he said.

"Samantha put those images of Dominic and, soldiers on the screen please."

Images pop up around them on 7 of 10 viewers. That's when the metal objects were released from her as she watched the viewers too with an intriguing look and, then fusses with her hair and, she said.

"That was fascinating and, the feeling of it. Well, it's hard to explain."

Pictures of Dominic show him as an Olympian and, later as a Colonel in the alliance fighter's brigade. An enemy of the United States and, free world.

He started out with a raised voice and, realized that he didn't want to alarm his bride and, then he began to lower his voice and, he said.

"Why would he attack me and, you too Amyl ion? I surely don't want you involved and, you got hurt today."

He was running his hands through his hair. She knew what was going

28

on with her husband and got up from her Captain's chair and, approached him and, stood for a moment with a gorgeous simple smile and, slinked down on his lap and, put her arms around his neck and, hugged him for a long time with her head on his chest and, almost laying down on him. He responded in kind with a long hug and, was rubbing her back and, he said.

"Samantha bring up the area around the house where the fire fight was and, find any images of soldiers and if you could get their faces on the viewer, please?"

"AYE, AYE Captain. It's difficult at this speed."

"All ahead stop Samantha."

"AYE, AYE Captain."

"That will help you get a fix on their faces let us know when you do."

"AYE, AYE Captain."

She looks up to him with confidence and, said.

"I will fight alongside and, for you."

He thought back about his words earlier that flows out so, easily for her. Something he never thought he had but, she is pure inspiration to him that only a few people experience. A sensation came over him that he'd never do that again and, he said.

"Bones of my Bones and Flesh of my Flesh, now it is said let it be written in our hearts."

Their bonding is coming along very good that they know what to say and, both said.

"Amen."

Slowly they release each other she gets up and, sits in her Captain's chair turns and, face each other and, contemplated what they said and, their commitment.

He wanted to explain to her what was in his heart and, said.

"A short while back I was in the hospital recovering from exhaustion and, my hands were badly lacerated, I fought for my life and, I collapsed at the Olympic stadium finally climbing out of an escape hole that it must have been a mile long. Right there in the middle of the stadium with crowds cheering as I emerged."

She looked at his hands and, got up to look at them closer as she held them in her hands then she sat back down as he continued and, said.

"I had them repaired on the ship here to remove the scars."

She's very relaxed and, serious and, said.

"They look very good I can't tell or, I can't see any scars."

He looked at them and, his mind flashed at the blood and, flesh hanging off and, it disappeared and, he said.

"The gold metal that I won and, the fierce competitor that I'd won it from it was life or death to him. We competed in the 200 meters, the Javelin throw, the high jump, shooting lasers at the moon that had targets on it, but what really mattered to him was coming out of that cave with the grizzly bears to escape from."

Her head went back and, eyes getting a little bigger at the thought of a bear encounter and, she said.

"Why would they have a competition that calls for an escape from grizzly bears that would otherwise kill you?

"I thought it would be a good challenge for me considering the talents my parents gave me and, hardly anybody did it."

She is very interested now and, she said.

"Can you tell me the whole story of the competition?"

"Well, you jump down this hole on the ground and it sits at an angle so you start sliding down right away and, you're sliding along down this long tube. I was having a blast when I slipped right out of the hole and, it must have been a mile long I thought. I landed at the bottom of what appeared to be a cave and, right on a dust pile. I got up dusted myself off and, cleared the dust from my eyes when a couple of grizzly bear cubs appeared and, they thought it was play time, but here comes papa and, mama bear coming after me and, there thinking I was going to harm their baby's. Well, they come charging and, stop and, raise up on their hind legs and, their eyes were red and, maroon like they were piercing inside of you that holds you in suspension and, then they kill you. I was falling back and, said to myself well this is it I'll shove my fists in their mouth and, down their throats, but that light above me gave me an idea as I was falling back. There were big rocks and, boulders round about. I got behind some rocks and, planned my escape. I ran and, jumped on one of the cubs back and, then jumped on papa bears back with my feet and, pushed off as hard as I could. Papa bear was just standing there wondering what was going on with me moving around so fast. I guess I took them by surprise at what I was doing. Luckily when I entered the hole in the ceiling, I grabbed a hold of some jagged edges but my feet and, legs were hanging out. I looked down to see where the bears were? There standing, while I'm trying to look and climb towards the light. Mama bear was starting to swing at my feet. I looked up to grab what I could, it was do or die now. My fingers were beginning to bleed, but I reached for the knobs that were just all the way up to the top. I slipped several times and, had to regain what I lost. I was getting exhausted by now and, my hands are bleeding more now and, running down my arms. I was getting to the top and, I put my right hand out on top and, rested for a while I thought when someone grabbed my wrist and, arm but, their hands slipped from the blood on my arms and, eventually were able to pull me to the top and, held me up. My thirst for life paid off. The bright lights came on and, I looked to where I was and, the crowd was cheering in the Olympic stadium. That's when I collapsed."

She was shaking her head and, captivated and, said.

"The loss of blood probably helped you pass out. WOW, my heart goes out for you. There must be more?"

"They rushed me to the hospital and, I came to a couple hours later my hands bandaged up and, I was barely able to open my eyes. The nurse was there tending to my hands and, taking the first wrappings off and, folded them and, laid them to my left at the bedside. She smelled incredible and, seemed to fill my lungs that gave me a euphoric feeling of ecstasy and, restored my strength. She grabbed my left arm with her hands and, looked up at me and, our eyes met. It was you Amyl ion as you are sitting here in front of me."

That's when her tears came down her cheeks listening to this story. He grabbed his handkerchief out of the back pocket and, gave it to her. She wiped them away and, said.

"Our God has shown me to you ... before I was even created. Absolutely fantastic! and, thanks for the handkerchief."

"There's more, as we were looking at one another your pupils dilated big that replaced your hazel iris's then back to small with your wings on the side of your eyes that go past your eyebrows and, you said to me I got to go now and, we'll meet again in the short future! I promise! She left out the door and, I knew what I had to do."

"And what is that my husband?"

31

"Get back to the space ship and, finish the upgrade to equal the power of our governments new space ships."

"That is an incredible story!"

"There's more, then the Doctor comes through the door and, ask how you feeling I said never better he looked startled and, took my vital signs and, I ask the doctor where did the nurse go that was here?

The Doctor smiled and, looked at me like. We'll what have you been doing and, he said.

"There hasn't been any one in here for over an hour and, have you hallucinated before?"

"I didn't know what to say so, I thought as quickly as I could Oh, I was asleep and, had a dream. After thinking for a moment, The Doctor said Yaw that was it ... Okay your released and, you can take your bandages off tomorrow."

There is a pause as the doctor put information in his tablet and, Maximilian said.

"Doctor could I do a little work around the ship?"

"Yaw but, take it easy."

"The Doctor was looking at the first layer of bandages folded that you placed at the bedside and, he must have looked at them for 5 seconds as he pondered and, thought ... well that couldn't be and, then left out the door. That doctor was contemplating what I already knew.

I ask myself what happened to the other guy at the stadium? So, when I got back to the ship, I asked Samantha and, she said, he was badly mauled by the bears at the Olympic stadium and, they rescued him and, then was picked up by Raven Hades in a space pod and, from there to a space ship and, they all left to Earth 2. Little else is known about his recovery and, probably nothing good will come out of their relationship and, he promised vengeance because Dominic Roku did not win the gold medal."

Samantha said.

"Captain Amyl ion you are integrated now with Captain Maximilian and, I wait for your orders."

"Oh, Maximilian this makes me feel ... well it's kind of chilling to hear and, I love you so, so, so, very much."

He thought of something that was in the back of his mind and, she gave him a look like hhmmm he's thinking deep about what to say and, he said.

"I want to get up and, draw up at the bridge [The Oath of Naturalization]. AAAHH, here we go so, captain stand up and, raise your right hand."

She did what he said with her face about to experience a new thing and, he said.

"Repeat after me."

This is what she said.

"I hereby declare on OATH, that I absolutely and, entirely renounce and, adjure all allegiance and, fidelity to any foreign prince, potentate, state or, sovereignty, of whom or, which I heretofore been a subject or, citizen; that I will support and, defend the constitution and, laws of the United States of America against all enemies foreign and, domestic; that I will bear true faith and, allegiance to the same; that I will bear arms on behalf of the United States when required by the law; that I will perform noncombatant service in the armed forces of the United States when required by law; and, that I take this obligation freely with-out any mental reservation or, purpose of evasion, so, help me God!"

He stopped and, her face started to light up at this and, covered her mouth with her right hand that had now opened at such a wonderful thing. They walk towards each other with his big smile she started to show tears. He has his handkerchief out for her as she snugs into his chest and, grabbed his handkerchief and, caught the tears and, he said.

"YES, yes. Congratulations you are a United States citizen now with a number for identification that you'll find at the bridges file for you."

She didn't know what to say and, they went back to their chairs with a satisfying closed lipped smile and, Samantha said.

"Captain's the viewers are displayed."

They get up and, walk over and, she is on the right side of him and, they see Dominic Roku on the site of the house surveying the damage. The next viewer Dominic is looking at the dead soldiers and, there isn't any more now left under his command. The next viewer shows his face with scares of the bears that mauled him.

"Maximilian is that him your competitor at the Olympic stadium?"

"Yes, and, his face doesn't look very good with those scars now and, it looks like he has a vendetta. I must say that Samantha was deadly with the fire power that she laid down for us at our escape and, most all were killed by Samantha with each of us getting several a piece ... Oh, by the way they cancelled that event at the Olympics."

"Well, I'm glad of that because that was crazy."

Samantha said.

"There is an intruder on board captains!"

The location on the viewer shows a flashing red light on the person as it approaches from behind them. The intruder had managed to get one of their laser guns off the counter when they weren't looking.

They turn around and, now she's on his left side and, the intruder soldier said.

"Don't move and, be very careful."

CHAPTER 6

They collected their thoughts as to what to do with this surprising development and, he said.

"How did you get on board?"

The soldier takes off the mask and, helmet with the left hand and, she shakes her hair loose and, the soldier was a good-looking woman but, what was she doing on the wrong side of things and, the soldier said.

"I heard everything that was said."

They took a glance at the laser gun that she had while she was talking and, must have grabbed it off the counter and, they saw that the safety was on and, the soldier said.

"I was sent ahead as a scout."

But, as soon as the soldier said that it was then that Amyl ion landed a left hook on her jaw which turned her head and, shook her brain momentarily and, the soldier turned back to face them and, Amyl ion had already stepped in front of Max to protect him and, gave her a straight right knocking her front teeth out. The soldier fell backwards with her lights knocked out. Well try to hold her back now and, then she finished her off with a right-hand hook to the cheek, and, the soldier crumbled to the floor and, she jumped on top and, started pummeling the soldier with lefts and, rights. As she was doing that she hollered out and, said.

"Don't you ever point a gun at my husband!"

He intervened by slowly grabbing her arms and, pulling her off and, said.

"Okay, Okay, okay."

Speaking softly to her because he didn't know how she would react … and, only seeing this for the first time and, he said.

"Amyl ion you're going to kill her!"

Lifting her up very cautiously she rises to her feet and, said to her.

"Amyl ion ... hey calm down, the sun has set on her and, take some deep breaths and, blow out."

He releases his hold on her and, she was so, charged with emotion like she had just won a championship fight and, she was walking around for a while and, looking at the soldier on the floor. He walked over to her when she stopped and, just stood there by her side. She turned to him with her arms wrapping around him and, hugged him with her head on his chest for a while and, she started to breath in and, out just like he said too as she calmed down. He put his arms around her and, stroked her back and, he said.

"That was some amazing work you did and, I was absolutely sure about you being a Warrior."

"Maximilian MY Baby Oh, I Love you and, I just did what I had to do for you. I would have put her in the dark permanently."

He was thinking I have in my arms the most incredible woman and, what do I say to her God? Instantly a thought came to him and, he wanted to check her knuckles and, hands for damage. Her mind was busy with all this excitement and, she said.

"What do we do now my husband?"

"Well, my champion ... let me see your knuckles and, hands please?"

She raised her hands as they were looking at each other for a moment. He was holding her hands and, telling her that he loved her with his eyes and, his smile. She smiles back and, some time went by and, she said.

"Maximilian you're not looking at my knuckles or my hands."

He had to say what he was thinking in the back of his mind to break the spell she had on him at this moment and, he said.

"The laser gun did you notice that the safety was on?"

Her face is so, serious and, spoke with conviction and, she said.

"YES, that was kind of dumb of her ... and, she was focused on talking and, the safety was on that's when I had to come in like lighting."

After a pause he is still smiling and, reaches down to give her a great big kiss and, she returns the kiss by jumping up and, wrapping her arms around him with standing on her toes and, they must have kissed for several minutes and, she was loving every precious second and, the sounds they were making as nothing else matters.

That's the way love is, isn't it?

They slowly release and, they touch noses and, there just so, very happy and, he said.

"Very well then let's tie her up."

They stoop down and, they searched the soldier's pockets and, found her credentials. Just a picture of her and, a small line running across the bottom that has all the soldier's information. They look at it and, glanced at her on the floor and, he said.

"She doesn't look like that picture anymore and, you sure did number on her. Okay, captain if you would please place this in the slot next to the Green Froggy on the bridge and, ask Samantha to decipher the data on the bar, and, after you've done that tap the Green Froggy's head a couple of times for a squeaky sound."

He is smiling at her as they get up and, she walks on over to drop it in.

She runs her finger across the small line and, it's as if she can read it. She shrugs her shoulders then drops it in the slot and, taps the Green Froggy, [Squeak-Squeak] it goes and, she said.

"Oh, how cute."

The soldier comes to with some groaning and, obviously she is in pain. She walks back over to him and, they look at her and, she said.

"What are we going to do with her?"

He bent down to look at her and, she bent down too and, he said.

"Samantha prepare the face alignment scanner it appears this soldier has a broken nose, swollen eye, missing teeth, and, a broken cheek bone."

"Aye, Aye Captain."

"Let's pick her up Captain and, take her to the nurse's station and, put the brace around her to stand her up with her face in the [face alignment opening]."

They put her face in and, the soldier gave out a sigh of relief and, Amyl ion said.

[While they were talking an image tries to appear on the viewers that the captains couldn't see. There were swirling colors of red, grey, orange, black and, pink. The swirling cleared up and, it was Satan bent over looking into a portal in outer space at here and, there trying to find them to destroy these two from being a future King and, Queen. He was grumbling and, snarling and, he looked demonic with his dark red skin and, long nose with black goatee and, hair. The twisted horns on top were red and, pointed out to the front left and, front right and, about 18 inches long. God had blocked him from finding them and, the three female succubus's were standing by [Labrina, Sabrina and, Zabrina] and, all you could see was there naked mid-section down to their knees with small pants. One of them came to his side with just her thighs showing and, Sabrina said.

"Be patient my lord you'll find them and, kill them."

The other two agreed and, talked between themselves and, Labrina said.

"Send one of us and, we can seduce him and, then you can have her to yourself. She will be a great addition to our hell]."

The portal goes back to its many colors and, in a few seconds the viewers in the ship go blank. They stop just for a few seconds and, glance around and, in their mind, they thought [no that couldn't be] then resume their conversation and, she said.

"That was very uplifting for me Maximilian when you called me Captain and, why did she do that sigh of relief?"

"It numbs the pain that she is going through and, then repairs the nose, replaces teeth, straightens bones, reduces swelling, seals open wounds and, there is no signs that anything had happened to her face. Amyl ion would you ask Samantha to send a red cross ship to this location to pick up a recovering female from her injuries please and, I'll pick up the laser gun with the holsters and, put them in storage. Then let's prepare a pod to launch with a beacon flashing so, the red cross can pick her up."

She thought about this responsibility as he left to the storage room and, the enthusiasm that came from with-in. Personally I [the author] just enjoy her at this new found role … and, look forward to observing their relationships and, she said.

"Samantha, could you send the red cross to these coordinate's please there's a recovering soldier from being beaten up and, the soldier needs a follow up on the repair of her face!"

She had contempt for the soldier and, you could tell by the tone in her voice because she pointed that laser gun at her beloved. He comes back from the storage area and, overheard her and, they come together. He picks her up under her buttocks and, gives her a couple of spins in the air. She loves it with a squeal of her own and, is thinking about what a change from the intruder to this wonderful moment and, it just smoothed it over and, what a beautiful man that I truly know that he loves me. He walks over to the Green Froggy and, he reaches with one hand and, gives it a couple of [Squeaky-Squeaks] and, looks at her and, laughs a little bit and, he said.

"[Beaten up]?"

They look at each other for a while, smiling a little and, she starts to laugh which made him laugh and, having a good time and, he said.

"Let's prepare ourselves for the trip to Earth 2."

He slowly lets her down but, not without one more spin with a kiss that can't be beat. Her head was spinning a little and, said.

"WWHHOOAA, HA, HA, HA, HA, HA, HA, HA Oh, Maximilian ... HHMMM."

She puts her hands on her head for a few seconds and, she follows him a few feet and, she sees an engraving on the metal frame doorway going into the bridge area and, she said.

"Captain I've got to read this."

He comes back to her and, they turn as she reads it while he looks on and, she said.

"MADE IN THE U. S. A. WITH GENUINE METALS FROM SELECT PLANETS OF THE [SEVEN SISTERS] I. e. PLEIADES PLANETS."

She turned to him and, said.

"They must be special metals?"

He thought of saying but, not as special as your creation but, changed his mind and, he said.

"Different than on earth 1 and, we will have a lifetime of searching on this planet for new metals. Captain the ships history will have the location of the area where the metals were excavated."

She turns to him and, he placed his hands on her shoulders under her black shiny hair and, she flipped her hair back and, placed her hands on his hands very lady like and, he said.

"The metals from those planets make up the ship and, interact with each other that makes it go straight up, hover and, zoom away in any direction at the controls or, verbal command."

She loved him speaking to her in this manner and, she said.

39

"Truly a remarkable creation."

When she said that she watched his face change into thinking of her. He placed his right hand on her left cheek and, said.

"Yes, a remarkable creation … truly!"

She smiled that rocked the ship and, she grabbed him and, he said.

"WOW! That never happened before."

They released and, placed his hands on the side of her shoulders and, she said.

"I understand more about myself now. With even these connections of planet rocks."

He grabbed her left hand turned and, went to the bridge and, he said.

"Let's talk about it later please."

Her face had a look of fascination at this and, could hardly wait to talk about it more as she stood by his side.

He presses 4 buttons on the bridge and, a bed is revealed after a portion of the floor slides away and, is just a couple of feet away from the bridge and, she said.

"What's that for?"

"We lay on our left sides, the glass covering goes over us, a cloud of life supporting mist comes out and, were transported through time till we reach our destination."

"Okay but, I want to be around your arms."

He looks at her and, smiles and, said.

"Amyl ion I'll be whispering in your pretty ear all through the trip."

"Maximilian your words will go right to my heart and, satisfy my soul."

He thought in the spur of the moment and, he said.

"There's a few Christmas songs I'd like to sing to you as well, what do you think? do you want to join along?"

"Christmas songs Maximilian!!!?"

She put her hands on her thighs and, bent over in a way that she was very excited to do just that and, gave out a cute deep throated laugh and, she said.

"Oh, Maximilian that would be just heavenly."

Then the red cross sends the signal that they are ready to receive the pod and, contents. She goes over to where the soldier is and, raises her voice and, said.

"I'll get her ready and, put her in the pod while you set the coordinates for Earth 2, please my Captain."

There's a pause ... and, she said.

"The soldier is passed out from the sedatives and, ... I have to carry her."

"I appreciate that my love and, do you need any help?"

"No, and, it's my pleasure Captain."

She is so, happy because she loves him so, very, very much.

She picks up the soldier and, carries her and, tries to get her to walk but, can't and, carries her with her arms around her to the space pod area in storage and, places the soldier in side closes the lid and, presses the send button.

CHAPTER 7

[I'm thinking that Amyl ion wanted to get rid of her right away] and, he said.

"Samantha set the ship on course to Earth 2, 12 valleys of the 99 hills and I'LL tell you when to go."

"AYE AYE Captain."

She walks back to him with a curious look while fluffing her hair with her fingers a couple of times and, said.

"The red cross will send the pod back when the patient is unloaded and, how does the ship know where earth 2 is at?"

"It's common knowledge on this ship and, just a few others in the space force know about it ... like the President and, two of the highest-ranking officers in the space force."

He turns and, faces her and, there is a pause and, he reaches with his right hand and, places it softly on her cheek and, rubs her lovely lips one time with his thumb straight across and, leans down to kiss her. They put their arms around each other with hers around his neck and, he squeezes her against himself. They release a little and, she lifts her arms up smiled and, said.

"Take me to the shower please my husband."

He picks her up with his left arm around her lower back and, his right arm back under her knees and, said.

"Gladly my bride."

As they start kissing while he is trying to navigate to the shower he bumps into the walls and, they start laughing while there trying to kiss.

[I would love to see this play out on the Big Screen, but, only with the right people and, if I could have a chance of choosing her].

They make it to the shower and, he said.

"Oh, our top part of the uniform's lets gather them up and, put them in the repair slot for the clothes."

When that is done, he said to himself now where was I? He picks her up again and, takes her to the shower and, take their top clothes off and, there uniform pants while she is tickling him. He is trying to keep her hands away and, backing into the shower at the same time and, she follows him into the shower and, the door closes automatically. The water and, soap came out they scrub each other and, there just talking and, laughing. The time comes when they rinse and, the warm air dry's them off. They stumble out the shower she jumps on him and, wraps her legs around him as he carries her to the bed. There excited now as he lays his bride down and, they start to unwind. She anticipates what is about to happen as she fluffs her hair to look good for him then lays her arms out to her sides on the pillows and, gets a soft drunk look as he is searching to enter her and, as he does, she takes a deep breath and, starts a journey to her land filled with pleasure. After a while she comes around to opening her eyes and, he said.

"Hello ... it's so, good to be with you."

They have conversations between her pursuits of entry to expressive heavenly cosmos. They finish having their heavenly cosmos together and, Samantha is recording all that they say. They will draw upon that in the future to listen when they get older and, reminisce. They go to the bathroom to clean up after their love making and, he said. [COPY-RIGHT 2021 BY CARROLL HOLST. ALL RIGHTS RESERVED].

"Let's get dressed and go to Earth 2."

She had a flash go through her mind about the past and, said.

"I wonder what it will be like?"

"My darling I wonder too but, in the meantime would you please step on the top of my feet."

As he takes her by the hands, he thinks she wouldn't mind if we did this naked and, she stepped on his feet and, totally trusts him. Then he starts shuffling his feet and, moves his arm around her lower back and, moves his other arm out with his other hand while holding hers and, moves to an imaginary beat and, she said.

"What is this my darling?"

"I call it the Crown of Rejoicing."

"Alright I get the hang of it."

"Okay you want to take your feet off now and, we can move to the beat and, ask Samantha to play a dance song or, anything you like."

So, she put her hand on her chin and, looked at him as she felt free and, told her what to play.

The music starts [Nu Shooz-I Can't Wait-Official Video] [Haddaway-What is Love [Remix] shuffle Dance Music Video [2019].

They had a very good time as she brightened up the room with her black hair jumping around. She said to him at one time.

"What were you going to whisper in my ear?"

"Could I have another dance please?"

She laughs with pleasure.

Well, they finished it up with a hug and, a long kiss then she said.

"Let's go to Earth 2."

"Samantha are the top of our uniforms ready?"

"Yes, they are."

He goes over to the exit door for the clothes and, gets his and, her uniforms. She is right behind him as she went to get their pants from the other room. They look at them and, they put them on.

"Wow, we look like Captain's again and, you look very handsome my husband."

He is looking at her and, thinking I must proceed on but, I want to make love to her again.

She walks up to him and, said.

"Maximilian what are you thinking?"

As she smiles and, looks into his blue eyes and, he said.

"I want to make love to you."

She smiles with closed lips and, a demure look then puts her hands behind her and, wiggles a little bit for a while fluttering eyes and, she said.

"We must go to Earth 2 Maximilian then I'm all yours and, your all mine."

He thought he was too anxious and, said.

"Yes, we must go now ..."

"HM, HM, HM, HM yes, we must go now HM, HM, HM."

He could hardly break away from his deep, deep yearning for her and, he said.

"Samantha prepare our scales and, then measure the right amount of nutrients for our drinks on our long trip."

"AYE AYE Captain."

So, he steps on the scale first and, the viewer shows [217 LB'S 6'1"] and out comes the drink. He looks at her and, drinks it down.

"MMMMMMM, My Darling would you please step on?"

She steps on and, the viewer showed [112 LB'S 5'3"] and out comes the drink. She looks at it with a questionable look and, said.

"We got different amounts how come?"

"We get the proper amount of nutrients for Male and, Female and, depending on our size."

She drinks it down and, no problem because if he went MMMMMMM then it must be good.

"MMMMMMM, this is good and, are you sure that this is not a love potion you're giving me?"

He thought in an instant ... now I like this and, I'll just play along.

"Yes, that's what it is a love potion because I want all of your life 1,000,000 percent."

"Okay then I want 1,000,000 percent of you too."

"Agreed."

"Agreed."

"Let's shake on it to make it binding."

He then spun her around and, is delighted and, they had a goodtime with that one.

They finally step into the bed below the floor and, there trying to stop laughing. They get in position and, snuggled and, he said.

"I got something for you."

"What's that?"

"It's a poem I wrote for you."

"I want to hear it."

He pulls it out of his back pocket and, said.

"Here goes ... [If you could Bee behind my eyes; would you whisper this is how I love with 100 replies; I can't explain these hills if you could Bee behind my eyes; would you turn to me as you whisk by; forgetting the asphalt as we roll to declassify; I love these hills I can't explain why; If you could Bee behind my eyes; we could go back in the morning beholding the splendor that has been reassigned; this is how we love]."

"Why Maximilian that was very, very beautiful and, I will cherish it all my life."

She kiss's both of his hands and, whispering she said.

"I Love you!"

Her face was filled with a delight of security for herself and, the future that they will share and, then she took in a breath and, exhaled and, he said.

"Samantha close the lid please and, let's take a trip through the ocean as we sleep."

"AYE, AYE Captain."

Then he tells her.

"This will be a part of our Honeymoon."

Samantha said.

"Enjoy your trip of hibernation, will be there before you know it."

The glass covering slides quickly and, there sealed in. Then the light steel blue gas starts to come out and, is filling the area while they lay.

She closes her eyes and, said.

"Maximilian [If you could be behind my eyes]."

"AHH … Amyl ion that was good and, as a matter of fact that's where I'll be."

Then he repeats the same.

"[If you could be behind my eyes]."

He closes his eyes and, is thinking about the future and, he wants to do the best he can for his wife … and, now a Captain.

Samantha controlled their destination and, the ship blasted through space to Earth 2 at the 12 valleys of the 99 hills.

The music starts [I'm your Captain/Closer to Home-Grand Funk Railroad Better Quality].

While they were lying in the h-bed their minds came to realize after the darkness disappeared, that the mammals and, fish appeared and, had noticed them to encouraged the couple on. They were gliding in the ocean and, noticed that they didn't have their clothes on. Well, they just enjoyed that and, put one arm around each other and, continued to swim. They looked to their left and, there was a school of yellow fish dancing up and, down. They looked to there right and, a blue school of fish coming in front of them and, they passed right through and, they were smiling and laughing. Then they looked behind them to see if anything was there and, there was some strange fish tails that had ducked behind a large coral reef and, they shook their shoulders like oh well that was nothing but, when they turned around, they collided with a giant grey whale head on. The whale saw them coming and, blew out some ocean water to soften the blow on their heads. The two of them bounced back a little and, grabbed their heads and, started to laugh. The whales had their way of laughing as well. A kind of a mixture of cry's and, whimpering and, their eyes closing a little now and, then. They looked around as they glided along on their dream journey through the ocean as the whales faded away. She points to the bottom of the ocean and, said.

"Let's go down to the bottom and, see what's there?"

He looks around and, sees no danger for her and, agrees with nodding his head and, said.

"Amyl ion how's your head feeling?"

"Okay but, I think we better look where were going from now on and, we might get eaten up."

They both laugh and, agree then they noticed again that their uniforms were not on but, they had some ideas.

Grabbing each other's hands, they embrace and, started to kiss. She wrapped her legs around him and, proceeded to have intercourse as they sank lower and, lower to the ocean floor. It was their Honeymoon and, who says you can't have sex in the ocean with your spouse.

There were schools of fish that took notice and, some that didn't, but the whales listened and, drew near but not to be seen. They were both having a very good time and, freedom of the positions to enjoy sex.

The restrictions sometimes of being on a surface of any kind limits your mobility but, maybe it's a perspective of one's point of view.

There were four female mermaids that were going back to their husbands in their secret passage way when they heard her first of many groans and, sounds from her first orgasm and, they stopped as they glided along and, listened very carefully and, the one with the brown and, white mixed hair pointed the way to the sounds. Our beloved thought they were alone but, the 4 mermaids hide behind a large coral reef with the growth from the ocean floor giving them some good cover. The second one had two toned hairs too with it being streaked with green and, yellow. Then the third had olive and, black streaked hair. The fourth one had red and, orange-streaked hair that' their all waving in the water around their shoulders and, stomach level. There fins were all different shapes and, colors which made for a beautiful display of mermaids.

[In times gone past they would have said … oh, there different races].

CHAPTER 8

They watched them intently at the way they have sex and, look at one another and, smile and, when they communicate the water waves from their foreheads to the one there talking to. In between one of her orgasms they had a brief word or, two and, they went to kissing each other and, Amyl ion peeped open her left eye and, could see the four of them watching and, I guess a little smile showed up because she had a dimple show up on the side of her cheek. She didn't care and, trusted the mermaids and, didn't tell him about it until much later or, I think she just forgot well ... anyway she didn't want her husband's interest being roused up. She had several orgasm's and, he had a couple too and, what a honeymoon. The mermaids watched them until they left and, they went on their way to their husbands talking back and, forth about her shaking with the waves of their communication over lapping and, you couldn't tell which one was talking to who. They were imitating her with similarities of the way her body would function under her orgasm's.

They had their fill of this once in a lifetime honeymoon and, he said.

"Amyl ion how would you like to see the highlights of the Pacific Ocean first?"

"Well of course my darling."

She was absolutely intrigued by the idea and, said.

"Hey Samantha ... take us to the most important sights on the bottom of the ocean please."

"AYE, AYE Captain ... you'll like AZ sector, the wall will come up shortly, just go in the direction you two are going in and, the wall will appear."

They see it appear and, get closer as the wall has pictures of aliens from

49

other planets and, their children as well. He thought no one in history has recorded anything like this and, with a startling discovery he said.

"Oh, their portraits from maybe this galaxy and, maybe distance galaxy's."

They were perfectly preserved because there was fish that would keep the wall clean by eating the corrosion that would develop on the surface of the wall. They glided along the wall and, noticed many different forms in their bodily structures. Then there were tattoos and, markings on their arms, legs, and, back. If they were on their back, they would be facing the ˙ other way and, he said.

"Samantha what are these markings on their skin?"

"To distinguish what planet, galaxy, nationality they were and, what alien language they spoke."

They looked at one another and, both said with over lapping conversations.

"These are gravestones! or, one long wall or, maybe both … when was the wall put up?"

Samantha said.

"No documentation has surfaced when the wall was put up and, there is more, the markings on their skin were later put on to signify what was there cause of death and, their descendants, purpose of life, children, goals and, achievements.

They start laughing and, looked at each other and, said.

"[Hasn't surfaced]."

He just barely got that out and, wanted to complement Samantha and, he said.

"That was good Samantha."

"I knew you would like that one."

Amyl ion looked around after laughing and, she said.

"Is this all there is to it?"

"No, it's a large circle and, in the inside is a collection of space ships from galaxies around the universe."

She thought that this would be very interesting and, said.

"Well how do we get in there?"

Samantha said.

"Just believe that you can walk through that wall and, you will be on the other side."

Well, they believed and, went forward and, the next thing they knew is that their bodies streamed in and, out and, they were on the other side of the wall. The look on their faces were like they discovered something that nobody has ever seen before and, they were right about that and, he said.

"Let's see the old to the new."

Shockingly out of the dark green ocean 2 large black and, blue stripped sharks cruised by them. They thought they were being attached but, the sharks were merely passing by to investigate and, as they passed by, they noticed that they had camouflaged bodies. The rings around them were black and, blue with jagged edges and, there were about 9, or 10 of the rings and, he said.

"UMM Samantha just tell us in what direction the closest and, the newest space ship is and, maybe the 3 of us can get it operational."

"AYE, AYE Captain."

Samantha is searching but, there is a delay.

Amyl ion looks around and, she sees more shark's circling overhead maybe a half dozen now. The front of the sharks to the back of the tail are all striped and, she said.

"Could you hurry up please Samantha?"

"Right ... just turn to your right and, go about 300 feet its similar to [27-Trips], in size and, shape."

Well, they started walking and, soon that changed into a fast glide. Then they noticed that their uniforms are back on. Very quickly a big shark came right between them and, knocked them to the ocean floor. Sharks usually bump into you before they actually bite into you. He grabbed her hand and, took off as fast as he could with her right behind him. Looking back never occurred to them now after the last head on collision. They reached the space ships just in time. There were gray ships, silver ships but, couldn't decide which one.

The urgency of this was unparalleled because of his love for her and, he said.

"WHICH ONE SAMANTHA!!!?"

"Go to the next row it's the charcoal one."

The ships were squeezed tightly together and, they made it through alright and, as soon as they did there was a thud, and, crash behind them. Turning around quickly to see what that crash was. A great big sharks' mouth was jammed between 2 space ships. They were staring with their eyes wide open at those teeth that would have shredded them to pieces. There was more circling overhead now they noticed.

The great striped shark was trying to free itself now. They reached the charcoal one and, they're underneath it and, he said.

"Let's look around on the bottom for some kind of handle or object that's not uniformed to the body of the ship."

"Okay I'll go on over on the other side."

As soon as she said that he grabbed her arm and, said.

"WAIT!"

She knew that was very important because of the way he grabbed her and, she responded with a surprised look on her face. His face was showing no don't go and, she said.

"What is it Maximilian?"

He with the realization that he responded so, quickly and, that he might have alarmed her too much and, then trying to look calm for her and, he said.

"Well, I thought that we might look together."

She relaxed as he released his tight grip and, thought that he might have overreacted but, that was way back in her mind.

He put his other hand on the underside of the ship to feel and, slowly released his other hand from her arm and, she said.

"I'd like to put you in my pocket."

There both feeling around now for any unusual object that would help get them inside of the space ship and, he said.

"That could be a title of a song."

The curiosity that she showed was helping her with the situation they were in and, said.

"I'll have to look into that."

They looked at each other and, laughed a little.

"Amyl ion you just created the hook to a song's beginning."

There still feeling around thinking what was just said between themselves when they heard a hissing sound and, stopped to listen and, she said.

"Where is that coming from?"

They turn around and, with shock and, awe … there was the biggest snake in the world slowly approaching with its head just a little off the ocean floor and, it too had rings of black and blue just like the other sharks. A poisonous one of course by the shape of the nose and, eyes. The tongue was darting in and, out and, sensing the situation with the head coming up and, it must have been 15 feet from the tip of its nose to the top of its head. He slowly wrapped his hand around her arm and, pulled her behind him. The giant snake was still rising and, pulling its body in a position to strike if need be. The snake was thinking and, looked at one then the other like [What are you doing here]?

They were backing up and, had to crouch very low to get on the other side of the ship. The legs of the ship had sunk in the ocean floor to the point where they had to crouch and, they knew instinctively that the giant snake couldn't follow. While they were moving backwards, she bumped her head on a rounded object and, slowly looked up and, tapped her hand on his shoulder. He looked at her and, she was looking at the bubble coming out of the ship's hull. They look and, see that there are 5 indentations on the bubble with arrows pointing in the direction to turn and, he said.

"I'll watch the snake as you place all 5 fingers in the slots and, push … then turn it in the arrow's direction."

She places her fingers in the slots and, begins to turn it but, it wouldn't go and, she turned harder and, harder until she was giving it all she had with a long grunt and, it finally worked. The hatch from the bottom of the ship slowly opened up with just enough space for them to crawl into.

He mumbled to her with caution as they watch the snake and, he said.

"Stay behind me and, let's start moving towards the side of the steps and, please don't make any sudden movements. When you get to the side of the steps, I'll hide you and, you crawl up inside and, go very slowly and, look for anything that might look like a handle, button or switch to pull the steps up."

The snake is beginning to lower itself to get a better view of what's going on.

He is waiting and, anticipating when she will say or, do anything so, he puts his arm on the steps and, uses hand gestures as to say well how's it going. He even uses a tapping sound like using 4 fingers in a rolling fashion to say I'm waiting. Eventually he turns his head just enough to see the bottom of the floor of the ship. She is looking at him with her lying on the floor facing him 5 feet away with her hands saying I don't know. He winks at her and, nods his head to say Okay. He slowly backs up watching the snake and, the snake is moving side to side surveying the situation but, can't crawl under. He is thinking if I make a mad dash now the snake will try to come in as fast as it can and, move the soft ocean bottom away. Then he realizes the opening is too small for its head to fit to get inside, so, he slowly starts to crawl up the steps and, moves his eyes to take a quick look and, sees what he has to do and, looks back at the snake but, it had already gone. He goes up the steps as fast as he can to look for her and, goes to her side as there both looking now to find that button, handle or switch to pull up the steps.

The shark that had got itself stuck between 2 space ships had finally freed itself and, lurking around the steps and, the snake was crawling over the top of the ship. They were both stirring up the ocean floor now and, they saw the diagram of the steps and, reached for it at the same time it was another 5 fingered slot bubble you press and, turn. He was pressing and, turning while she was placing her hand on top of his hand to make sure it turned and, it did and, the hatch closed. Well, the 2 of them were so, excited that they got that done and, were bending forward with their hands on their knees and, breathing out with the sounds of relief at what had just happened and, came and, held each other until they knew they had to try to get the ship operational. If at all.

The first thing he was looking for was an oxygen release valve to put pressure in the compartment if that is how the aliens did it. Pushing out the ocean water. They would press this or, that or, turn this or, that until she saw this blue dimmer of a light on a panel, the size of her finger and, said.

"Hey look at this."

He looks and, under his breath he said.

"There is energy in this ship."

Their faces are showing an elevated response that things are going well ... so, far and, she said.

"Well, what are we going to do?"

"Well God hasn't brought us this far for nothing."

Then they said as if a great idea had just come to them and, they said.

"It's the next step at releasing the oxygen and, it's telling us what to do."

They look at each other and, she said.

"Maximilian you press it."

He brings up his wife's hand.

"[May I have your hand in marriage?]"

"Yes, you May."

With that he placed his index finger over his bride's index finger and, moved them close to the blue glow on the panel.

By now the snake was moving over head on the ship by the sounds of it and, pushing the legs deeper in the ocean's soft floor.

They finally touched the blue glow and, you could hear the sound of air as it was rushing out of the ceiling. They put their hands over their ears because the pressure was building up. They had to wait and, wait and, watched the last portion of water disappear in several holes in the floor and, immediately the holes closed up. They look at each other and, it must have been an eternity it seemed and, he said.

"Where is that Green Froggy at now?"

She was quick to respond and, gave a smile and, said.

"[Squeaky-Squeak]"

CHAPTER 9

There laughing and, releasing that tension that had built up and, start walking towards each other rather hurriedly and, bang into each other and, hug the hug of hugs with the side of her head on his chest. There arms are going up and, down the backs of one another.

Pause ... Their inner feelings were expressing the bond that they have for one another. At some time, they have to release and, try to get the ship operational. Finally, they come apart and, she removes her head from his chest but, ... no not yet. Then their hands grab the backs of their heads and, SMASH a KISS one more time of great happiness and, exhilaration.

Meanwhile back outside the snake was wrapping itself around the ship from the topside edge to the bottom side edge. The sharks were circling around the snake and, keeping their distance knowing that it was poisonous and, the sharks were poisonous as well because of the black and, blue rings they have. The snake was tightening its grip and, darting it's head back and, forth at the sharks as if to say' [Don't get to close].

AHH ... here we go there talking now about a reserved power in the ship but, there in a small entry part of the ship. They look at the door that must be the main part of the ship so, they open the door and, to their surprise he said.

"HAA this is just like [27-Trips] with 3 Captain's chairs."

She looks at everything and, said.

"Maximilian the cabin is all clean."

"Yaw like a self-cleaning operating room ... what I mean is a command center."

He offers a Captain's chair to her and, they sit down and, collect their thoughts as they hold hands. They release and, swivel in their chairs and, look around and, he said.

"We have to get off the ocean floor."

She points her finger at something and, said.

"What does that do?"

He thinks of his past experience and, said.

"Well, these ships are pretty much universally the same let's get up and, take a closer look he glances at her with a curious look and, a pause and, said.

"Tell me more about your descent from the heavens and, your conversations with God."

She turned sideways looked down and, leaned against the bridge and, touched her chin then looked at him and, said.

"Well one question I ask was where did you come from … then God said that you are of the blood line of Japheth.

They pause and, think … and, both start to speak at the same time and, both said.

"Well, you go first."

He was curious about this and, couldn't believe it as they sat down, and, he said.

"Please you go first I want to hear about this Japheth person?"

She's delighted to tell him and, said.

"Well … Noah had 3 Son's, Japheth, Ham, and, Shem when they landed on Mount Ararat."

"Was Japheth married?"

He already knew that but, he wanted to hear her talk and, enjoyed their conversation about what God told her.

"Yes, to Adataneses and, their descendants spread north on the continent of Europe."

"WOW! You've got a good memory"

She was enjoying the heck out of this because of their unusual marriage and, knew they were very blessed and, she said.

"So, God has planned you and, I to go to earth 2 at the 12 valleys of the 99 hills, and, be the King and, Queen and, start a family there and, I'm so, excited to get started!"

He curled up his bottom lip and, nodded his head up and, down and, he said.

"Yaw that's pretty much it we don't know all his plans but, you are made by God and, not born. God could have put either one of the other descendants with you and, I'll tell you this right here and, now that I am going to do everything I can to love you with all of my heart."

They pause and, ponder and, she said.

"Let's get the hell out of here!!!"

They jump up and, start looking at the language of things and, diagrams and, images. There talking to one another while searching and, searching. They come to figure things out and, stop and, look at each other and, he said.

"This little gadget goes first."

Then she moves it and, a voice comes on but, they couldn't make out the language and, she said.

"This ship has a voice command like [27-Trips], look for a list of languages or better yet say [ENGLISH PLEASE]!?"

She blurted that out but, no answer.

There talking over one another again and, stop and, he said.

"There is no translation and, obviously it said that with what we did was not the correct procedure and, that it knows what steps we should take to get the hell out of here."

They have a belly laugh and, she said.

"So, if we do the right step, it will say a different word."

"Right."

She presses a red button which to their surprise shocks the snake with an electrical charge and, it slides off the top of the ship with a screech they could just barely hear. It landed on the ocean floor stunned but, trying to collect its thought's and, they've figured out a way to get off of the bottom of the ocean. A control knob set up for only getting off the ocean floor and, out of the water and, once there cleared of the water there's a main control next to it but, they wanted to see where that snake was and, searched for the viewer control. They finally find it and, they looked under and, on top and, there the snake was laying on top of a ship next to them and, he said.

"Once we get cleared of that snake and, get out of this ocean, we can set course for our new home."

They braced themselves to blast off so, they sat in the captain's chairs and, he sets the control knob and, take off but, the snake followed and, wiggled right behind the ship staying in its draft. They watched in the viewers that showed all around the ship and, the sharks were trying to stop the ship as well by getting in front of it to block it. There were massive amounts now and, couldn't blast off like they wanted to. The snake was still trailing behind and, at this point beginning to open its mouth a little and, getting closer as if to stop it from leaving the ocean.

They were waiting to clear the ocean and, the ship was humming now keeping up the speed that was set before launch. The sharks were all in front and, the ship was beginning to vibrate. They're waiting for the ship to clear water and, watching the viewers with the ship not letting up even though pushing all those sharks out of the way. The snake was getting closer and, opening its mouth a little larger and, they can see the dawning of the light at the ocean's top. There watching the viewers and, the sharks and, snake with everything that's coming to its final conclusion and, the day light is approaching and, splash, whoosh goes the ship right out of the water carrying and, pushing dozens of sharks with it and, they think that there free but, the snake comes right out of water with them cause it finally caught up to the ship and, that big mouth is about to catch the edge of the ship and, they hold their breath to see the insides of that big mouth in the viewer and, it catches hold, driving the fangs in the ship and, jolts and, shakes the ship. They're ejected out of their Captain's chairs with that big bite and, the ship carries the snake a small distance until the weight of the snake was almost too much for it. They landed on the floor and, apart from each other. The ship is pointing straight up and, the snake is just three quarters out of the water. By the looks of this it is a stale mate and, the ship is still thrusting. He is holding on to the bottom of one of the chairs next to the bridge and, she is just below his feet hanging on to a pipe that came through the floor. The alarm has gone off and, smoke or, steam is gushing out here and, there. It's a real scary scene and, the room turns an emergency blue and, flashing white lights. He looks down at her and, she looks up to him and, she's scared half to death. Some moments pass by looking around and, at each other and, he loudly said.

"The electrical charge Amyl ion on the bridge there above me I can't let go so, climb over me and, hit the electrical charge and, that will get rid of the snake."

She was dangling in the air with her feet swinging around as the ship is swaying a little and, pointing skyward. She is switching onto another pipe coming out of the floor that had emerged slowly that is closer to his feet and, she cried out.

"Maximilian help me … Oh, do something!!!"

"Take a couple of deep breaths and, relax and, think what we got to do."

She takes a couple of deep breaths then rolling her eyes and, thinking inside what she said and, was that necessary and, said.

"Okay I'm ready."

"Good, grab that pipe that just came out and, climb over me and, hit the electrical charge button."

She starts to grab his shoes then the ankles and, pulls herself up his pant legs left hand then right. She grunts with each hand and, gritting her teeth he smiles a little and, he said.

"[COME ON YOU CAN DO IT]!"

She musters up what she can and, grabs his belt and, takes a couple of well-deserved deep breaths. She grabbed his mid-section and, shimmied up to the top of his uniform with her arms and, legs. She gave a congratulatory smile for herself with a breath of satisfaction. He watches her as she takes one leg after another and, puts it on his hips and, now she can push and, pull herself up better then reaches to his ear and, said.

"God hasn't brought us this far for nothing."

She gives him a kiss on his cheek and, exhales with a lunge for the button on the bridge and, taps it which shocks the snake right off. The ship is free and, goes through the clouds and, starts to level off and, they hold one another on the floor. They put their fore heads together and, gave a sigh of relief as they were clutching each other's head and, neck when their eyes slowly began to close.

At that very same moment the fog clears away in the hibernation chamber and, the oxygen pours in. Then start opening their eyes and, their back on the [27-Trips] in the hibernation bed where originally, they went to sleep. She looks around and, the glass covering slips away. She looks at her husbands' arms that are still around her slides her right hand on his right arm to feel it and, she turns a 180 and, he's just coming around too. They look at each other and, hear the familiar sounds of the ship. They look around and, talking to each other how it all was a dream. Well, slowly they begin to laugh and, catharsis take time for the cobwebs clear up.

He asks Samantha, as he scratches his head and, tries to shake his dizziness as he sits up and, she stays lying down and, shakes her head a little too and, she said.

"Where are we?"

He thought I hope we're at our destination and, Samantha said.

"We are nearing Earth's 2 Atmosphere."

She looked at him with a pleasing face and, he said.

"WOW, that's great … Okay then when we reach 219 miles from the planet give the ship a cruising speed of 20,000 MPH around Earth 2."

"AYE, AYE Captain."

He was excited and, expressed to her his feelings rubbing his hands together and, he said.

"Well, My Love, we are here and, that ought to give us enough time for us to get things in order."

They climb out of the hibernation bed and, stand facing each other to stretch and, yawn and, she said.

"I'm hungry what have we got to eat?"

His stomach growled at the thought and, they laugh and, he said.

"Oh, I know what you mean."

He starts doing some push-ups on the floor and, she takes to noticing that with her head bobbing up and, down. She's thinking HHMMM now that's a good idea and, gets next to him and, starts following his and, she said.

"I can feel my heart pumping."

They do 12, 10, and, 8 push-ups with 30, seconds of rest in between. They face each other lean their head on their palms. These two just cannot be apart from each other because she reaches out to him and, they wrap themselves together and, he is on top but, just his top part and, she has her leg around him and, he's kissing her cheek and, gets to her ear and, talks to her but, I can't make it out.

He has his hand under her head and, the other on her belly. She is giggling and, he starts to laugh and, this goes on for a while.

Well, don't they know that they have to get going and, the people are waiting for their arrival.

She has her hand in his hair and, she must love it and, he stops and, kiss's her cheek again then he said.

"I Love You, very, very, very much and, I'm crazy for you."

Then goes for her lips. She presses hard and, places his hand on her breast and, squeezes to her delight and, she starts to have a slight spasm. He was going to release the kiss so, she could have freedom to breath but, breathed in through her noise and, took that deep breath and, held him firm on that beautiful kiss that helped her along that kissing journey. Her stomach is rolling and, after she had her trip, he knows when to release that kiss because he understood her. She is blinking her eyes and, smiling which turns into a happy laughter of sorts. She is thinking WOW just through a kiss and, pressure on my breast I can have this happen. He thought to himself God made her and, this is the most incredible thing and, I love given her pleasure. She's smiling rolling her head from side to side and, back at him and, said.

CHAPTER 10

"WHOA that was wonderful."

He's smiling gets up and, puts out his hand she quickly takes it. They hug when on their feet and, catches her breath a little.

He steps away and, places his hands on her shoulders then on his hips and, his face said watch this and, starts doing leg squats and, she raises her arms out and, gave a look that said okay then jumps right in and, follows along. They do 12, 10, and, 8 squats with 30 seconds of rest in between. He observes her and, loves taken care of her and, someday she'll be self-sufficient. In the future they'll build a large exercise room to work-out in and, he said.

"Samantha prepare us some scrambled eggs, red peppers, bacon, strawberries, blueberries, with a vitamin, and, mineral drinks please."

Well, they clean up the mess hall table while sipping on their drinks then sit back down looking at each other [slurp, slurp] and, both said.

"Thank you, Samantha."

"You're Welcome. Captains I have the information you ask for about the intruder."

He conveyed a look that meant you answer with a smile and, she said.

"Go Ahead and, put it on the viewers and, tell us what you have please."

"Her name is Major Sasha Sokolov serving under Colonel Dominic Roku. She is of multiracial descent of Scandinavian, African, Hispanic and, Asian. The Major was picked up at the red cross ship by the Colonel and, the pod in which the Major was jettisoned in is now back and, in possession of the [27-Trips] again before we left. The non-detection shield blocked them from finding our location. They met up with Raven Hades, and, by all indications and, sources I can gather there heading this way. There is more information about her at the bridge."

[A side note] Satan can possess Raven Hades body at will to do evil deeds and, leave his body with raven still having some wicked powers.

Max began to worry and, one thought was. What a gathering of danger we are in for and, he said.

"Samantha what do you have on this Raven Hades?"

"Only that he picked up Dominic and, Sasha at the Olympic Stadium, and, the meeting that they all shared, and, the attack on you two that failed with the intrusion on the ship. There is nothing more that I can pick up."

"Very Good Samantha."

They sip some more coffee [and, there joyful thoughts of arriving have slipped away and, he said.

"Well for one thing Dominic has a vendetta and, number two that it appears there is more involved in this and, three there on their way here."

She sets her cup down and, clears her throat and, grabs his big hands and, rubs them and, she said.

"There trying to stop us from reaching Earth 2 cause look at our dream and, the attempt on Earth 1 to kill us."

"Yaw your right and, the devil can get into our dreams ... how amazing."

She fussed with her hair and, looked at him with beautiful hazel eyes, wings, eyelashes, eyebrows, shapely lips and, she said.

"There probably planning another attack on the planet when we land and, most likely try to hit us here in orbit." He had to break the spell she cast on him then to protect her and, he said.

"Right ... Samantha launch the latest sonar and, search as far out as you can and, set up the most recent reflector shields. Then let us know when it's set up?"

"AYE, AYE Captain."

"The President was so, kind to let me upgrade the ship because he knew I was going to Earth 2, and, that I had a good premonition and, Oh, ... the new lasers ... but, no one is supposed to know."

"I'm glad you told me."

"Captain you should know everything about the ship and, ask anything at any time or, you can look at the list at the bridge."

He gets up and, she grabs his arm when they get around the edge of the table and, wraps it around his. She gives him a kiss on the cheek. They clique coffee cups take a drink with eyes glued to each other and, her with that gorgeous smile she said.

"Thank You Captain."

He takes her to the place where all the information can be seen and, utilized, at the bridge with all the explaining he can do in a reasonable amount of time and, he said.

"May I ask you what other thing did God say on your descent from the heavens?"

Sweetly came her answer with a voice so, loving, kind and, she said.

"Why Maximilian you can ask me anything and, I'm so, glad you asked me for another one cause our bodies belong to one another. Well ... that is my body is for you to enjoy and, that your body belongs to me too."

"That's right because that's what the word said."

Samantha breaks in and, said.

"Captains the new reflector are operational."

Meanwhile we get a glimpse into Raven, Dominic and, Sasha's meeting and, Raven said.

"I want you Colonel and, Major to kill Maximilian and, this wife of his. They must not be able to fulfill their destiny."

The place on his Raven Hades ship has a large dark room that's eerie. Flames with dark red, blue and, yellow all around that you can hear Zombies walking to and, from one place to another and, acting like there miserable souls and, bumping into each other and, snarling and, growling. Then there is the monster's and, the creatures with wings behind his throne but, Dominic and, Sasha aren't paying any attention and, by the look on their faces there scared to be sure. He is in a sharp suit that's black with red lapels and, an orange shirt with a blue tie that fits just for that time of era. He has dark red skin with slicked backed curly black hair. His eyes are black and, his face is sculptured or, chiseled like a demon with a long nose and, goatee with a devilish smile. He has a neckless with a medallion on it that has a symbol of death of skull, crossbones with a burning flame of hell that's actually burning and, he said.

"I must have Earth 2 and, you two will rule the people as I give out the plans to fulfill my plans."

Dominic and, Sasha said.

"As you wish."

Then they put their fists over their chest as a salute.

Meanwhile back to our Captains. After they review the new upgrades, she said.

"Baby, how did you acquire these weapons and, new technology?"

He smiles and, thinks to himself HHMMM, I really liked that when she said, Baby. He feels that it came deep within herself and, not just a flippant expression with it going right inside and, sticking and, he said.

"My dad and, mom served in the space force alongside a man and, woman that's the President of the United States and, the First Lady. They knew each other so, well that they could trust one another."

She is listening with keenness and, she wants to learn all that she can and, she is like a sponge and, he said.

"Well, it's kind a hard to explain."

"I think I understand Max the bond of spirit and, mind even though there not blood related."

She gets closer to her husband and, looks up at him and, said.

"Baby ... not to take away anything from your dad and, mom but, I think of what happened back on Earth 1 is probably one of the most incredible miracles there is and, that it's of you and, me."

She reaches behind her husband with her hands and, places them where the 2 short ribs were taken by God to make her and, she said.

"[Bones of my Bones and, Flesh of my Flesh], we have a bond of Spirit, Mind, Soul and, whatever else we can think of."

He thought that was an incredible statement and, he said.

"I believe an invisible cord is attached to us that only our God can see."

She stood on her toes and, softly said.

"Kiss me."

"With the utmost pleasure my Sweetheart."

They kissed until they were satisfied and, he said.

"Let's sit in the captain's chairs and, do you want to do a Captains Log?"

She thinks for a moment and, said.

"I'd like that very much."

He looks at her and, there's a kind of quizzical expression on her face and, smiles and, she said.

"Maximilian could you explain a little how it goes?"

"Just make a list in your head of the highlights of what happened sense your beginning's that is, your creation and, our highlights until now." She brightened up with excitement and, said.

"Can I mention our dream?"

"Yaw sure Sweetheart but, before you begin tell me more of your conversations with God on your descent from the heavens."

"When we meet the people on Earth 2, we tell them about the inscription on the stone wall next to the ring of fire that burns continually until The Black Rose is thrown into it which they already know about and, the land will be restored like a wave of Gods hand. Then they will believe that we were sent by God to be the King and, Queen and, that their prayers are answered."

With an intriguing look smile on his face, he said.

"Really! ... God told you that?" she rubbed her right hand across her forehead then pointed her index finger up and, she said.

"Oh, by the way we have to toss the Black Rose in the ring of fire at the same time."

She smiled that she remembered it and, placed her hand down and, he said.

"Why that is incredible and, it's like a fantastic story that you and, I will be living right through it and, making history."

She smiles and, the expression on her face is of joy, peace and, they sit in their chairs. She puts her hands together and, relaxes and, looks at him and, she's so, happy.

There is a pause ... Max said.

"There is a date indicator on the wall, just say the date before the Captains Log, and, the voice recorder will pick it up."

She gathered the information and, said.

"Captains Log September 14th, 2228 Sunday. Jewish History month. Amyl ion, Abara, Abebe. Created October, 26th, 2227 Friday. The captain and, myself survived an attack by progressives to destruction with anarchists. Then I was made Captain, we dreamed that our lives are in danger, we time traveled to Earth 2 to search for The Black Rose ... STOP."

His smile grew and, moving his head left and, right a little bit thinking what a bold, and, powerful, name and, he said.

"That's a beautiful name God gave you."

"Oh, Maximilian it's incredible. What with all that's happened our future together. I like it very much and, guess what? I like you very much. What is your complete name Maximilian?"

"Maximilian, Mathieu, Milan, the 3rd. I really enjoy being with you and, I like you very much."

She smiles that would stop all wars, drops her right hand, with palm up. He reaches for it turns it over and, kisses it then gets up to pick her up from the captain's chair and, takes her to the bedroom. She has that look of you can do whatever you want with me and, I am all yours. Their looking at one another and, she is getting an intoxicated glow and, starts melting in his arms. He takes his sweet time gazing at her. Her pupils spread to turn the iris into a Black Rose and, see's the edges of the Rose Pedals in the left eye were green and, the right eye edges of the Black Rose are red and, knew all too well his wife was drawing him in with her magic eyes and, she could only do that to him because of their blood connections. He read her like the true woman she is and, made just for him and, he said.

"[If you could be in front of my eyes]."

"Hurry Maximilian I'm about to explode, then take your time, I won't withhold."

The bedroom has purple walls a dark red floor green bed and, white pillows.

He takes her to the edge of the bed and, sets her down and, starts to take her uniform off. She proceeds to lie on the bed with a pleasurable expression. She watches him undress as she fluffs her hair to look good for him. He crawls from the edge of the bed and, she reaches for his erection and, places him where she's at fast idle. They start to kiss and, he turns towards her cheek as he's kissing all the way to her ear with whispers.

I can't make it out but, maybe Samantha did and, I hope I'm there when they review their whispers in the future.

He's slowly entering her she groans and, takes a deep breath arches her back and, starts to roll and, convulse.

He gets on his hands and, straitens his arms as he watches her go through an expression of satisfaction inside and, waits for her to subside, and, said.

"Hi welcome back."

"HHIIEEE its fantastic to be here and, it hurts Oh, so, good."

He wanted to ask her about the stone wall around the ring of fire and, the inscription but, waited awhile. Finally, after she had several more expressed satisfactions, he asks her softly and, sweetly and, said.

"The inscription on the stone wall, what does it say?"

"God told me this many times so, I wouldn't forget, it said.

"[Seek, Seek the chosen hand, it's in a Descendants land, Seek, Seek Japheth's hand, into her hair facing you she stands, See the Black Rose in her eyes, draw out now and be Wise]."

She placed her fingers in his hair playing with it and, then she closed her eyes and, took a deep breath and, slipped into another dark explosion.

CHAPTER 11

Nothing more is known sense they were whispering in between the times that she was having her distinguished shock wave. He finally has his as they scream together. It's one of her most intense ones because he's fast and, furious and, some day in the near future he will plant the seed that will fertilize her egg and, produce a boy the coming Prince.

God knows when the time will be right.

They get up from the bed and, he said.

"Amyl ion yaw know, it's just amazing that you and, I, well we get to do this whole thing. The trip we had and, our future because I am so charged."

He takes her by the hands and, pulls her into the shower the door closes and, there talking away. They soap up scrub each other and, rinse off the blower dries them off and, they step out of the shower and, slip on their uniforms and, face each other next to a counter and, she said.

"Wow, yaw we have been in hibernation for 10 months and, 19 days, because I saw that doing the Captain's Log."

He wanted to take her back to earth 1 that she never experienced. So, many places to enjoy for a good time and, he said.

"Someday we'll go back." She grabbed a brush on the counter combed her thick hair [swoosh, swoosh] it went as she turned her head to get it all as she thought and, said.

"Or, sometime."

They laugh he winks and, she throws a kiss he catches it on his chin as he moves his head.

She takes him by the hand.

"Max lets go and, sit in the captain's chairs."

"That's the first time you called me Max."

"That's alright, isn't it?"

The Green Froggy was between them and, she didn't notice it because she is so, focused on her husband or, sometimes not on the surroundings. He touches the Froggy twice [Squeaky-squeak] it goes. That meant that it was okay and, she said.

"When did you put the Froggy there?"

"When you were in the restroom for a while."

She swings from a playful mode to a serious one and, said.

"We must take Froggy with us wherever we go. Samantha show us images of the planet of the wild life, people and, is there any detection of Raven, Dominic, and Sasha?"

Samantha brings up images on the viewer and, they are shocked at what they see. There talking back and, forth. The one-half side of the planet must have had a 100 or, so, of volcanoes sort of in a row that are actively flowing out lava with smoke and, ash reaching only a certain height and, then carried along towards the ocean. A dozen or, so, are dormant with the continent in the center of two oceans. There was some lush vegetation and, could be habitable in a couple of places and, he said.

"That lush vegetation there in the center of the continent we're going to have to visit it to see what it's like and, map this planet."

She was all intrigued with this and, her mind is filled with curiosity and, she said.

"Samantha, could we have a couple of tasty fruity drinks with protein please I got to have something comforting."

"Thanks, Amyl ion that was a good idea."

"Samantha how much time would it take to check out the other side? and, what about Raven, Dominic and, Sasha?"

They look at each other and, shrug their shoulders and, smile cause there waiting for any information on those 3 people and, the other side of the planet.

Samantha said.

"I could increase the speed of the ship until we reach the point where the ship is able to pull in the images and, proceed to cruising speed."

Max was familiar with the ship and, said.

"Very well then."

Mechanical hands and, long arms bring down the drinks from the ceiling. They grab them and, the hands zip back up and, she said.

"Thanks for the drinks Samantha."

"Captains, Raven Hades, Dominic and, Sasha have come into the detection field from their ship."

Max took a sip [slurp] and, said.

"Are they able to pick us up yet?"

"No captain."

Amyl ion is learning about this terrific ship and, she said.

"How come we are able to pick them up but, they can't pick us up?"

Max was pleased with her analytical probe and, said.

"We were given advanced equipment from the President."

She rubbed her forehead with the fingers and, thumb of her right hand and, said.

"When will their equipment be able to detect our location?"

Still pleased with her probe Max said.

Samantha interrupted when the information arrived and, said.

"In 7.2 minutes."

Max jumped to the immediate concern and, said.

"Samantha, we have to find those 12 Valleys that are nestled in those 99 hills as soon as possible please."

"AYE, AYE Captain."

Finally, out of all the viewers one pops up and, shows a Griffin Monster flying down and, landing on a zebra carcass. They're sipping on the drinks [slurp, slurp] lunge forward and, spray out a portion of their drinks onto the floor. It was immediately cleaned up by the automatic floor cleaner with arms, hands with towels that moved very quickly. They're mouths are open Max spoke first and, she said.

"What in the world is that?"

"Where did that come from?"

They jumped up from their chairs and, got a closer look with their mouths still open and, staring at each other wrapping arms around themselves and, Samantha said.

"I found it, the 12 valleys."

Then the 12 valleys appeared, on the viewers 1 at a time popping up, they look at them very quickly and, he said.

"Samantha, can you find an entry for the ship on the side of a mountain close by one of the 12 valleys, a cave I mean to hide the ship in."

Amyl ion with a surprised look on her face said.

"Oh, you're going to hide the ship in a cave?"

Max with a serious look said.

"It's the only thing I can do under the circumstances. Captain what are your thoughts?"

She didn't have time to respond when Samantha said.

"Six minutes to detection and, there is a cave nearby but not big enough for the ship."

She grabs a hold of this situation and, said.

"Can we get to the location as fast as you can and, when you do, I want you to blast the back of the cave out so, the ship will fit in please."

The ships sounds were of a humming and, propulsion and, Samantha said.

"Hang on."

They quickly jump back in their chairs and, the ship takes off to the location and, he smiles with satisfaction … because he is very pleased with his partner and, said.

"Very good Captain."

She is beaming that he complemented her on the decision she made and, he said.

"Samantha when you're inside the cave melt the ceiling so it doesn't come down on the ship and, use the non-detection shield and, close the front opening with rocks or melt the rocks but, leave a small opening for myself and, Captain Amyl ion to squeeze through please?"

"AYE, AYE Captains."

The townspeople saw a saucer shaped object come down from the sky but, couldn't tell what it was and, ran into the valley to tell the Senior Officials and, Mayor what they saw. When they were telling them they stopped and, listened and, heard the rumbling of the mountain. That was the sound of the ship digging itself in. There for a moment the doubting Senior Officials facial expressions changed and, decided to take a look at this phenomenon.

There finally in the cave and, its sealed up except for a small opening that they can go out and, in with and, Samantha said.

"5 minutes to detection and, with the shield up in the cave Raven Hades ship will not detect us."

Meanwhile back on Raven's ship he speculated on what to do and, he said.

"I have Creatures that will stop them from being King and, Queen on this planet and, I'm going to set them free."

Raven found a landing spot just north of [27-Trips] about 13 miles. He knew the planet well since he planted creatures of all sorts there. Stepping off the ship he summoned 2 of the Griffin Monsters and, in a couple of minutes they landed by him. They looked very majestic with their lion's hind legs and, tail, brown wings with black feather tips. Large eagle talons, neck with green feathers, ears that pointed backwards, golden eyes with green iris's, black beak with yellow tip and, he said.

"Find the 2 that is called Maximilian and, Amyl ion and, kill them they will be wearing silver uniforms."

They flew away Squealing and Squawking.

Raven also called his Dragon as it's going to be a full moon the next night and, release it. Raven stands quietly looks into the sky. He knew he could communicate to Draco anywhere on the planet and, said.

"Draco Occidentalis Magnus …"

In a cave close to the captains Draco's eyes opened and, knew there was an assignment from Raven. Draco took a little air in his nose and, breathed out through his mouth with a grumble that could be heard throughout the cave and, outside the entrance. The birds in the trees nearby the entrance of the cave flew away but, not the black crows and, ravens. There Squawking to one another, a meal is coming up and, they were waiting for some easy pickings. There were several piles of bones and, skulls of many assorted animals like cattle longhorns, horses' heads, and, human skulls, the birds had almost picked them clean.

Meanwhile back in the [27-Trips] they were looking at the viewers and, she noticed a Pride of Lions gathered around a shady area and, the trees looked rather small and, she said.

"Maximilian UMM, hay … look at this."

They look at each other he sees her puzzled expression and, thinks this looks pretty odd. Turning to the viewer again they study the area and, he said.

"Everything looks smaller around the Lions."

He can hardly believe his eyes scratches his head and, glanced at one another. In their thoughts, they're thinking is that large Lions and, she said.

"Samantha, can you get a measurement on the height of these lions?"

"Several are standing and, the averages are 6' 2" Tall to 6' 7" for the Males and, 5' 11" Tall to 6' 1 for the females from the ground to the top of their shoulders."

"WOW! this is incredible."

He looked at her with a look of new discovery on his face. She smiled back with her mouth popping open and, in disbelief gave out a short breath of air and, said. "[Huh] can you believe this? WOW."

They sit down in their Captain's chairs and, kind of laughing and, glancing around the other viewers and, looking at one another with a stunned look on their faces and, they are both talking to each other but, it's hard to understand what they're saying with their overlapping conversations that goes on for almost a minute and, Samantha said.

"Captain's I have something of interest. I just picked up a pride of Lions that has walked through a village or, it may be their normal path as the Pride travels across it. More observation is needed."

The viewer picks up the Pride and, there's many citizens putting their hands on them as they pass by, or some don't pay any attention like it's just another day. A child happens to dismount and, then went on her way into the store. The female Lion acknowledged the dismount by turning her head to look at the child and, kept walking and, the child said.

"Thank You Apple blossom see you next week."

The lion nods her head in return.

He puts his hands through his hair and, combs it back and, blurts out an old expression.

"[HUH ... BY GEORGE! there tame my sweet lovely wife]."

She is softly laughing at her husband and, very amused at watching him with this discovery. There waiting for the next viewer to show something. She gets up from the captain's chair and, starts slowly to sit in his lap and, he reached to settle her down. She put her left arm around him and, waiting for the next visual on any screen and, he said.

"I've got to meet these Lions and, your invited." She smiles bounces a little raises her lower legs and, places a beautiful [smack] on his right cheek and, said.

"I thought you would never ask."

She watched as he leaned at her right hand, she gave it to him to kiss. With such care it went [smack]. She responded in kind with grabbing the side of his head and, kissing his cheek several times and, they smile with satisfaction.

CHAPTER 12

Meanwhile the village Senior Officials from several valleys had gathered together and, was going to search out this sighting. They left in their horse and, buggy transportation with a few of them that had the bigger wagons at four horses a piece and, they have a long way to go in the development stages in society but, then again maybe it isn't so bad it depends on how you look at things.

[Personally, I would really, really, really be in Maximilian's shoes but, I must confess anywhere with Amyl ion].

The viewer comes up with another picture of Raven standing outside his ship and, she said.

"Raven Hades can't locate us here now and, we have time to try and, meet the people and, Samantha where is the nearest location of the people?"

"There heading in this direction with an ETA of 45 minutes."

She was disappointed at the speed and, said.

"Why so long Samantha?"

"Horse and, wagon 3-to-5 miles an hour when loaded."

Both wanted to leave and, she said.

"Do you want to go outside Maximilian?"

His face was troubled and, said.

"As long as we have our laser guns you never know what we're going up against."

They go to the storage area and, he grabs a couple of portable viewers and, gives one to her and, they put it in their back pockets.

He was thinking to himself that he must look out for his wife and, couldn't bear the thought of anything happening to her as they were putting on their holsters with the laser guns with one on each hip. They look at one another there both thinking that now were getting down to business as they can see it in their eyes.

They look at the viewer that shows the inside of the cave and, also see that its clear outside and, they see the exit and, he said.

"Samantha lower the hatch please."

They walk down survey the ship and, cave then walk to the exit and, walk outside about 15 or, 20 feet. They take a deep breath and, they can tell the difference in the air and, they HUMM and, she said.

"Hey you can actually taste it."

"YAA, like its enhanced oxygen and, when we get back on board let's do some research on that."

She is on his left and, they look at the land with the surrounding area with its rocks and, boulders of various sizes from large to small and, the hills with its high chaparral brush, sycamore, and, oak trees. He pointed out how burnt it was in patches and, some areas were still green and, he said.

"That seems odd and, look way over there it looks like what use to be a ranch."

She takes a couple steps to look and, said.

"Yaw, it's all burnt down to the ground."

[Out of the blue as I write I got a déjà vu]!

Two Griffin Monsters appears over the mountain top and, one surprise's them but, the other one stayed on the edge of a rocky peak watching the attack. The Griffin comes between them from above and, there to far apart for the Griffin to do any damage with those deadly talons or, the ripping beak but, manages to knock them down on the ground with its big wings as it flew down upon them. She landed on her left shoulder cut the uniform and, her skin was cut open a little on some sharp rocks. However, the Griffins claws were able to just reach the guns on their hips on the inside of one another and, knock them away from them and, now they were out of reach but, they had 2 left and, they reached for them as the Griffin Monster was turning around and, facing them on the ground and, coming right at Amyl ion. She raised her gun and, fired but, the Griffin Monster just absorbed it and, it took a step back but, she kept firing and, firing and, each time it would just take a step back. He was watching this and, thought our guns are on stun and, looked at his gun and, adjusted the capacity to kill and, hollered as he was waving his hands and, said.

"Hey Ugly Over Here … YA-YA, that's right … look at me not at her."

The Griffin Monster took notice of him, with a squawk from the Griffith as he was stepping in front of her to draw the attention away and, wanted it to focus on him and, it worked. It charged him and, started to fire repeatedly and, the Griffin Monster couldn't take that kill switch on the laser gun and, was rolling backwards. He kept firing at the chest area and, it was coming apart and, the blood splattering out with a hole showing right through it and, he thought that was enough and, it was dispatched. He turned to look at her and, still having his gun in his hand. She was already back on her feet and, observing very closely and, watched her walk past him. She too adjusted the capacity to kill on the gun and, he saw that she had a psychological response or, a little shock a little pale, with pupils dilated and, irregular breathing too. She was walking towards the Monster and, firing and, firing as it was flying in pieces. She stopped at the Monster still firing. He walked up next to her shielding his face from the flying pieces of it and, she was catching a few pieces of feathers flying on her. She turned her eyes a little and, noticed him standing there and, stopped firing and, brought her gun down to her side with the release of anxiety and, realizing it was over and, the Monster to her was dead and, in pieces. He put his laser away and, puts his left arm around her and, said nothing gently turning her around and, started to walk away. They take about 5 steps she turned around and, fired once more he too turned and, fired once more and, thought maybe that will bring her back from the state she's in and, looked to see a cut on her left shoulder.

I must say you never know what a person will do when your attacked by a Monster that is trying to kill you and, that we all hope that our instincts will take over … especially the ones like progressives, lying politician's, leftist, Marxist, socialists, anarchist's and, the list goes on.

They looked at one another and, she was sniffling a little and, wiping some tears away and, softly laughing at herself that she fired one more time at the Monster. That God's gift of pure blood instantly brought her back unlike a regular human and, she said.

"I must look like a mess."

Both start to giggle and, grew into some laughing, carrying on about the spattering of their uniforms and, he said.

"The thought never crossed my mind … and, as a matter of fact I love it when where in battle."

"Oh, Maximilian Thank You and, I do adore you and, your so, wonderful to me. … I think your right about that being in battle thing … because I feel the same way."

The music starts [Eddie Moneys-Think I'm in Love].

He was thinking she's Okay I don't have to worry about her with the color back in her face her eyes are normal with her breathing calmed down. They go back to pick up the two laser guns that the Griffin Monster knocked out of there holsters and, put back in. He pulls out a handkerchief from his back pocket and, gives it to her. He didn't notice it but, a piece of paper fell out as he gave the handkerchief to her but, oh, she saw it and, said.

"Hey Maximilian some paper came out from your back pocket." He's more concerned about her and, looks behind him and, said.

"There's a cut on your shoulder I'll have to look at it right away on the ship."

He picks it up she looks at her shoulder and, proceeds to put it back but, she is curious and, looks at him and, he thinks Oh, she wants to know what it is and, she said.

"What was that?"

"Oh, it's a poem I'm working on."

He thinks I will finish it and, say it to her at the right time. She thinks I bet that's for me I know it is because he is so, crazy about me as she looks at him. She's humbled puts her head down a little. She's done wiping tears away and, gives the handkerchief back and, she said.

"Captain could you please wipe that cut with the handkerchief for now please."

He finishes up and, then she takes the handkerchief and, starts to wipe the few pieces of flesh from the monster off his uniform and, some bloody spots on his face.

"Thanks, now let me wipe the pieces of feather off you and, you got a few spots on your face and, neck."

He proceeds to clean her up and, enjoys his touch while looking at the remains of the monster and, she said.

"WWOOWEE there is certainly nothing left of that thing."

He wipes her face from the handkerchief that's wet from her tears. She stands there and, offers her face and, she is turning her head and, he goes to her neck and, she lifts her head so, he can see better. They just forget everything and, they bond together with whatever it might be. He thinks what a beautiful woman as he cleans her. She thinks I love this man and, what can I do for him?

He's done at cleaning her up as best that could be done except for their blood stains on their uniform's and, puts the handkerchief in his back pocket and, she said.

"Captain how come the guns were on stun instead of kill?"

"YAW, well I was thinking about that too ... they automatically go back to stun as a safety precaution."

"Oh, WOWW we got to remember that one ... HUH Captain?"

The other Monster was still on the hill watching them with his evil beak and, eyes showing anger that it just lost a friend and, wants to get even.

They come together put their arms around each other look into their eyes laugh, smile and, breath out sighs of relief that this was over with and, he's concerned about her wellbeing and, he said.

"Let's sit on some nearby rocks I want to check our laser guns and, how you doing?"

"I'm doing pretty good ... YAW."

Then they heard the horse's hoofs and, wagons wheels and, decide to find a hiding place behind a big rock. They have just one laser gun out a piece. He pulls out a portable viewer from his pocket as there behind the rock and, watch them get closer and, about 20 paces they stop cause there the ones that saw the ship. The lead wagon with its two horses come to a halt after the man holding the reins said.

"[Whoa, Gladys, Whoa, Bess,]."

The wagons are about half a dozen or, so, stop and, the dust slowly cleared away.

One of the leaders said.

"Now men and, women just to let you know we mean them no harm but, that doesn't mean we can't protect ourselves we have seen this before but, nothing ever came from it and, remember we have our wives, and, some children with us."

The captains are peaking and, listening then start talking among themselves back and, fourth and, she said.

"I don't think they'll hurt us."

He nodded his head in agreement and, said.

"Their peaceful people and, when we stand up, we just say greetings friends."

She had her doubts and, said.

"YAA if we stand."

There's a pause … and, he said.

"I'll go first."

He slowly stands up takes a deep breath and, exhaled and, said.

"Greetings Friends."

He still has his laser gun in his hand but, it is shielded by the large rock. They all turn their heads with some straining to get a better look. They look at his uniform with puzzling expressions. Some of the children pop their heads out from among the adults. One of the Senior Official's looked at the Dead Griffin and, with a relieved smile looked back and, said.

"Did you kill that monster?"

"Yes, we did my wife and, I."

He was trying to coax her to stand up with his other hand she played with his fingers and, finally, she stands.

Somebody in one of the wagons at the back said.

"Well look at that."

Someone else said.

"Their man and, woman and, by the looks of it they had a little rumble, tumble with that their Monster and, I declare them as our friends, you can rest assure of that Mayor."

There standing together and, smiling at everyone trying to present themselves as friendly.

One of the boys looks up to his parents and, said.

"She's pretty."

The father doesn't say anything but, the mother does and, she said.

"Yes, she is … well son they're both a good-looking couple."

She smiles at the boy and, most all of them said.

"[Yep, they speak English too]."

A man on a horse said.

"[Well, Jumping Gee Haus a Fat]."

That man with a smile convinced their okay took his hat off to wipe his brow with a handkerchief and, said.

"Well come out from among that big rock there and, let's all of us say welcome to the 12 valleys."

The mayor and, the rest said a few words with excitement in all their different ways.

"Welcome to the 12 valleys."

So, they came out from the big rock put their guns away and, they were holding hands. She raised Max's left arm so, she could slip under it and, be be-side of him with arm around her neck and, her hands are holding it in front of her chest.

One of the men with a cool Stetson gage black hat on a strawberry roan horse with a circle badge and, that said sheriff on his brown vest with tan long sleeves steps down and, he said.

"Looks like you 2 have had a little run in with this here Monster by the looks of your clothes. Let's see if we can clean you up a bit."

CHAPTER 13

He motions over to some of the woman and, they start coming forward. The captains take notice this older man is wise and, knows what he's doing and, see his two guns with one on each hip. Max notices his light blue riding chaps that come up to the hips with it only representing coming from the Comanche peoples. Their very good horsemen but, he has the dress code of the day with short hair. Max took a closer look and, sure enough that's a pair of Colt 45s single action army, cattlemen with a soft grey patina look to it and, he said.

"Hello sheriff and, I believe Comanche ... am I right?"

"Why yes how did you know?"

He just points to his riding chaps and, smiles and, the Sheriff said.

"Oh, the riding chaps well we are the only tribe that wears them and, that was very good and, you and, the miss's must come to the office and, visit along with my wife."

The captains shook hands with the sheriff.

Several women come over and, said to Amyl ion.

"Hello, dear would you please step over hear by one of the wagons we got water and, some first aid and, it looks like you're bleeding a little on your shoulder."

The captains look at one another like what's this because their lost with-out each other. She looks at the woman while walking then turns her head with a gorgeous smile at Max and, said.

"Their friends ... UUMMM don't go away Maximilian"

"Oh, yes, the best ... I'll be watching you every second"

The other woman come over and, are just fussing about her making her feel good and, welcomed. The men walk over to Max and, stuck out their hands one by one for a handshake. He acknowledged that shook hands with them and, exchanged names. He was thinking that we'll have plenty of time to talk. The men wanted to talk about how they killed the Monster along with how does your guns work?

The women were cleaning her up and, saying you are so brave and, talking about her uniform and, how interesting it was and, one said. "My dear your figure reveals so, much how do the men maintain their composure around you?" She thought to herself after glancing at their bonnets and, there long dresses that they do have a point but, kept silent and, took a drink of water from the cup and, all the while they just looked at one another like the people weren't there nor, could they hear much of what they were saying. Something had to change. Eventually they left the people around them and, it was like hey where are you going on their faces. They came together in the middle between the people and, horses with their arms around each other and, he said.

"Lady's and, Gentlemen we've got something to tell you … sweetheart, you go first."

She didn't hesitate and, felt perfectly comfortable and, said.

"Okay, I am Captain Amyl ion, Abara, Abebe Milan and, this is my husband."

She smiled at them and, you could have seen the 4th of July fireworks.

Then looks up to him and, said.

"Sweetheart, it's your turn."

"I am Captain Maximilian, Mathieu, Milan the 3rd."

They stand side by side look at one another to think and, pause and, they're right on que and, both said.

"We have come to look for the Black Rose."

The men and, woman start saying things amongst themselves and, one of them said.

"Well, our prayers are answered and, there is work to be done we must get rid of the Dragon, and, there's the other one of those creatures that you killed right up there."

That man pointed to the top of the edge of a large boulder. After that was said the other Griffin Monster flew away from its perch after watching and, listening and, all the people watched it fly away. Going back to Raven Hades no doubt. The scattered body parts of the dead Griffin Monster started to dissolve and, hissing with smoke coming up from the carcass and, it left a burnt mark on the ground and, of course everyone heard that sound and, looked over to watch the carcass parts dissolve.

Then a strange thing happened with the sheriff's horse and, sensed Amyl ion in a way of the way horses think that she was not like all the other humans and, began to act up. The sheriff looked at his horse saw it beginning to move his head up and, down grumbling from his throat and, hitting and, dragging his right front hoof in a way as if he was conveying to Amyl ion and, talking right at her. Inside this horse's mind he was thinking I know you; I smell you and, that you're a pure blood. A heavenly creation not as the humans. Everyone now was starting to pay attention especially the sheriff along with her and, Max. The sheriff looked at Amyl ion and, his horse and, he never saw that before and, the sheriff in his special abilities with spirituality perceiving things as a plains Indian can and, he said.

"Maximilian, Amyl ion my horse King David is talking to your wife and, I've never seen that before." Putting their arms around each other and, he bounced her a little at his side and, said.

"Someday sheriff we'll explain."

She was glued to King David as was King David and, started to approach one another with everyone watching. They met after 20 feet or, so, separating them and, she lifted her arms to greet him. King David was making horse sounds thinking it's so, good to meet with you and, don't be a stranger please come to the ranch and, meet my family and, go for a ride. When she got to him, her face was a glow and, she used a very mellow toned voice which conveyed she's trust worthy, and, I would never hurt you and, she said.

"Hello … King David Ooh, your so, beautiful and, I just love you … you are such a sight to see with the way that you are made with your shining black mane I want to be with you again … I promise."

She put her left hand on his nose and, moved it up his head slowly while her right hand on his neck and, went to hug around his big neck. She released while they looked in their eyes. Well, his left eye.

He put his jaws on her back-left shoulder with sort of laying his head on her shoulder as a sign of trust or, maybe that was a horse hug. Then he moved his head from her and, motions for her to get on the saddle and, she said

"I promise I will come to visit in a couple of days and, we won't need this equipment on your back, head or, mouth, I will just ride on your enchanting body.

Pause ... "We have to go now I'll see you later."

King David raised his head up and, down like he knew how to answer her. She walked back to Max with a look like she just got a Christmas gift. She kind of collapsed into him on his side or, was it a crash and, wrapping her arms around him and, looked at King David. They hugged he kissed her head moving side to side just a little. She will figure out later that when she rides on King David bareback all you have to do is grab the mane and, turn him left or, right with your legs too and, that's where he will go. With other commands she'll learn along the way.

The sheriff walked over to King David and, softly said.

"That was quite a conversation you two had and, yes, I like her too ... and, you know the spirit is in her."

He looked at the couple for a few seconds and, feeling the presence whispered in his native tongue to himself but, I couldn't make it out and, he said.

"Maximilian, Amyl ion you must come to our home and, visit with me my wife and, family and, go for a ride in the countryside and, you'll forget everything."

They nodded to accept the invitation and, one of the women came forward through the crowd and, asked Amyl ion.

"Where do these creatures come from?"

They're very intently listening to her and, sympathizing with her but, said nothing. They look at each other and, back at the woman and, Max said.

"We will do everything we can to get rid of these Monsters."

The woman gasps out a few breaths and, said.

"They keep us in fear for our lives and, then there's the children that are being terrorized they're going to grow up scared inside with nightmares, and, that beast takes our cattle, sheep, chickens and, our pets but, won't take the pigs."

Then one of the men said.

"It tries to burn up what it can on a full moon and, comes out again tomorrow night."

The conversation abruptly ends and, out of one of the wagons in back

87

a young man began to speak and, they all turned to look and, he carried on for a short time and, he said.

"Amyl ion … Amyl ion … Amyl ion."

Everyone got quite and, the mother of this man was climbing out of the wagon and, helping her son get out and, the young man's father came over to help from the crowd. The mother of the young man said.

"Thanks, Pop, for coming over and, helping me with our son."

The young man couldn't be stopped he was so, drawn to her and, he said.

"Thanks Pop and, Mom for letting me get down"

The father of the young man looked over at the captains and, said.

"Our son wants to meet your wife Maximilian."

The captains look at one another and, nod. She slowly moves to stand in front of Max and, said.

"I will meet your son."

He puts his hands-on her shoulders close to her neck. The father and, mother escort their son because he's blind. The captains see he's blind and, she thought that something special was about to happen and, felt the presents of God coming over her. The family reached her which felt like an eternity moving through the crowd. Max was thinking this young man doesn't get out much and, wanted to meet someone new. The other thing was about what could we do for him? He senses that he's like a younger brother.

[A Side note]. In the future this young man will have a part in the development of the valley they had just come from.

They reach Amyl ion and, stand 3 feet apart. The young man was born with no eye balls. She stretched out both hands and, said.

"My hands are out in front of you."

The father said.

"Go ahead son and, grab her hands."

The Mother watches and, senses something with a curious turning of her head and, a mystifying face. The young man without hesitation takes her hands and, said.

"Hello, it is very good to meet you."

Her heart goes out him and, said.

"The pleasure is all mine, I'm sure."

The young man spoke with dignity and, said.

"The Grace that is coming from you is like no other on this earth and, I shall get to my point now for I know you will be hard pressed in your future responsibility's ... and, that your name is Amyl ion I know ... but, I was thinking in the wagon and ......"

The mother said.

"He is very good with names."

The young man has a studious and, steady look on his face and, he said.

"I split your name in a different way. I separated the L from the Y and, joined it to the I in ion."

[He pronounced it Yun].

I hope you readers got that?

"That comes up with Lion ... Amy Lion."

Well, Max was just amazed and, said.

"That is very fascinating."

She blinked and, agreed with him and, the people were talking amongst themselves. That's when she started to pull the young man inch by inch closer and, closer he didn't resist and, began to see the top half of a woman that only a blind person can see in their mind and, this was going to be a miracle. He directed his thoughts to his father and, he said.

"I see a woman coming into view pop and ..."

"Go on Son."

She is still pulling him closer until their faces are 18 inches apart. The young man is seeing the image getting clearer and, clearer until the full image is in his brain. He describes it to everyone with a loader voice.

"I see a woman with long wavy hair and, bright glowing eyes in the hair about a couple of dozen or, so, that match's her eyes and, I believe she has wings on the side of her eyes. Hey mom do other woman have those wings?"

"No son no one else does just the woman that stands in front of you."

He knows that this is special and, gets a sensation through-out his body and, said.

"I will go on ... she is standing there smiling her hair is moving with the eyes in her hair as well. Yes, as if in a breeze that comes over me when I rested under an oak tree after working in the sun."

Then her voice is heard in his head and, she said.

"[Believe and, see]."

Even though no one heard that voice. Then the vision of her saw her lips move this second time and, she said.

"[Believe and, see]"

Then without hesitation the young man's vision came and, was able to see and, the first thing he saw was Amyl ion. They look at each other again she said. "[Believe and, see]."

Everyone heard her that time with her lips moving and, the young man saw them too. She realized that God had transported her voice to the young man's inner hearing the first two times like a small echo.

The young man was blinking his eyes and, looking at her face, wings, hair then down to her feet and, back up and, smiled. He dropped his hands looked at Max and, turned to his father and, said.

CHAPTER 14

"Hi, yaw Pop."

Then to his mother and, said.

"Hay Mom."

He turned this way and, that way and, said.

"I see you all."

Someone hollered out with great surprise and, said.

"[Jumpin Gee Haus a fat]."

The young man turned to the one that said that and, fast as drawing a hand gun from a holster that your life depended on stretched-out his arm pointed his finger at him and, said.

"Kenny Ray there you are ... you OH! buffalo soldier."

He drew out his Winchester model 94 from the saddle holster with a spin cock in the air to put a cartridge in the camber and, said.

"Yaw that's right Billy, now let's go hunting for some monsters that have been terrorizing you and, folks."

Billy's parents are just so, excited that their son has received his sight that they can hardly believe it and, there walking back to the wagon and, said.

"Dad, mom I can climb on the wagon by myself now."

Billy when climbing in the wagon said.

"Kenny Ray when I get home, I'm going to clean my guns and, dip the tips of my bullets in pigs' blood and, we'll go hunting.

"That'll be just fine Billy let me know when you're ready."

Billy's parents are having a good time laughing and, carrying on about their son and, Max looked at the mayor and, said.

"We have our space ship hidden in the mountain here and, we have someone chasing us and, we can't risk leaving it out in the open nor, can we go to the valley yet."

The mayor thought how can that be and, took off his hat and, scratched his head and, said.

"Okay that's fine."

The Senior Official raised his arms to all and, said.

"Everyone let's all head back to our one valley and, throughout the night well organize the heads of the other 11 valleys and, plan this attack out. Captains your invited and, I'll send a couple of the Lion's over to pick you up at 5 in the morning they'll be waiting for you and, our valley starts just past that large rocky peak many miles away."

Then he points in the direction and, the Senior Official was thinking to himself and, took it for granted that they already knew about the Lions of how tame they were and, that they can talk, reason and, communicate to humans and, Max said.

"We will be ready."

Because it came so, easy for them to say yes about the Lion's both remember the scene of the civilians and, how they interacted with them. The town's people all left as they stood there watching and, most all of them were waving.

Amyl ion was thinking to herself I can't wait for this. He's thinking too what precautions should I take for her and, the ship in the cave and, Raven Hades, what was he up to?

She turned to face him and, she's jumping up and, down about Billy receiving his eyesight and, telling him things that was making her so, happy and, she puts her hands-on his arms and, slips them down to his hands and, gets close with a wiggle for a while. He picks her up with his arms under her buttocks and, holds her up in the air and, spins her around a couple of times. She's just loving the moment and, she put her arms around his head and, fingers in his hair and, she's hugging his head and, he whispers in her ear and, kissing it and, she's giggling with her eyes closed and, breathing in and, out with the sighs of being over whelmed with excitement and, she thinks that she is in 7th heaven. This goes on for several minutes as they enjoy each other to the MAX. Pardon the pun. She gets serious now even though he was willing to carry on with their play making and, she looks at him with her hands in his hair and, said.

"Max the ship ... will it be safe? we must make it secure and, our detection shield must keep working for us hear and, we must extend it out to the meeting tomorrow, I don't want this Raven Hades to find us because we got a job to do."

He thought how she's taking charge of some things and, helped her along and, he said.

"I look forward to riding on the backs of the Lions with you tomorrow and, please don't worry."

He spun her around a few times and, she gave out some joyful squealing laughter to express how much she enjoyed the fun they can have and, he's laughing too and, having a great time. He loves her with a love that only he can give her cause she came from his bones. He doesn't know this but, he will love her deeper and, deeper as the years go by.

Just then a red light came on the viewer with beeping that he had on his belt. She reached down and, grabbed it and, they looked at it still in his arms. The viewer showed that it detected 2 figures that were approaching about 96 Feet behind a large boulder at the edge of some smaller rocks apparently to look at what they were doing. He slowly lowers his beloved to the ground she got serious and, she said.

"Let's do this ... I got an idea."

Max thought about her cunning and, he said.

"What's that?"

"Well, we can pretend that were walking away from them but, we will be circling the 2."

"I like it."

They put the viewer away and, walked towards some rocks that would shield them as they hustled at the location and, drew out their weapons and, the viewer again to make sure they were still there but, there was no trace of them. They must have moved to another location. They adjusted the viewer and, found them again and, she turns to their location and, said.

"We got to go this way and, we must be slippery and, cunning and, surprise them ... let's go."

He was admiring her as she knew what to do. They darted over some smaller rocks made their way between several other bigger rocks and, crawled on top of a flat boulder very quietly to look down on the 2 and, sure enough there they were trying to find them on their own viewer and, they were tapping it a little bit to try and, make it work but, couldn't. That's when they jumped down about 10 feet away and, surprised them. It was the Colonel and, the Major and, the captains said.

"Don't turn around and, hold your hands up ..."

There was silence for a moment and, he motions with his index finger over his lips at her not to say anything. She nods her head in agreement and, Dominic said.

"We have come to talk to you both and, you can see we don't have our weapons drawn ..."

Silence again ... as they watch them ... then they turn to each other and, knew it was time to try and, trust them and, he said.

"Okay ... we will put ours away as well."

He glanced at her at his side and, could tell she was hard focused and, she said.

"Turn around slowly and, with your hands up Colonel Roku and, Major Sokolov."

She was thinking that we've got the goods on you and, know who you are and, her face showed it. They turn around and, the captains were thinking alike to be cool and, be ready for anything. Dominic and, Sasha looks at one another and, back at them. Dominic gave a facial expression to Sasha as if to say you go first. Sasha said with a little bit of anxiety because it took a lot of courage to say what she wanted to say and, she said.

"We've had a change of heart and, want to leave the hold that Raven Hades has on us and, move to one of the valley's because we just fell in love with the land and, want it restored too and, to rid the terror of the monsters."

Sasha turns to Dominic with a sigh of relief with her body language and, he acknowledged it was his turn and, Dominic said.

"I heard of the facial repair you have on your ship of the [27-Trips] and, I was wondering could it erase the damage done by the bear claw on my face?"

The captains were thinking and, looked at one another with facial expressions showing a little distrust and, could this be a trap but, then Dominic said.

"Here take our weapons that should make it convincing."

With their hands still up, Max motions with his laser to raise your hands higher and, he said.

"Okay I'll take your weapons and, keep your hands up."

He walks over and, thought if they make a move for their weapons, I'll blast them into eternity and, I must protect my wife. She was thinking if they so, much as move to their guns they'll wish they hadn't.

He pulls their weapons from the holster's and, walks backwards to her and, places them on the rock ledge nearby. Dominic and, Sasha noticed that Amyl ion has a cut on her left shoulder but, they kept silent and, she said.

"Well, what about this Raven Hades does he know where you are?" Dominic said.

"No, he thinks were on a reconnaissance mission and, we were going to make it look like that we were killed and, that there is no trace of us." Max curiously said.

"Dominic, does he think you 2 are dead now?"

Sasha quickly spoke out of turn and, said.

"No."

The captains look at one another with curios faces that this must be legit and, Max looked at them and, said.

"Wait a minute don't move I want to talk this over with my wife."

He gently takes her right arm and, she turns as they walk far enough so, they couldn't hear what was said. They stood facing one another and, both said.

"Well, what do you think?"

Max kept silent for her to go first and, she said.

"What are we going to do with these two?"

His protective side came out and, he said.

"I don't know if we can trust them because I love you."

Their saying this and, that with overlapping conversation and, carrying on with whispering and, hand motions and, at one time she is tapping the palm of her hand in the other one trying to make a point and, reached up with her hand touching his face which meant I don't want anything happening to you. He reaches for her hand and, kiss's it and, they place their hands back down. They said a few more kind words.

Dominic and, Sasha is watching this play out and, seems that they have forgotten all about them. The captains are smiling at times with serious faces and, he sees a piece of a twig in her hair and, pulls it out and, flips it to the ground and, casually said.

"The ladies missed that and, they were supposed to have cleaned you up."

[They continue whispering]. She starts to swipe his hip and, thigh with her hands to get the dust off his pants and, Dominic nudges Sasha she looks at him and, he smiles looking back at them and, Sasha said.

"Yaw … aren't they wonderful."

A little bit longer it's coming, Dominic, Sasha clears their throats and, coughs and, that gets their attention. The captains stop talking look at them and, they look as if … what do you want? Can't you see we're busy. They go back to talking and, finally stop and, Max said.

"Samantha, can you hear me?"

"Yes, Captain."

"Can you see me and, Captain Amyl ion?"

"Yes, Captain."

"Can you see the 2 figures in front of us?"

"Yes, Captain."

"Could you make them disappear on the detection screen?"

Pause. Domonic adjusts his stance and, said.

"What's the purpose of that?"

Max responds back with a question and, said.

"Will Raven Hades be concerned if you disappeared and, or, appear dead?"

He knew the answer oh so, well and, he said.

"No, he would erase us from the memory banks."

Sasha wanted to be consistent and, said.

"Raven would believe that we were dead."

Samantha comes back in and, said.

"Yes, I can make them disappear on the detection screen." The captains are happy with this and, Amyl ion said.

"Well, then if you would please lay on the ground Samantha will capture that image and, send it out and, you'll be frozen in time as dead."

Dominic and, Sasha lay on the ground as dead and, Samantha said.

"It's done their image has been sent out."

Max was wary and, said.

"Okay you can get up now."

They were so relieved as they got up from the ground and, dusting themselves off and, Sasha said.

"Thank you and, we will start our new identities later when we get to our new destination."

The captains gave their weapons back and, were all talking and, you couldn't make out what they were saying except for Dominic and, he said.

"Sasha and, I have a place picked out in the center of one of the valleys."

They get to the mountain and, Max said.

"Samantha the 4 of us are coming in."

"AYE, AYE Captain."

CHAPTER 15

Later Dominic gets the scars removed and, he look's good and, they get some food and, provisions of whatever they might need with sleeping gear and, blankets. They had some departing words as they escorted them to the beginning of trees about 100 feet or, so, away.

The captains get back in the ship and, he takes her by the hand to the bedroom as she said.

"Samantha close the hatch please."

They relax lying on the bed a little exhausted and, thinking of the day and, she said.

"There's still some time left in the night … Maximilian are you hungry?"

"I could eat a horse."

She cracked up laughing and, both giggling, joking with each other and, seriously I don't know why they can't look at her wound. They slowdown from there joking and, she said.

"How about some salmon and, veggies of your choice?"

He's troubled about her wound with a little blood still oozing out and, he said.

"I really should look at your shoulders."

She wasn't concerned about it and, felt nothing and, she said.

"Well, okay but, in a little bit please."

So, they got up ate and, cleaned the place. He wanted to take their uniforms off and, put them in the shut for Samantha to clean and, repair her shoulder tear where she got hurt and, he said.

"Amyl ion I want to clean the uniforms and, check your wound so, please come to the nurse's station with me and, I want to undress you and, clean the cut on your shoulder."

She went with her husband with a smile as he took her by the hand and, he observed her and, sat her down and, said.

"I'm going to take your top uniform off and, look at your cuts and, it's beginning to bruise."

He proceeds and, pulls her uniform up and, off and, starts to examine her.

She was thinking Oh, I'm going to get pampered he gives me so, much comfort and, the kindest man there is. She kicks her lower legs forward and, back leans on her hands on the edge of the examination bed as he fixes some soap and, water while watching him. He comes back over to wash the cut and, is gentle with her they smile at one another. He rinses the cut with water and, dries the cut off and, looks at her and, said.

"There was 6 or, 7 slashes that scratched along the top here and, made it look like one big cut … Okay, I'm going to raise your uncut arm and, you can resist a little while I push it down and, you tell me if you feel any discomfort."

Her species is incomparable to a regular person that other-wise it would have hurt and, she said.

"No, nothing unusual my special Doctor."

She was so, cute raising her lower legs one at a time playing a little she felt so, at ease.

He raises her left arm and, said.

"This is the side that you first landed on and, I wanted to check your motion and, now that it is up, I'm going to press down on your arm and, I want you to resist and, tell me if it hurts? Or, does it feel weak?"

"No, nothing unusual."

He's done with checking her resistance and, he's satisfied with the results that both her arms are the same in strength.

[They forgot about the scanner healer. I think I know why. They're so, attached they did it the old fashion way of bonding and, she said].

"I didn't feel anything unusual with your tender care."

She's just enjoying all this attention.

He puts a bandage on her shoulder and, said.

"I want to wash your cut in the morning, noon and, night."

She smiles very pretty for him. He smiles back and, cleans up a little bit at the sink and, said.

"I'm going to take my uniform off and, put it down the shut for Samantha to clean along with yours."

She removes her pants watches him take his clothes off she can't keep her eyes off him and, he said.

"Let's get some regular clothes on while Samantha is cleaning our uniforms."

Their forming into a good team and, she said.

"I'll grab the uniforms and, put them down the shut and, ask Samantha to clean them up."

He wants to get her more involved with responsibilities and, he said.

"Let's go around the ship to check things out."

After doing that they laid back down on the bed with her nestled in under his right arm and, her head on his chest with their eyes closed and, enjoying the moment and, he was thinking about the Griffon Monster attack. There both thinking about the events of the day. She was thinking about blind Billy and, how he had received his sight.

Meanwhile Raven Hades back on his ship had begun calling up from the Abyss a Female Succubus to see if she can seduce Maximilian and, to join her in her realm but, that was a lie. When she kisses it's the kiss of death but, first she must bring him back to the Kingdom of a forgotten realm of hers. Sabrina appears from behind the clouded, smokie background as she breaks through the cloud as it rolls mystically around her where there lurks strange figures waiting to be called. A beautiful seductress with wings of dark reddish maroon, and, dark brown wing arms for support when she flaps them to fly. Her straight red hair with a little wave and, long enough to cover her bare breasts. Long black gloves up to her upper arms and, a bare midsection, a black belt with green emeralds and, red rubies, and, the buckle with a S on it for Sabrina. Her pants if you want to call them that was very small and, black ... kind a like panties. High heel red boots that went almost to mid-thigh. After walking with a strut that could seduce any man on the spot. She stops and, waits with her right hand on her hip with an attitude and, said.

"Well, who is he this time?"

Raven heard the confidence in her voice and, said.

"I want you to take Maximilian to your Kingdom you'll know how and, where to find him."

She has a look that would seduce the Devil himself. She leaves like a swift trail of nothing that was there.

Later on [27-Trips] she was starting to climb on him and, they still had their clothes on she puts her arms around his head and, she's on her knees and, shins. He welcomes the move and, puts his arms around her and, rubs her back. She lay's her head between the pillow and, his left ear and, starts to talk and, eventually she was whispering and, starting to get a little emotional with the whispering and, happy crying and, breathing a little erratically with her body moving emotionally and, kissing his cheek and, he pulls out a handkerchief from his back pocket and, gives it to her and, she laughs and, takes it because he always has one for her. He laughs with her and, kiss's her cheek, lips and, some of her tears feel on his cheek. She wipes her tears every once in a while, and, wiping the tears from his cheek and, wiping hers again. He's caressing her back and, moving his hands up and, down with a few words once in a while. She's still whispering and, kissing his cheek but, that seems to slow down and, she begins to breathe a little normal now as if to say it's coming to a close and, she starts to wipe her cheek's one more time and, he raises her head with his hands and, kisses her on the lips and, she responds. After a little while she goes back under his left arm and, lays her head on the side of his chest and, said.

"Maximilian thanks for the handkerchief, I am so, happy with everything [WWHHOOAA] and, being with you and, we'll get to see the Ring of Fire tomorrow that burns eternally." He squeezes her tight and, said.

"Yes, and, it's going to be a busy day with the Lion's and, the meeting with the town's people I hope Billy is there?"

She tapped his chest and, rubbed a little and, said.

"WOW Billy received a new set of eye balls right before our eyes and, everyone else."

He smiled with a positive conviction and, said.

"I believe that our God is going to do special things through you with the years ahead of us."

Well, they talked about Billy for quite some time then did a Captain's Log and, took a shower with jumping back into bed on their backs and, set the alarm with her lying close to his left side.

"Amyl ion my love in the morning I want to show you the Javelin's the President gave me you'll like these."

"Okay."

She waited for 5 minutes and, rolled on her right side to look over at him and, he had his eyes opened and, noticed she was watching him and, he rolled his head to look at his beloved and, she gave him a smile he couldn't resist and, rolled onto his left side and, put his right arm around her and, they scooted real close and, he began to kiss her warm lips and, they groaned at the touch and, she was breathing a little more than usual as she put her left hand and, fingers in his hair and, they put their hands together and, squeeze them together. He slowly release's their kiss and, gets up to straddle her and, she rises as he takes her top off and, goes to take her pants off. She is lying there naked with her legs closed and, he goes to the front of the bed and, she fluffs her hair to look good for her husband and, lays her arms out to the side on the pillows as he takes his clothes off. He stops and, looks at his beautiful wife and, thinking to himself I am the most blessed man to be married to her. She knows what he's thinking and, giggles a little and, then puts her arms straight out to beckon him with her palms almost facing up and, they turn left and, right and, the fingers roll to tell him to come to her. He slowly puts his knees on the edge of the bed as he starts walking towards his lovely Bride. She notices that he is now at full erection for her and, he is almost there as he crawls and, she rises up from the bed and, looking at him and, she grabs his erection with her right hand as she puts her left arm around her beloveds neck and, draws him closer and, she opens her legs and, their lips meet and, she guides his erection in her as he lays on top of her and, he loves kissing her puffy lips but, not only that they swell and, get warm just a little more while love making. She's breathing with sounds of ecstasy and, there twisting each other's lips together. They release a little and, there kissing becomes a touch and, release as she has her groaning's with anticipating another escape. She's already rolling a little in her stomach. He starts to rise off of her with his arms straight and, going to watch this beautiful creation, as he slowly strokes her and, her eyes are half closed. She opens them just a little more to look at his face and, she takes a deep breath and, begins her agony of pleasure burying her head in the pillow as she arches her back. He is totally with his Queen as he enjoys every second, of her boundless energy. Then she puts her hands on the sides of her head and, turns her head from side to side and, coughs out like crying because it hurts. She is in the depth of being captured with her convulsions that gnashes at her body. He continues to watch and, she takes her hands off the sides of her head and, slaps them on the bed just one time next to her and, lets out a little air and, breathes in again. He realizes now that she is in the middle of the torturous isolation or, perhaps she is peaking. She begins to arrive on the other side after about 25 to 30 seconds of this and, he patiently awaits as she breaths out and, she begins to lick her lips and, giving out sighs of ecstasy with opening her eyes and, looking at him and, smiling with a look of innocents and, rolling her arms around like she's free to fly and, he said.

"Good evening my love."

She blurts out with a belly laugh and, she said.

"Good evening WHUUUOOHH."

There both having a good time and, she relaxes her pretty arms on the pillows and, smiles as he stops stroking her for a moment and, said.

"How is your shoulder feeling?"

"It feels fine and, my husband I can't feel a thing HA, HA, HA."

She is not able to talk much she's in feelings of joy and, tranquility and, he said.

"May I kiss your lovely shoulder to make it heal faster?" She plays at her answer while rolling her head with a innocent smile and, she said.

"Please Maximilian, put your warm, warm full lips on my shoulder I want to feel the healing of your kiss on me … MMMHHAA"

Little did they know that the prophetic statement about her cut healing faster would do just that and, in the morning her cut would be completely healed with no trace of anything.

She raises her one hand to put on his head as he lowers to kiss her shoulder and, she watches with eagerness and, gives him her shoulder. He kiss's it and, lays on top of her feeling her hard breasts with the weight of his body and, she's sighing with enjoyment and, humming as she is all a buzz at all of this. He begins to stroke her again and, it would be about a couple of minutes or, less before she campaigns in her mind to have a detonation all over her body. They had several more campaigns. In between one of her campaigns she said.

"Max why do people talk about their ethnicity?"

He raised up and, straightened his arms and, said.

"Oh, I think you're wondering about Sasha's I. D. card that revealed all her mixed blood?"

"Yes, you never mentioned it."

"Well, HHHMMMM I was raised with my parents never mentioning that or, the schools totally absent of it and, all my friends were ...... Well just friends."

She moved her hands up and, down his arm's while he slowly stroked her and, she said.

"Oh, okay uummm like lying politicians would always bring up people's race?"

He thought I hope I can say the right words to her and, said.

"I'm glad that you said that because that's the way the democrats identify people. Well, I mean their racist's and, say they'll help but, actually suppress."

She has a studious face and, said.

"So, just let people develop on their own and, don't draw any attention because were all human."

He was amazed at her and, said.

"That's right my love."

He admired her intelligence and, how fast she catches on. Then he drifted back to her creation that day and, was stunned at such a new magnificent human species. She watched him in his thoughts above her and, she said.

CHAPTER 16

"I know what you're thinking."

He smiled and, she placed her sweet palms on his cheeks and, felt her warmth and, she gazed into his eyes for the longest moment and, he said.

"I LOVE YOU."

After saying that she showed signs she was going to start convulsing and, closed her eyes dropped her arms with a deep breath and, had their winning election together sounding like they were going to die. That completed their love of the night and, finally went to sleep.

During the night just after midnight he woke up for a few minutes because he thought of something to right with the old pen and, paper right at the tip of the corner of the bed. She opened her eyes just for 5 seconds and, smiled and, went back to sleep. She was thinking Oh, he's under the inspiration and, writing it down.

The alarm went off and, they slowly wake up and, he sits on the edge of the bed for a minute and, she climbs on his back and, whispers in his ear.

"Good morning my husband."

"MMM, Good morning my wife." [September 15 2228 Saturday]

He starts to stand up and, reaches behind her legs and, picks her up and, starts walking towards the restroom. She is giggling and, squeaking with her cute happy laughter and, he is bouncing her up and, down a little and, sings a short little song for her as they make it to the restroom. There all cleaned up as they come from the restroom and, see that their uniforms are ready and, there sitting at the exit shoot and, they put them on. She asks Samantha for a pair of golden hooped earrings and, a two-toned wide scarf to wrap around her head and, to make it a bold purple and, orange striped to hold her hair down. She's beginning to look even more stunning and, Max is all the more fixed on her.

They just finished breakfast and, she wanted an old writing devise as well as him so, they looked around and, couldn't find one. He told her let's put it on the counter above us and, draw upon it, when necessary, under the inspiration. When there in town they'll ask the mayor for some old writing material and, Samantha said.

"Large Animal's coming into the Detection Zone."

They look at each other and, drop their mouths open with excitement and, she said.

"When is the ETA?"

"38 Minutes ETA captain."

He gets to the edge of the chair and, said.

"Samantha we will be leaving with these Large Lions and, meeting up with the town's people so, keep track of us and, God willing nothing should happen to myself and, Captain Amyl ion and, we will return later in the day and, Samantha guard the ship at all costs."

"AYE, AYE Captain."

They look at each other as they sit in their Captain's chairs and, they both reach for the Green Froggy and, there hand's take turn's tapping the Green Froggy to make it go [Squeaky-Squeak]. He wants to look at the cut on her shoulder and, said.

"Amyl ion take my hand I want to look at your cut and, wash it with soap and, water."

He proceeds to take her at the nurse's station and, he has her sit down on the examination bed and, he stands in front of her and, takes the top of her uniform off as her firm breast's bounce taking his time to see her shoulder. They smile at each other she just loves it when he fusses with her and, you can actually see her glow with contentment. He takes the bandage off very slowly she looks forward and, the bandage is off. He can't believe his eyes and, said to her.

"My Sweetheart take a look at this."

She looks and, draws in a deep breath of air and, she said.

"Maximilian it's gone and, there is no trace of anything but, how can that be?"

He sits down in the chair opposite her and, is thinking and, looking at the wall with his hand on his chin and, elbow on the armrest. She gets up from the examination bed looks at her shoulder in the mirror for a while and, she said.

"I got it!!! … you wanted to kiss my shoulder to make it heal faster."

She walks over to him and, starts to sit in his lap and, he puts his arm around her and, with their mouths open a little and, he said.

"The cut healed because we wanted it to and, [that my dear sweet wife is the power of suggestion] but, let's not forget that you were created by God in a very remarkable way and, with the evidence already seen you have God working through you for his purpose. Well, many purposes."

"Maximilian, we have all these years ahead of us and, God will perform many miracles through us I do believe … what do you think?"

"That my dear wife is exactly right and, I can hardly wait for the next one."

They both sit there for a minute and, she has her arms around him and, there speaking to one another very quietly with her head on his shoulder. There thinking how wonderful a life they have with the blessings of their God.

He remembered they have an appointment with the Lions and, said.

"The Lions will be here shortly."

The lions were having fun on their trip and, would leap over one another as they gallop. Go around big rocks and, meet with a leap in the air and, roar. They came to a shallow stream of ice-cold water from the mountain took a drink. Time to take off and, they leap as long as they can just two times cause didn't want to get their paws wet. A tree nearby is where they stopped laid down to lick their paws and, when that was done, they started running again.

Max looked at the clock and, there was some free time and, she said.

"I want to see these Javelin's first if we have time?"

She said it so, sweetly how could he deny her and, devoted to his wife she gave him kiss on the cheek and, [that was the clencher].

They get up he helps her put the uniform on it's a little difficult with her breasts takes her by the hand and, she's enjoying this pulling her along with a little squeak and, they reach the storage area. They stop at 2 Military box's that are side by side and, there marked [E.G.C.J.] and, she said.

"What does that mean?"

He notices she's very inquisitive and, he said.

"[Explosive, Guidance, Control, Javelin]. Samantha release the security on box number one and, I'm going to open it."

She moves her body to look in anticipation and, she said.

"How many are there?"

Max looks at her and, smiles she wiggles a little and, he said.

"12 per Box."

The box opens with an air release sound and, he said.

"Captain grab 1 of those rounded condensed monitors or, viewers and, I'll take 2 and, you take 2 Javelin's."

She puts the viewer in her back pocket and, said.

"I like the color blue to match the sky."

She is thinking I know you throw these and, what does all the marking's mean and, she said.

"I know what you're thinking let's go outside."

He grabs 2 Javelin's and, they take off and, he said.

"I'll demonstrate it to you very clearly."

She can hardly wait and, quickly said.

"Samantha lower the hatch please were going outside the cave."

"AYE, AYE Captain."

There outside and, he put's one on the ground and, so does she. He lay's the one Javelin in his hand's parallel to the ground and, motions to her to do the same he explains and, said.

"Hold in your left hand and, balance it somewhere in the middle and, I'll hold mine in my right hand and, you follow my actions as I explain and, repeat after me."

She straitens her stance and, turns her focus on and, said.

"Okay captain."

She was thinking I like this. He pulls out the tracking tablet flips it open with his thumb and, said.

"The Screen appears as you see it hear about a foot in diameter."

She flip's hers open.

"Now do you see the Javelin on the screen?"

"Yes and, it is very clear and, I can still see the background."

He listens to her voice for any change and, he said.

"Good, it will follow the Javelin for 21 Miles and, back so, its total range is how long?" He waits for her to respond to the question.

"42 miles."

They smile at one another. She was thinking that he is a very good instructor and, is patient with me.

"That's it's total range."

He points to the Tip and, said.

"The most advanced Chromium tip with the highest explosives and, it will penetrate double brick walls."

He points to the triggering mechanism.

"This is where you squeeze with your index finger and, thumb and, hold that, which releases the 4 little wing's that pop up right there at the tail end which you just saw and, while its inflight the wings will move as you guide it with your finger on the viewer. Now then I can't release this right now because it will take off so, you reach under the Javelin here with your other hand and, push this button in to hold the triggering mechanism in place until you're ready to release and, throw the Javelin."

She's captivated by now and, he sees her like a sponge.

"Okay, here is the eye just behind the tip which see's what you're guiding it to."

He pauses … and, he said.

"Any questions?"

She reviews in her mind for a while and, she said.

"Captain, … I have no questions."

She gives him a look of trust and, smiles.

"Okay, now we go to the one jet in the back here …"

They look at it and, he said.

"Be careful here … Because when you release the trigger mechanism from your finger and, thumb the jet comes on and, you lean away from the jet exhaust … very important …"

"I know you don't want me to get burned … right?"

He gave her a nod of his head and, closed his eyes for a second telling her … that's right and, he said.

"So, now you have the tracking tablet in your left hand and, you start tracking the Javelin as soon as you release it and, using one of your fingers or, thumb you can guide it anywhere within its range. That Orange Glow there that you see is you on the Screen."

He puts his Javelin on the ground and, she does too, he comes in close to her casually and, said.

"The explosive device is activated once it is released and, you have to run the fuel out to deactivate it so, I suggest hitting your target and, the range one way round trip is 42 miles, if it runs out of range and, out of fuel chances are someone will pick it up and, we don't want that so, I suggest hitting the explode button on your tracking tablet."

She is paying strict attention to him as she looks at him.

He shows the explode button on the tablet to her and, he said.

"Captain that's about it."

They put the viewers in their back pockets.

"WOW ... Maximilian that is an incredible device."

They draw closer hold each other her arms around his neck and, his at her waist side. He was thinking how incredible it is that I can be serious with her and, yet she is the love of my life and, maybe someday I will understand more about this gift or, maybe just take it just like it is with loving her with all my heart and, doing the best I can at taking care of her. Looking at him she smiles and, moves her head a little up and, down closing and, opening her puffy lips. Does it again he's deep in love with her she looks into his blue eyes, face and, hates to break the moment but, looks at her watch and, they have a couple of minutes before the lion's show up and, she said.

"When did you get these Javelin's?"

"Oh, about 6 Month's before you landed beside the [27-Trip's]."

"Oh ... and, it's quite interesting that you competed in the Olympics with the Javelin and, how is it that they were developed as a weapon and, the technology put into such a fun sport?"

"Well, my father taught me early on as a child how to use a Javelin and, through his imagination and, his creative abilities drew up a blueprint and, gave it to the President his best friend and, a short time later presented him with a gift of 12 from the army."

Samantha said.

"Captain's the lions are 2 minutes away."

He tapped her hips and, said.

"Let's get back in the ship and, watch on the viewers."

They pick up the Javelin's and, start to jog back to the ship they enter the cave and, she said.

"Let's leave the Javelin's just inside here on the inside next to the opening of the cave and, take them with us when we leave. You never know. I like it because it feels so, natural."

He thought in the back of his mind she must have had a Sixth Sense about leaving the 4 Javelin's at the opening of the cave to take with them when they leave.

[I must say he is going to be right about that Sixth Sense of hers].

CHAPTER 17

"Okay … Yep that is probably a good idea."

While they were jogging back to the cave. Sabrina is sailing down into the upper clouds and, accidently runs close by the griffin monster and, her long hair covers her naked breasts and, she said.

"I'm after the man."

Griffin squawked like good and, it said.

"That's right I got the girl. Climb on."

There distain for them was all over their faces. Looking up into the sky from the ground a small image appears with 4 wings and, it's them going through a big white cloud. They look for the captains she points at them they extend their wings to glide and, drops down on a tall rock top. She flaps her wings to get off and, gets next to it and, she said.

"We can trap them in the cave."

They see a movement up the trail a little and, duck down. It's the two lions and, their enthusiasm dropped because they wouldn't stand a chance against those two and, they look at each other and, she said.

"Well, I guess we will have to wait because something is about to occur."

Their faces put on a blank face as they waited.

The captains sit in their chair's and, wait with him giving the Green Froggy a [Squeaky- squeak]. She loves it and, she gives it a [Squeaky-squeak].

The viewer show's a count down from 10, to 1 second's and, then they come around a rock formation. The male first and, then the female. They smell and, sense that they were there and, lay down on all fours with paws and, forearms out front. They noticed that a dead Griffin Monster had dissolved and, left a burnt marking on the ground they turned up their noses and, looked away. There in a sort of squatting position and, waiting for them to show up.

The captains look at them on the viewers and, stare. She is thinking what magnificent animals and, soon we'll be outside with them and, he said.

"Baby what time is it I can't take my eyes off them?"

She glances at the time and, giggles because all the information is on the viewer and, all he had to do was glance at the time on the viewer but, she quickly thought Oh, that's okay and, said.

"Can you believe that it just changed to 5 am?"

They grab each other's hand's and took off. They come to the door and, look at one another he gives his bride a kiss she happily gives him one back looks into his eyes and, her face is glowing which tells him that she's very excited to be going into town on the backs of lions and, he said.

"WHEW ... Let's go."

They grab the Javelin's at 2 apiece. They step out the exit look and, smile. The lion's look at them from looking somewhere else and, the male lion said.

"Hey kid's we were wondering where you were?"

The lions were smiling back and, the male said.

"If you would let me introduce you both to my lovely wife, Apple Blossom."

The male lion turn's his head at her stop's and, said to her.

"It's your turn."

The female lion could hardly wait and, she said.

"This is my handsome husband Green Tea, he's crazy about me and, never lets me out of his sight."

The lion's stop speaking wait for them to say something and, Green Tea said.

"Apple blossom I guess these humans can't talk."

Apple Blossom laughs a little and, said.

"YAAYAA, cats got their tongue."

Well, that did it for them because they just started laughing and, released the tension and, calmed down and, Max after hearing that loose introduction he responded in kind.

"This hear is my wife and, she's [Bones of my Bone's and, Flesh of my Flesh, Amyl ion, Abara, Abebe]."

Then she said.

"This is my husband, [Maximilian, Mathieu, Milan the 3rd] and, he too is [Bones of my Bone's and, Flesh of my Flesh]. We haven't officially been married by a preacher and, when we do my last name will be Milan."

The lions move their heads up and, down and, Green Tea said.

"Without further ado we have got a way to go so, hop on."

Apple Blossom said.

"Those spear's there in your hands are you going to take them with you?"

They nodded their heads and, he said.

"YAW we might need them."

Green Tea said.

"We understand with the dragon and, other thing's flying around just let us know when you have to use them and, well get out of the way."

Max said.

"Where would you like to put us?"

Green tea nuzzled her a little and, said.

"What do you think Apple Blossom?"

Her tail went by his face a few times and, she said.

"Well, I thought that you would decide? Sweetie how about Maximilian on you and, Amyl ion on me."

Green Tea thought this is incredible she smells like a pedigree of humans. I've never met one and, said.

"I believe I would like Amyl ion on me, how's that?"

"Okay that's finally settled get on Maximilian."

The lions took a great deal of interest that it was so, amusing. Amyl ion is the more amused because of the majestic character with their appearance and, caring for the decision-making process.

She gets on Green Tea and, he can sense that she will be totally at ease on his back and, said.

"Amyl ion you're a natural so, please relax and, enjoy the ride."

"If you only knew how much I'm going to enjoy this."

Max spoke to the lions and, said.

"We just love you both and, we think we're in a dreamland."

Green Tea turns to Apple Blossom and, gives her a wink. She smiles back and, Green Tea said.

"Hang on to some fur, balance your spear's we are going to get up and, turn around and, going to start out with a walk and, increase to a gallop and, go to half speed and, what do you think Apple Blossom?"

"Perfect, let's get up to speed and, take the shortcut."

Max said.

"Samantha close the entry door and, you're in charge until we get back and, track us along with our beautiful friends here."

Apple Blossom said.

"AAHH that was sweet Maximilian."

The two lions didn't say anything when Max talked to Samantha, about their communiqué with the ship because they knew that they came in a space ship and, it was hidden in the cave and, their friends witnessed all that had happened and, told them about it and, Samantha said.

"AYE, AYE Captain."

Well, they go through the steps as the lion's rise, turn around and, walk, gallop and, half speed.

The music starts [He's a pirate, Main theme] [Best theme of the century] [Extended].

What a beautiful thing it is to see. Green Tea and, Amyl ion together running and, dodging large rock's and, jumping over bush's and, Apple Blossom right behind until they get on a straight path. Apple Blossom pull's alongside and, winks at Green Tea, she pulls in front for a while pull's back until their side by side. The captains a beautiful sight leaning forward a little as if on a race horse and, her black hair is flowing behind her. The two lions are making a straight Bee line to the nearest valley with tall trees, bushes and, rocks going by. A few dips in the path down and, up the big cats jump over fallen tree trunks and, more rocks in front they leap on one and, jump on the other one to cross that treacherous 1/2 mile stretch and, avoiding the road most of the way. There's a shallow stream a little further ahead that's about 80 feet wide and, the lions knew that they had to cross it ... or, leap over which they could at stretching their abilities and, Green Tea said.

"WWUU, WWEE I can feel the blood rushing through my head ... let's get a drink of water okay my blossom?"

"Okay ... and, you two stay on top there might be grizzly's around here."

That got our beloveds attention and, looked at each other and, looked around as the lions slurped some of that cool water coming down from the snow caps many miles away. The lions could smell the bears as there down wind and, thought they were safe. The two bears come out the other side of the river from the brushes and, have a couple of cubs. The lions raised up their heads and, the bears wanted to cross in that direction. The bears size up this pretty quickly because they have to protect their cubs and, begin to charge the lions in the water. The lions being around 6 feet tall at the shoulders and, the bears when standing are 8 feet and, Apple Blossom said.

"Hang on you two we have some business to take care of ... right my love?"

"Right ... don't let them stand up and, swat them away."

The lions leap at them to stop there running at them which stunned the bears the lions stood on their hind legs with a royal yell and, lighting cat strikes of left and, rights that they employ knocking the bears down and, went rolling in the water. The bears in their minds were thinking that they were just bluffing and, thought they would stop halfway in the water just to say to the lions don't come any closer to our baby's. Our beloved was all amazed at this and, watched the bears proudly walk away to their cubs and, Green Tea said.

"Let's go shall we ... times a wasting."

The lions look at their riders and, Apple Blossom said.

"Hay ... kids you, okay?"

They relaxed with a gushing out of some laughter and, Max said.

"HA, HA, WOW I guess were okay ... you two are amazing what do you say Amyl ion?"

"WHOA, ... I'm almost speechless ... that was great ... and, you took it right at them."

That's something Amyl ion will never forget [when attached take it to them and, reverse it]. The lions thought well yaw what else could we do and, slowly start going and, resume their way to the valley. In the lions minds they thought that it was just natural to fight that way and, a little way down while there riding Max said.

"Amyl ion, what other thing did God say to you on your descent from the heavens."

"I'm glad you asked we are going to have a baby boy in 21 Months after our coronation."

He looks over at her and, smiles and, thinks HHMMM, let's see 1 Year to Reign, and, 9 Month's for pregnancy, yep that's it 21 Months. While the lions are at half-speed many black crows and, raven's squawking and, crowing fly by to keep up. They wave up and, down in flight with their white tipped wings and, tails. The lions and, captains look around and, smile at this magnificent sight then they're gone.

Meanwhile as we view way above them and, see them riding on top of the lions.

What's this? Sabrina, the female succubus and, the other Griffin Monster appear above them and, follow along with the two lions at half speed where they can't see way up above. Their flying separately and, obviously there planning their attack.

The lions were slowing down to a gallop and, then a walk and, Apple Blossom said.

"Were gonna rest here for a while."

Green Tea said.

"There's a rest spot over to your right under the shade tree with water and, some fruit's." They slip off the lion's backs with their 2 Javelin's apiece and, Max said.

"That was one of the most incredible things I have experienced in my life." Amyl ion combs her hair with her fingers and, said.

"Yes and, I just loved it you both are the best friends that anyone can have we must do something for you whenever you want."

The two lions thanked them and, Apple Blossom said.

"We are going up the hill there to talk to some of our friend's about how were going to stop a friend from destroying herself and, maybe if the law enforcement will look the other way then maybe we can save her life so, we will ask them."

Apple Blossom starts to cry and, Green Tea sees that she can't go on and, he said.

"Yes, we want to take her away from the area that's destroying her."

Apple Blossom wipes the tears with the side of her forearms and, said.

"We've got a place picked out to take her away and, explained it to her that several friends had a dream about losing her life and, she agreed most assuredly to accept our love and, consent to go away for a while so, we got to go now and, be back in a little bit."

Max and, Amyl ion smiled at them and, they all departed in their separate ways with the captains walking over to the shade tree and, laid down their Javelin's on the table and, began sipping some water after dipping the cups into the bucket. There both silent as they think about the ride they just enjoyed and, how they took care of the grizzlies. He looks into the reflection of the water as its stop's rippling and, sees the other Griffin Monster hovering overhead and, his eyes got big and, he gently pull's her next to him and, thought that was unusual and, she said.

"What is it Maximilian?"

He keep's looking in the water nods his head to look as they sip she looks at him he whispers into the cup and, said.

CHAPTER 18

"Look into the water's reflection but, do it slowly."

She slowly turns to look into the water and, sees the Griffin Monster and, draw's a breath with her eyes getting bigger and, slowly return's the drinking cup to her lips and, said.

"What are we going to do?"

He's thinking to himself and, remembers they didn't bring their laser gun's.

Sabrina drops from the sky appears alongside the Griffin Monster hover and, talk moving her hands, arms as there planning the attack together.

Max decides we can't let them get on the ground with just two javelin's a piece and, he said.

"Okay this is what we got to do."

She listens very intently.

"If we can stick the Javelin into a mass body part and, squeeze, to release the trigger."

Max didn't have time to finish what he wanted to say for they attacked dropped down on them and, he said.

"Let's go and, get out into the open."

They drop the cups that banged on the table and, started running and, she said.

"Stay close to me Max."

"You got it ... fight with the one Javelin and, keep the other one close to your feet."

"I got it ... and, we can't let them get on the ground!"

Oh, how their connected with their sounds of yelling and, fighting the Monster's with the Monster's sounds heard by Apple Blossom and, Green

Tea. Taking notice of this walked to a ledge and, watched with unbelief raising their eyebrows looked at one another blinked their eye lids.

The lions see the monsters coming down and, without hesitation the captains turn the attack on them and, the monsters are kind of surprised. There trying to land but, won't let them and, all the while trying to stab them in their body mass. The 2 Monsters are flying up and, down, up and, down. Then the Griffin Monster knocked the Javelin out of Amyl ion's hand's and, she was surprised and, backed up to stay clear of the claw and, the beak that would have struck her. The Monster was coming down on her and, she was a couple of feet away from her Javelin and, that was too far away on the ground for her to reach and, time was of the essence. Max saw this and, took his right foot slipped it under his backup Javelin and, with a shout he said.

"AMYL ION!!!"

She looked tossed it at her and, it went sailing she caught it fell down backwards with the Javelin pointing at the Monster [instinctively]. The back of the Javelin went against the ground and, the Monster fell on it with the point penetrating several inches. The Monster was surprised looked down to see the Javelin in its chest she moved her fingers to the trigger squeezed released with a shout and, she said.

"GOOODDBBYYEEEYYAA!!!"

The Javelin took off propelling the Griffin Monster in the sky. She looks at Max and, he was looking to long at her because Sabrina knocked his Javelin away which landed close by Amyl ion. She dove for it before her body or, the javelin hit the ground, she flicked it towards him and, said.

"MMAAXXX!!!"

Sabrina took her eyes off of him for just a second watching Amyl ion and, that's all it took. He grabbed it by the trigger with his right hand and, shoved the Javelin in her side while squeezing and, releasing the trigger. [A slick move I have to play it again]. The Javelin with Sabrina takes off to the left a little and, gradually went straight up and, he said.

"Grab your tablet quick let's detonate the Javelin's.

Amyl ion had it opened and, touched the discharge and, the Griffin Monster blew up about 75 feet in the air. She looked over at him opening his tablet pressing the discharge and, Sabrina blew up about 50 feet in the air.

The lions were watching all of this happen. The Griffin Monster goes up explodes Female Succubus goes up explodes as their heads went up and, down watching the body parts fall to the ground. [Plunkadee, plunk, plunk, splat, splat] and, Green Tea said.

"We better go down and, see how they are."

The captains stayed sitting on the ground watching the body part's falling and, their kind of stunned for a while and, he said.

"That's the first time you called me Max."

She smiled at him and, he was very glad to see that smile from her.

The lions are coming down the hillside realize they've got to get up meet the lions and, start to get the dust off their uniforms again.

Their journey into town is almost complete.

The body parts on the ground begin to burn up and, leave a charred resemblance. They grabbed the one Javelin that they had apiece and, came together and, embraced with breathing a sigh of relief and, no words were spoken yet. They just stood there and, the lion's walked up to them.

They couldn't leave that spot and, Green Tea said.

"WOW ... are you all right and, how did this all begin?"

Apple Blossom said.

"That was a terrific fight Maximilian and, Amyl ion we are so, very glad you came out all right."

She was on his chest and, facing the other way and, slowly she turns her head towards the lion's and, said.

"YAA were okay thank you for your concern but, please excuse us we want to be alone for a minute and, then we will continue on."

The lion's nod their head's and, walk away a little and, lay down on all fours.

He grab's her and, buries his head in her hair as she reaches up with her arms around him she start's whispering and, rubs her hands over his head and, kiss's his cheek as she is standing on her toes this goes on for a minute and, they kiss on the lips looks her in the eyes and, he said.

"Okay we're ready now let's go on our trip to town."

The lions were looking at one another and, thinking after that ordeal who could have a change like that and, be ready to go. They walk up to the lions they look exhausted gathered their strength and, Max ask's the two lions as he puts his arm around her and, said.

"How is your friend with her life in danger?"

Green Tea took to the answer before her and, said.

"Well, the local authorities said they understood and, other law enforcement agencies agreed and, they said that they would look the other way. She is in the City of Love with her dad, mom because they quit their jobs looked for careers in that area and, wanted to be around their daughter every single day morning, noon and, night with hugs and, kisses for they felt she didn't get hardly any of that as she was growing up and, they realized their neglect. Most all her friends now come around all the time. She was over whelmed with everything and, we believe that did it for her so, she is alive today because of that."

Amyl ion puts her hand on his stomach and, other arm around him as she looks up to him then at the Lions and, smiles that would stop a dictator from mass murder. Well come to think about it there is no more dictators on earth 1.

"We are very happy to hear that."

As he looks at her and, then back at the lions and, said.

"We would just love to meet her."

Amyl ion's mind flashed how she read on the ship's memory banks of history and, thought we must find ways to stop dictator's, communists, socialists, Marxist, leftist, anarchist, democrats, progressives, drugs dealers from coming into power and, killing innocent men, women and, children and, wanted to talk to her husband about it … now she had to focus and, Apple Blossom said.

"Well, kids the next valley is only 9/11 minutes away that's where you 2 want to go and, they'll be waiting for you. We timed it so, let's go if everybody is ready?"

They mount up on the 2 lion's and, the lion's get up to half speed. The music begins again and, Max said.

"We noticed abandoned bee hives along the way and, some on the ground what happened to the Bee's?"

Apple Blossom knew that one and, said.

"The dragon burn's up much of the land in hopes of driving every living thing away or, killing every living thing."

They look at each other and, with a stern look and, there both thinking now we got one more thing to do and, that was to kill that dragon and, Amyl ion said.

"I hear that it comes out tonight, is that right?"

"Yes, with a full moon and, nobody will be around ... believe me."

They finally reach the edge of the valley and, come into town and, walk a little way's until they are at the city hall as town's people look on and, wave with whispers talking to each other the mayor walks up and, said.

"Hey how you doing?"

The mayor is concerned and, comes up to the lion's and, said.

"It's good to see that all of you are alright. How are you Apple Blossom and, Green Tea."

Green Tea said.

"Never better mayor."

Green tea said.

"What have you been up to?"

Apple Blossom looks at the two of them and, gives them a look as if to say well you know what we've been doing and, Green Tea said.

"I got to talk to you they just killed 2 flying Monster's."

They talk for a little bit.

The mayor welcomes them they slide off the 2 lion's and, give a big hug to each lion. They shared their thanks with many words towards the lions about the bear encounter. The senior officials are waiting at the door and, the mayor said.

"Won't you please come inside we have food and, drinks.

A young man comes over to the lions and, gives them a slab of beef a piece and, the lions grab it with their mouth and, wink at the boy and, turn around and, walk away. Max and, Amyl ion walk through a crowd of people and, they notice billy as he comes through the crowd to meet them and, bringing a girl with him and, said.

"Maximilian, Amyl ion we just heard you 2 just killed 2 more Monsters."

They look at each other and, dialoged she said he said.

"WOW news travel's fast around here ... how are you doing Billy?"

Then Billy pull's his girlfriend to him and, then in front with his hands on her shoulder's and, is immolating what Max does to his wife and, introduces his girlfriend and, said.

"This is Lavita."

"Hi Maximilian and, I am very glad to meet you and, your most beautiful wife."

The two lady's touch cheeks as Max is standing behind her she puts her hands-on top of Max's hands when he placed them on her shoulders and, she said.

"I was wondering is it okay that we call you Bill and, Lavita?"

Billy liked that and, said.

"Yes, that would be fine … and, I really prefer Bill anyway."

She was thinking as was Lavita with a little code between them. Maybe it would be better to call him Bill to be more grown up and, Max said.

"Listen we will have plenty of time to visit and, I feel awfully rude but, we must go to the meeting."

Bill agreed and, understood how important that this meeting is to everyone and, said.

"Of course, we will see you later."

They walk through the crowd with her arms around his left arm and, the people are gathered around them. They see their uniforms with dirt here or, there. In a couple of minutes, they make it to the door and, shut's as they walk down the hall but, it reopens and, the people come through the door and, there expressions were smiling, rushing to catch up to hear what was going to be said. He ask's her as they walk together and, still curious about things.

"Was there anything else that God said about our son?"

The music starts [The Police-Every Little Thing She Does is Magic].

She looks up at him smiles that would stop a hurricane. She's thinking YAA he's taking interest in our boy to be. She raises her body and, twists a little cutie left and, right with her derriere walks on her toe's hands on his arm for support and, starts talking in his ear.

"The day I give birth a stranger will come by and, visit in the door way of the hospital and, he'll say. It's a beautiful day and, do you have any names picked out yet?"

"Is that it?"

"No, there's more when he leaves the doctor will come in. Okay you can go home in a little bit."

"You will say [Hey Doctor] who was that man in the doorway?"

The look on the Doctors face was like a smirk and, said.

"There hasn't been any body in this hallway it's restricted and, there's police officer's and, deputy's everywhere."

He stop's and, start's kissing her and, releases to look at her kiss's her again, again [SMACK, SMACK, SMACK] just like that. She puts her arms around his neck when he starts still standing on her toes, they hold that position for almost a minute [SMACK, SMACK, SMACK.] The mayor and, one of the senior officials were watching this when they came out from the conference room and, were looking for them. They stop smile the Mayor nudges the senior official as they grin and, they know. They stopped kissing and, she turns to them and, said.

"Were ready now."

They walk in and, someone show's them were to sit and, she really wanted to sit on his lap but, didn't then dinner was served. They finish eating and, she break's the silence.

"We want to see the Ring of Fire."

CHAPTER 19

They all look at one another and, knew that they were sent by God. The mayor spoke to the leaders of the valleys and, said.

"If were all done with our dinner, we shall all walk out the back door to the rock formation that's about 20 yards away."

They all quietly get up and, she wraps her arms back around his left arm. The captains get outside and, notice all kinds of nationalities. Max notices to his left a pile of what he thought was asbestos turned to the mayor and, said.

"Is that asbestos?"

The mayor looks at it.

"Yes, why do you ask?"

She looks at him curiously spoke softly and, she said.

"What is it Max?"

"That material is fire retardant."

Amyl ion starts thinking HHMMM what can be done with that? [It's in a form of chips about the size of a coin].

They're approaching the rock formation at the entrance and everybody stops except Max and, Amyl ion they watch still walking and, they get it. Walk in observing the Ring of Fire that it's about 9 or, 10 Feet wide and, the whole circle is in flames that are about 5 Feet tall or, taller as some of the flames go higher. They stand thinking how beautiful this is and, the colors so, bright. They can hear the faint sound of the fire with its crackle and, a slight hissing while it draws air that they can feel the air go by as the fire needs that fuel to keep going there was no other fuel [that is] wood and, she said.

"There is no heat Maximilian."

He puts his hand on her back and, then she puts her arms around his waist and, they both notice what appeared on one of the wall's an inscription but, was blurry and, waving so, as you couldn't make it out what it said with each letter moving like it was alive with the color's moving inside the letters of red, yellow, and, blue. She squeezes him and, look's up to him and, smiles that would stop an earthquake and, said.

"We got work to do."

They turn around hold hands and, walk out of the entrance of the rock formation where the Ring of Fire is and, she said.

"The inscription is there but, it's not legible yet."

He agreed with her in his mind and, said.

"We have to look for the Black Rose."

The mayor over heard them talking and, said.

"It's under one of the stones that's on or, in the Belly of the Dragon."

With the eagerness of a school boy waiting to spring into action Max said.

"Which one!"

She is right behind him with her eagerness as well and, said.

"How do we kill the dragon?"

The mayor shook his head and, said.

"AAHHH now that is a question that's been going on for decades and, decades."

Max with a blank face is thinking if I can get Samantha to do the ship's magic.

She really is getting to know him better and, turns to him and, said.

"What is it Max I know you're thinking of something?"

"I got an idea."

He turns to her with a bright face of discovery and, places his hands on her shoulders close to the neck she places hers on top of his. He looks at the mayor then back at her and, she's loving this and, he said.

"How many stones are there Mr. Mayor?"

"Well 4, I think."

The senior official brings his arm out from the crowd and, said.

"YAW that's right 4 Stones, the Diamond, Amethyst, Emerald, and, Ruby and, legend has it that the Black Rose is under or, in the Diamond stone."

The mayor with his firm face said.

"Bring back the stones to the Ring of Fire or, the conference room as proof."

There reading each other and, didn't take their eyes away thinking to themselves she's waiting with whatever it is and, he said.

"Amyl ion you see that pile of asbestos over there?"

She looks over for a couple seconds then back to him and, nods her head yes and, he said.

"Well, I think the ship can make us a couple of fire proof cloak's and, we just have to get some of that asbestos pile to the mountain and, are you with me?"

She thinks for a moment with enthusiasm she shout's out.

"Kenny Ray, Bill, can Maximilian and, I borrow your wagon?"

Their lost in the crowd and, one said.

"Sure, you can."

She moves her legs like so, far so, good and, she said.

"Okay then put in about 15 gallons of that asbestos in one of the wagon's please."

How she came up with that number the calculation she did it with … we may never know. He looked at her like how did you figure out that one … okay, I'll just trust her rubbed her neck with his thumbs and, he said.

"Men can you bring the wagon at the asbestos pile along with 3 buckets, please?"

Her mind is snapping into the conversation and, she said.

"Men take them to the side of the Mountain were we first met and, how soon can you get started …?"

They think for a moment as there still glued to their eyes and, Bill said.

"Well 30 minutes to get it loaded don't you think Kenny Ray? … Yes, and, it'll take us 2 to 3 hours to get there."

Max said.

"Will get Green tea, and, Apple Blossom to take us back I hope and, get there before they do with the asbestos. We will pay you very well later on."

He reaches up with his left hand and, puts it on her cheek with his thumb running across her puffy lips and, kisses her, she kisses back opens her eyes wider up at him and, smiles with a wiggling of her whole figure a little and, facial expressions showing [I am so, happy] and, he said.

"We have to plan and, rest when we get back because we will be up probably all night and, I just hope the ship can transform the asbestos into those cloaks for us."

Her face showed a compelling look and, said.

"Samantha make's our clothes and, repairs our uniforms for us she should be able to."

Bill is excited comes over to them and, he said.

"I always dip the tips of my bullets in pig's blood and, give them to Kenny Ray when he goes hunting for Monster's."

She was very interested with that and, said.

"Why is that I never heard of such a thing?"

"They can't enter the afterlife when their shot and, there is no chance of them ever coming back to this world or, any other world for that matter."

Bill was thinking to himself I hope they catch on and, starts to explain with his hands.

"Well ... if ... you ... dip ... the ..."

That's when Max said.

"I got it we dip the tips of the Javelin's in the pig's blood and, when they penetrate the body there gone forever."

Kenny Ray said.

"YAA, you got it now."

Bill clapped his hands twisted them said.

"Let's do this."

Kenny Ray said.

"Oh, there's one more thing and, the kicker is once the Javelin is in the dragon's body it cannot be removed no matter how hard the dragon tries."

Amyl ion put her hands in front of her with a thankful expression and, faces them with a sense of urgency.

"Let's get going gentlemen and, bring the wagon and, load the asbestos please. Thank you all from the bottom of our hearts."

Max said.

"We owe you a debt of gratitude to you all."

That's when the lions came into view she grabbed his forearms looked at them and, to her beloved she said.

"Maximilian guess who's hear?"
Everybody looks and, Apple Blossom said.
"Are you ready to go back?"
Max said.
"Did you get anything to eat?"
Green Tea said.
"We sure did, we split an antelope after the slab of beef that the young man gave us and, we must've been hungry."
The young man appeared again and, gave to Max 2 more slabs of beef in a sack for when the lions reach the mountain to eat because they loved their friends ... the lions and, she said.
"Well then let's go and, we can't Thank You enough."
She turned with her hands together again in front and, with just a little bow and, turning from side to side a little and, looking at everyone humbly and, said.
"Thank You."
Green Tea said.
"We know you can do it because the land needs to be restored."
The lion's lay on all 4s and, Apple Blossom with a smile said.
"You know the routine."
There on their way down the road and, she sees the many abandoned bee hives along the way and, think's when the land is restored the bee's will be back and, she wants to collect a couple when they get back but, think's I got the biggest responsibility right now and, I'm thinking about a collection. That's foolish of me. He looked over at her and, noticed she was deep in thought as they're riding along. He said to himself I got to ask what she was thinking about maybe I shouldn't but, then again, I should I'm so, crazy about her. They get to the rest spot but, nothing much was said there all thinking about what's ahead. The lion's take their rest knowing they have to trek on back. They lay under a cherry tree that has an empty bee hive in it with in his lap her head laying on his chest facing up at him. They drift away fall asleep he thinks of the ship wakes up and, said.
"Samantha, can you hear me?"
"Yes Captain."
"We will be coming to the ship in a little while."
She opens her eyes and, is listening in and, he said.

130

"Samantha, can you transform pieces of asbestos into cloak's that are the size of a 10' foot by 10' foot Blanket?"

"What's the size of the asbestos? Is it in powder form?"

"No, the size of coin's and, we need 2 cloak's that size to shield ourselves from a fire breathing dragon."

"Searching the data and, I need to know how much asbestos is there?"

Amyl ion puts her hand on his chest as Max tells Samantha 15 gallons and, Samantha said.

"That's enough the data show's now that the cloak's will be thicker and, Captains put on masks from storage before bringing it on board and, just a side note Captain's it's fire resistant of up to 1600 Degrees Fahrenheit."

She must be a little drowsy because her eyes are opening and, closing and, he said.

"Samantha knows we are together here?"

She whispers in a slumber state of mind and, said.

"Yes, Baby and, everything is going forward as planned."

She grab's his hand gives it a kiss. He thinks she needs some time to nap and, waits as he put his head back against the cherry tree.

Pause ... she opens her eyes a little and, reaches for his ear to spin her index finger around it and, he opens his eyes and, looks down at her and, thinks are these things really happening ... there she is my pretty wife and, he said.

"I Love You." She breathes in with eyes closed and, pleasantly said.

"I Love You too ... and, I feel rested so, we've got to go to prepare ourselves for tonight and, Kenny Ray and, Bill are on their way to the mountain."

They get up and, the lion's get up too and, she said.

"Samantha are there any cherry trees near the mountain with a bee hive in it?"

"Only one and, it's 1,983 yards or, 1.127 miles north of the mountain."

"That's too far I want this one here it looks just right for what I want to do."

She looks up at the bee hive and, he looks up too and, she said.

"Green Tea may I stand on your back please so, I can take the bee hive back to the ship?"

He walks over under it and, she climbs on his back and, asks for Max's knife. He tosses it to her and, she cut's it loose from the branch and, she has it in her hand and, was going to toss the knife back and, he said.

"Keep it on you my dear you may need it sometime."

She rolls it around in her hands and, said.

"It smell's good on the inside and, I'll have to clean it up a little."

She takes off her belt from the uniform and, it has a double belt to undo if needed and, wraps it around the bee hive and, attaches it to her belt loop. They all watch this and, she thinks to herself ... I've got to get serious they think I'm being silly and, she said.

"Let's go."

CHAPTER 20

They arrive back at the mountain, they dismount and, said to the lions.

"Thank You both and, that we love you."

Max held out the 2 slabs of beef to them and, Apple Blossom said.

"You will be careful, won't you?"

Max looks at his wife with a protecting face and, he said.

"Yes, we will."

The lions take the beef in their mouth they do an about face walking away. They too were going to turn around but, she grabbed ahold of his hand and, said.

"Oh, Maximilian I just want to stand here awhile and, watch them go until there out of our sight."

"MM, AAHHAA … I know what you mean."

Their watching as they disappear and, slowly turn around and, head for the entrance of the mountain. They were so, very grateful for what the lions did for them and, they will never forget it and, she said.

"Samantha, could you open the entrance for us please?"

The entrance opens like a round portal and, step in to look at the ship for a moment and, he said.

"I'm going to lay down."

"Okay I want to put these bee-hives in storage."

He takes her by the hand she tags along by Green Froggy they both give it a couple of taps and, goes [Squeaky-Squeak] she gets a happy smile after hearing that she shakes her hair around with her hand. She finds a place in storage on a box at chest high as he watches and, she places her hands gently on top of one. He feels she's dreaming and, said.

"I'm going to wash my hands."

She smiles at him as he left and, looks at the bee-hive and, lights flashed 7 or, 8 times as she glided her hands down the sides and, in her mind seeing the development in stages. The sounds of bee's buzzing and, whispering [QUEEN BEE] over and, over again. She hears he is done with washing his hands and, snaps out of its grip and, leaves flipping her hair with a twist in her hips with her legs having their own unique choreography. She meets him near the bed and, they plop down to rest and, plan the night out with her snuggled under his left arm and, he said.

"Samantha, can you locate the horses and, the wagon with 2 on board as they are heading this way and, give an E.T.A. please."

"AYE, AYE Captain ... 30 minutes E.T.A Captain."

They both look at the clock it's 11:45 AM.

"Maximilian, we made good time of the day considering we left early."

"Yes, we did and, they'll be here about 12:15 so, perhaps we can rest and, eat something. We'll need to unload the wagon and, bring the asbestos up in the ship."

Pause ... Samantha said.

"1 Minute till there at the mountain."

So, they leave the ship and, go outside. He walks over to a boulder sticking out of the ground like so, many of them are with her by his side they lean against it and, wait. She decides to move on his front facing the same way and, takes his hands and, wraps his arms around her belly looking for the horse's and, wagon to appear.

The music starts [Elvis-One Night with You].

He bends down and, starts kissing her ear and, cheek as he hums. She giggles and, he keeps kissing both sides with her giggling. She tries to squirm away but, she just loves it. Then he moves to her other ear whispers [I Love you 3 times] she put in a little seriousness and, said.

"The inscription ... squeal ... on the wall ... giggle, giggle, giggle ... at the Ring of Fire do you remember ... HA, HA, HA ... what it said."

They have to get serious and, he said.

"Could you say it please [SMACK, SMACK] and, I'll repeat after you. Please, please, please!"

He waited she said.

"[Seek, Seek the chosen hand, It's in a descendant's land]

[Seek, Seek Japheth's hand, into her hair facing you she stand's] [See the Black Rose in her eyes, draw out now and, be wise]."

She does a 180.

"We must repeat that together my love."

She put her hands on his chest looking at one another with her pupil's opening up the iris's disappearing turning Black and, the same 2 Roses appear as before Black and, the petals on one are trimmed in red and, the other is trimmed in Green on the petal's. Then her eyes go back to hazel. She puts her arms around him as he reaches down to draw her up as her body bends and, they start kissing a touch and release. They had to stop cause the horse's and, wagons appeared.

She turns around sees Bill, and, Kenny Ray. They walk over to the entrance of the cave as Max points at the entrance. Kenny Ray directs the horses to the entrance and, said.

"WHOA Gladys, WHOA, Bess."

They all greet one another and, Kenny Ray said.

"Where do we unload this here asbestos?"

They look at each other smile Max turns his attention to what they are about to see. He looks at them and, said.

"Gentleman what you are about to see we would like you to be silent for a while what's behind this rock formation."

He turns to her and, gestures with his right hand and, said.

"Captain Amyl ion if you would please lead the way."

"Thank You Captain Maximilian."

They're thinking that a professional approach to this is the right way which would help them keep silent. All 4 step in and, stop and, the captains watch their expressions as Kenny Ray, and, Bill are stunned at what they see inside the cave. She wanted things to move along and. Said.

"Gentlemen would you like to come aboard we'd like to show you where to put the asbestos."

Max said.

"Samantha we are coming aboard would you please lower the hatch and, there are 2 guests coming on board."

"AYE, AYE Captain."

Bill and, Kenny Ray was looking around in the cave and, Bill said.

"Who was that?"

Max knew it was his turn to answer that one and, said.

"That is Samantha the ship's overseer and, when we want things done or, need some information she can do almost anything except command the ship."

Kenny Ray was dumbfounded and, wondered that there could be such a technology as this and, said.

"This is absolutely amazing I can hardly believe it."

Bill said.

"Hey Captain Amyl ion what does the [27-Trip's] mean?"

"I thought you would ask that and, it is the name of the Ship."

Kenny Ray said.

"What's the size of this ... aaahh ... saucer Maximilian?"

"103 feet wide in all directions with it being 11.2 feet in height at the outer edges that are flat but, rounded a little at the upper and, lower edges and, has a slight curve on the bottom and, when the hatch or, steps are shut it is completely sealed. The top is a little more rounded but, not a bubble because the real bubble is centered inside with it completely sealed with no glass and, the way we see out ... well that's a secret. The thickness of it is 28.9 feet from center top ... to center bottom ... in the middle. The stars and, stripes you see on the starboard side in front of the [27-Trip's] there ... well it waves whenever the ship is in flight."

Kenny Ray, Bill was playing around like young boys pushing, slapping on their back shoulders with some dust each looking at the flying saucer right in front of them and, Bill said.

"I see about 10 more stars on that flag ... I suppose the United States is making positive progress."

She reached up to whisper in her beloveds' ear.

"I knew you were very proud of her and, the way you said it ... well I am too."

He thought to himself. Perhaps I shouldn't have said all that confidential information then whispered back to her ear and, said.

"My Love if you add the numbers together sideways what do you get?"

She looked up at him when he raised up and, she put her left hand around his neck and, contemplated with intrigue on her face and, placed her right hand on his left check and, tapped it with her fingers as she was adding the numbers like he said.

"HHMMM ... 4, 5, 6, 7, 8, 10, 18, and, 9 equals 27 ... HA, HA, HA, HA, HA, HA, HA ... that's amazing ... how did that happen?"

He smiled and, knew she would like that and, he said she said.

The music starts [Maxx-Get A Way Shuffle Dance]

"That's code in remembrance of President Trump draining the swamp back in the day."

"Yes, I just saw that info in the history banks at the bridge but, there's a time span missing of weeks or, months it wasn't clear. We must go back in time at earth 1 to crush the communists for them or, help them without anyone knowing … right baby?"

"Right! … that missing time span was when something mysteriously happened and, not recorded and, also there seems to have been some milk toast politicians in higher offices back then but, not the president and, the time capsule will take us back instantly and … My Wife you are brilliant!"

She lit up like a red, white and, blue fireworks display from his complement still has her hands on his cheeks and, she said.

"Then setting the date in the capsule like it said at the bridge and, I'll sit on your lap and, we get commfee and, in an instant we'll be there. Then fall asleep later tonight to rest."

"HA, HA your so, cute … we will start in D. C. when we wake up with turning the ship invisible and, remember there's only 24 hours available on the panel that slides in the ships brain."

"I remember … and, baby it will be exciting that we can kick the communists butt … side by side."

He puts his hands on her cheeks and, said.

"I Love fighting beside you … but, most of it will be on the ship with the lasers … and, if need be … we'll get off and, fight but, not to kill … just stun them to knock them out and, they'll think twice!"

"Alright I see … using the lasers to stun the crowds with a sweeping motion from the ship and, melt their weapons. Then we'll move across to New York, jersey along the east coast and, the mid-west at hot spots. Then to the west coast and, into Europe and, Russia."

"Then we sweep through Africa, the middle east and, the Asia pacific."

"We finish up with the rest of the Americas."

"I like it … and, we'll do our part for the United States and, the free world!"

"OH … one more thing we must take our lasers."

They laugh and, smash a kiss with a groan that echoed in the cave and, the two men slap each other on the arms as if to say look at this ... they lean back and, silently laugh. Well, they just had to wait for their love to play out because they heard of times like this.

They release and, want to get it over with and, finally enter in the Ship.

"Samantha scan our friend's and, you guys are always welcome aboard now."

Max points and, said.

"This is where we put the asbestos through this opening on the floor ... and, Samantha could you open the receiver?"

They stand there for a couple of seconds and, she said.

"Did you bring the 3 Bucket's?"

She still wants things to move along. He gets the masks from the storage area and, said.

"If you would please put these mask's on as you load and, unload up in the ship."

Kenny Ray took his hat off and, scratched his head and, wanted to get this over with too and, said.

"Well let's get going Billy."

She turned and, looked and, thought to herself where's one for me and, said.

"But, there's only 3 Bucket's."

They stop and, look at Max with a bucket a piece in their hands and, he said.

"Well maybe there's one in storage."

He was thinking old school that he didn't want her doing any manual labor like this and, when he came back, he said.

"I can't find one."

They look at each other as he comes back and, the captains place a hand on each other's cheek for a moment with the understanding and, the two men leave. She moved her lips to say thank you and, she said.

"Samantha the asbestos is going to be put down the receiver are you ready to receive?" "Yes, captain."

The three start bringing it in as she goes to do research at the bridge. The job is done and, the is hatch is closed and, they take off their mask's and, throws them away and, he stands by her side at the bridge and, bill said.

"Oh, I almost forgot."

He reaches in his back pocket and, pulls out a half pint of pig's blood and, walks over and, give's it to her. She gets out of the chair takes it the captains look at bill and, she said.

"Bill what's this and, it's all very dark red?"

CHAPTER 21

"It's Pig's Blood."

"Oh, Thank You ... UMM, and, so, we dip the Javelin tips in the pig's blood is that correct?"

"YAA or, drop a couple of drops on each tip and, smear it around and, it will dry and, once the Javelin enters the flesh it won't come out ... it's just an amazing thing."

Her body relaxed said.

"You guys already knew about the Javelin's, didn't you?"

Bill is excited and, said.

"Oh, yes Green Tea, and, Apple Blossom, told us."

Kenny Ray said.

"Mr.'s Milan ... we didn't do anything wrong did we about knowing about the Javelin's?"

"Absolutely not ... you gentlemen are the best."

As she smiled that would stop a space ship from taking off. She puts the bottle in both hand's and, clutches it towards her belly.

"Thank You Oh, so, very much ... I really mean that."

She looks up at him as he's standing there still and, they knew how important this was for the men to give this to them ... Max break's the silence and, said.

"Excuse me ... Samantha when will the cloaks be ready?"

"In 4 Hour's and, 48 Minute's."

They look at the clock it's 1:19PM.

Bill said.

"That's 6:07 well we better get going Kenny Ray we can't wait that long."

They both had a worried look on their face's as they said there good byes and, made their way down the step's and, looking at the ship one more time and, walked outside with them as they watched them climb into the wagon. They said their goodbyes one more time. They tipped their hats and, Kenny Ray said.

"Giddy up Gladys, Bess."

They watched as they rode away until they couldn't be seen … they looked at each other and, he said.

"We could really use the A. I. Robots back on earth 1."

"Why is that?"

"They can identify the billionaires very quickly that fund the communists and, anarchists in the world to withdraw their money to use to destroy governments, cities, and, monuments of history. They tried to bring down the United States along with free peoples over the globe. They could have given it to needy individuals."

"YAW … that leaves the human element out of it."

They hold hand's as they walk back inside and, sit in the captain's chairs. He's thinking she knows he's contemplating on what to do. So, she ask's Samantha for a couple of tasty fruit drinks with protein. A mechanical hand drops their drinks from the ceiling they grab the drinks and, the hands zip back up and, he said.

"That was a good thing you did … I needed that … how did you know?"

She smiled and, gave out a sudden gushing of laughter … that meant … I know what you're thinking. She took a sip and, uses her head, neck, eyes and, whole body with a coy smile.

So, there sipping on those tasty treats as he looked steadily at her and, he said.

"Oh, by the way we need an acquisition for a couple of A. I. robots."

She jumped to it and, went to bridge and, said.

"I can do that right now … and, keep talking please while I'm at the bridge."

She has her back to him sends the request to earth 1 sits back down while he's talking and, he sees she has it completed and, said.

"This is what I propose we do and, please say what's on your mind at any time."

She's silent sits back down and, knows how important this is and, he said.

"The dragon will come out sometime tonight when there is a full moon and, that it will strike at places that it hasn't been before such as barn's, house's, crop's that are close by us so, we don't have to reach out to far and, try to keep the dragon close."

He stopped took a sip and, wanted to see what she would say. He sort of had it planned out anyway but, held back. She is in deep thought for a good minute and, took a sip and, she said.

"If we can find the area's that the dragon will strike first, we can be standing by with the Javelin's and, with the cloak's and, we will be able to launch the Javelin's at the dragon."

She pointed her finger briefly at him and, said.

"Exactly."

They stop and, think. He ask's Samantha if she can locate the nearest barn's, house's, crop's and, livestock? … silence … Samantha comes back after a moment with the information they need and, Amyl ion said.

"Could you display it on the viewer's please with how far apart are they from one another?"

He added before Samantha could answer and, said.

"Could you locate the dragon in its cave or, it's hide out and, how close by to our location is the dragon and, one more thing, how close is the dragon to the barn's, house's green crop's, and, livestock?"

They wait with anticipation. Samantha comes back and, she display's the information on the viewer's and, said.

"Here is the layout from the dragon to the nearest locations to the farthest place away from the dragon … one more thing Captain's …"

They wait with their gut turning that there might be some bad news as they are surveying the viewer's and, Samantha said.

"The long body that is curled up in the area you see is glowing red on the viewer and, it is 2.43 miles, southeast of here."

Both look at the location of the glowing red pulsing motion and, looking at the distances of all the location's but, keep looking at the pulsing motion of what they hope is the dragon.

"Hey, I think I just saw it move."

She looks too and, there watching for a couple of minutes and, there observance pay's off. They have a sigh of relief and, she said.

"That's got to be the dragon because it just moved again."

He turn's his chair towards her she turn's too and, he said.

"Captain where do you think the dragon will strike first?"

"It would appear where the fresh crops have grown while the dragon was waiting for the full moon."

So, they look at the distance where the strike will be then back at each other and, he said.

"While it is day light, we place a couple of the Javelin's close by the crops and a couple at the next location just in case the dragon strike's there ... Amyl ion your thought's please?"

"I like it."

He goes on while she put her finger under the nose and, moved it back and, fourth and, he said.

"Now at night we carry 5 Javelin's a piece with cloak and, what do you think?"

She takes her finger away and, said.

"We have to get the dragon's attention first to get at least 2 Javelin's in the belly of the dragon close to the heart and, vital organs to be sure."

He smiles with the expression on his face of how things are rolling along very well and, he said.

"We've got 10 Javelin's left and, put 2 at each location so, that's 8." She raises her finger and, said.

"With 2 at the mountain close by."

She was thinking that to be on the safe side she wanted those 2 Javelin's close at the entrance of the cave to protect her husband and, the ship.

"Good and, one more thing I want to coordinate with Samantha the Javelin's all going off at the same time once there stuck in the belly of the dragon what do you think?"

She meditates for a moment and, said.

"That's a great idea because with as many Javelins that we can stick in the belly of the dragon we can signal for Samantha to blow them off at the same time and, no more dragon."

She raised her arms squeals with a celebration and, hopefully that's exactly what's going to happen and, he said.

"That's right, now I think that once we get that first one in the belly of the dragon the dragon will be focused in its belly. The dragon will focus on trying to blow fire down on one of us we have our cloaks with us that's when we have to go to work. I do mean stay alert at what we must do because the dragon will be chasing one of us so, one of us will be sending a Javelin at the midsection that first person will have the cloak for protection from its mouth of fire the second Javelin will penetrate the dragon. It focuses its attention at the second person and, so, on and, what do you think?"

"When we get as many Javelins in the belly of the dragon, Samantha will know which ones they are and, we'll have to give a code to say to Samantha and, she ignites them when we say, [Samantha Blow] sounds pretty good."

"Amyl ion are you scared?"

She got a little worried look and, said.

"Yes, I'd be lying if I said that I wasn't scared."

He raised his right hand to make a point and, with his index finger and, he said.

"If the code doesn't work, we blow them up all at once that are in the belly with our tablet so, we must get as many as possible in its belly."

They pause for a minute he twists in his chair and, said.

"Amyl ion what do you think of all this planning and, preparations?"

She ponders for a few seconds.

"I'm ready and, it all has to work ... Yaw know it's all pretty stimulating"

She's thinking and, he picks it up that she's in a thought process and, he said.

"What is it Captain?"

"Well, I was thinking what if we go searching for the dragon at the location and, kill it there with either ourselves or, take the ship there and, destroy the cave and, the dragon?"

He doesn't say a word but, is looking at the floor and, at her. Finally, with a deep breath and, a big discovery coming over her face and, she said.

"Captain we can't risk ourselves with not knowing the whereabouts', of Raven Hades or, risking the ship and, again not knowing what this Devil has planned."

He is silent ... then with a great big smile he said.

"YYEESSS."

She leaned back and, relaxed in her chair and, said.

"We must do this the way we first planned it and, then see what Raven Hades will do if anything."

He gave her a slightly stern face and, said.

"Hopefully that's when his plans are defeated, he'll leave and, the ship must be protected."

She agrees by nodding her head and, said.

"Samantha … Raven Hades still does not know our whereabouts', is that right?"

"That is correct captain."

They smile showing to each other that their discussion was very productive and, successful.

"Amyl ion well I guess we better get ready and, prepare ourselves and, are you up for a nice meal before we go and, perhaps rest awhile."

She gets it and, said.

"Yes, I want some spicy chicken, veggie's and, an apple."

"What no Blossom?"

She crack's a cry with laughter thinking that was so, good and, reaches for the Green Froggy and, it goes [Squeaky-Squeak]. Both laugh for a while enjoying themselves prepare their food. They finish eating go to the storage area and, put the pig's blood on the Javelin tip's and, coordinate with Samantha what is going down with the dragon. They grab a couple of bags for the stone's to be put in and, he grab's an extra knife. It seems that there all ready and, they look at the clock and, it's 2:23pm.

"Maximilian in roughly 3 and, a half hours the asbestos cloak's will be ready."

They sit back down in the captain's chairs and, he said.

"By the way these chair's will move when your thought process tells them to go across the bridge when you work at a subject matter to research or, manually control the ship."

She looks around study's the area and, thought that it would be more relaxing to sit than stand and, she said.

"Samantha when does the full moon come out tonight?"

"At 1:01AM at its peak. The tradition on this planet is called [Honey Moon]."

"Samantha are their other full moon names and, if there are Amyl ion and, I don't want to know them."

She smiles and, knows what he's thinking.

She was right there are more names for full moons and, he didn't want a distraction from the name of [Honey Moon].

"Yes, there are other full moon names."

Pause … There thinking that this could be there last night together.

Looking at one another she gets up rubbing her hips a little slowly goes to him in his chair sits in his lap her right arm around his neck places her head behind his head and, hum's a lullaby that she just created. She thinks I need him right now I'll soften his heart. Her left hand is on his right cheek and, he kisses her wrist. A couple of minutes pass by she moves to the front of him to straddle him places her knees and, shins on the outside of his thigh's and, start's kissing him on the lip's as he groans a little and, lean's back to balance herself and, take's the top part of her uniform off and, holds it for a couple of seconds in the air then drops it on the floor with a seductive look. She gives him a side look as she turns her head then wiggles her shoulders a few times and, stops for a few seconds then taking her hair pulls it to her left side and, brushes it with her hands and, twisted it. She opens her mouth and, take's his hand's and, places them on her breasts and, squeezes his hands for a moment. They close their eyes and, she release's her hands for 15 or, 20 seconds. She is already shuddering around her belly. She stop's and, gets up to stand in front of him and, raises her arms above her waving along with her body that said I'm all yours and, her face is very alluring and, drawing him and, said.

CHAPTER 22

"My husband please take me to the shower."

He picks her up as he always does take's her right to the shower takes the rest of her uniform off and, he takes his off tosses them on the bed close by and, jump in the shower. They come out approach the bed she wrap's her arms around him draw's her lips to his ear and, whisper's something but, I can't tell. He wrap's his arms around his precious wife listen's as she is caressing, stroking his neck and, hair and, she said.

"I don't want to lose you and, I don't want to lose all of this that we have."

He wanted to complete that statement of hers and, said.

"Happy Honeymoon Mr.'s Milan."

She was so, filled with contentment that she bent her knees to collapse on him with her head back and, she wanted to put it in concrete with a low soothing voice and, said.

"Tthhaaa tthhiirrd."

The music starts [Rachmaninov-Prelude in C Sharp minor Op. 3 No. 2]. VIDEO. Smoking hands.

Then her whispers become very quiet and, he starts kissing her very passionately and, he's got his left hand on the back of her head with his right hand on her breast and, pressing on her lips. Then whispers in her ear that I love you kissing her cheek then to her lips and, back to her cheek and, neck. They release she guide's him to lay on the bed with her right hand and, she mount's him with her arms around his neck and, head she continues to talk in his ear, her shinbones are on his sides searching for his manhood stops talking presses him in takes a deep breath as the hammer pounds through her body until she's no longer possessing her faculties.

Then starts to rise up with her hair hanging down as she is still pressing him in and, straightens her back placing her hands on her thighs and, when she has him almost all in, her hips and, body began to dance for him with arms limp she fled to the clouds with head back rolling and, took another deep breath. Extreme pleasure took possession of her. Pounding, pounding her relentlessly. She's obliterated in that minute but, has utter commitment he thinks she said.

"Don't go ... don't go ... don't go ... don't go ... don't go ... don't go ... don't go."

Pause ... The trembler released ... then thanked her don't go.

She materialized with her shaking to laugh with her man. A couple minutes pass by as they talk and, soon her disappearance has seized upon her again she dares not to stop.

The Music continues.

She sticks her fingers in her hair at times holding her head ... then back on his chest. When their peaking sometimes she's shaking her head with that coal black hair swishing around the trembler whispers in her mind Oh, have another one my dear. She peeks at him and, thinks how much she adores him times it when they reach the top of the waterfall with her pulling on his habitat that pierced her, she bore the extreme thumping in her frame. The beautiful sounds that she made were like she was practicing a mad dash up a stairway. Lost, lost, lost ... she's in radiant thirst clutching her breasts squeezing pulling them up gulping for more. They broke out into a sweat. What's left is her rich intensity of the highest waterfall that pounds at the rocks below.

Pause ... Both laugh real silly like ... in a minute they clean up come back to bed and, she said.

"Would you get on top please my husband?"

She thought about her body and, how it's lost strength.

I must say that when she calls him my husband it is with the utmost Love that comes from within her whole being.

They resumed slowly stroking her he said.

"I wanted to tell you what I discovered while I was reading one time why God gave you those beautiful wings as a permanent marking."

She has to clear her throat and, focus and, said.

"HHMMM ... what did it say I'm very interested because I'm between waterfalls."

148

"It's his protection for you and, to say to others. [You are under his wings]."

The music starts [Rachmaninoff-Moment Musicaux No. 4 in E Minor]. VIDEO smoking fingers.

She smiles with that information has that drunk look moving her head from side to side meaning she's waiting for the surrounding touch all over her skin. She places her finger between his eyes and, moves it down to the tip of his nose as she studies his face. They're going to finish up knows she's about to leave him placing her hands on the side of her head and, stares at him with a waving silken passion. He feels her bowels are burning and, no one is home. On and, on ... she's in her journey with convulsions and, knows she'll break no laws. He increases his speed to match the timing of her wide field of delight with groans, deep cries the dividing of her property has begun. He holds back a little to prolong her empire. Then he decides that it is time to give it all he has for her. There yelling like they're coming apart taking longer for the weld to bond all the way through ... just the way he planned it. This goes on until there fulfilled and, lay on the bed as dead. They recover and, think of the responsibility that lays ahead and, she said.

"Samantha, could you wake us up at 6:00PM please?"

"AYE, AYE Captain."

There on their right side him in front laying sleeping naked Samantha wakes them up and, he turns a 180 and, he said she said.

"Captain ... mmMMmm yes ... it's time to get in the capsule ... HHAAA! LET'S GO." The Music starts [Maxx-Get Away]

They jump up grab their uniforms and, walk and, talk to the time capsule. He slips as he tries to put his right leg in the pant leg and, falls. She's got her uniform on laughs lowly and, giggles she falls on top of him when her feet got tangled up with his. He turns with his hands catching her shoulders ... her hair bouncing and, brushing against his face and, they look in their eyes and, she said.

"That's what I get for laughing."

He didn't want to say anything laughs with her a little looks her face over and, pulls her down with a kiss she presses hard with twisting her lips to sink that one in their hearts. They release with a [SMACK] she sits up with a smile adjusts her uniform offers her hand out she pulls him up seals his pants and, slips his top on then they climb in. Both grab the handle look at each other and, laugh while they shut it together. She looks around for the first time not much room with the inside glowing a steel blue color he tells her what he's going to do and, said.

"We seal it with pressure set the time of year, month, day, and, hour."

"I'm getting on your lap ... woo this capsule is small ... there I'm good now."

He just takes it like it's a natural thing between them with his left arm around the back of her lower waist and, her right arm around his shoulders so, his right can use the devises along with her left and, he said.

"Here we go ... could you turn that time indicator and, I'll push the lever too hindsight 2020."

They look at the viewers all around them as they light up with a dozen they turn when they internally command them too. They'll be at D. C. in a second as they feel a motion of the capsule with their body's swaying and, there right above D. C. She can hardly believe it as they observe the rioters and, attempting to take down a statue. He knew of this from history a couple of centuries before. There 6 to 8 miles above as there hovering and, zoom in and, she said.

"Which group do we take out first?"

"This one and, then that one." The Music starts [Authority Song-John Mellencamp]

He points at the viewer ... they quickly make adjustments and, fire many red, white and, blue lasers to knock the Marxists on the ground and, then melt whatever they had in their hands as projectiles. They wait a few seconds to watch the results. The peaceful protestors started to run away in a panic looking in the sky but, couldn't see anything. The captains celebrated with excitement as they talk with overlapping words.

Their words cool down talk back and, forth quickly and, he said she said.

"Look there on this viewer at the old white house ... how do you know ... old photographs and, film I've seen ... there must be 2 dozen men in black surrounding a white-haired guy and, a short haired man ... oh, I remember the info just popped on the viewer ... let me read it too ... that's the 45th President and, General Flynn ... there looking in the sky for us ... should we show them something ... you're asking me? Yes ... okay let's go down and, just show them the flag and, the ships name … yaw I like that that'll be great … oh, one more thing … what's that … let's play the star bangled banner … wow let's do it I can't wait to see their faces."

There at the old rose garden in a blink of an eye and, the ship hover's sudden like 100 feet above them but, they can't see it and, the U. S. Flag appears and, it's waving [IT ALWAYS DOES WHEN IN FLIGHT]. That's all they can see and, the secret service draws their weapons and, the President said.

"Hold your fire!"

The bullets would just drop to the ground from the ship's resistance.

She touches the viewer and, the song begins … redone by a most resent male singer. Everyone on the ground looks at each other with surprised faces and, they put their weapons away placed their hands on their hearts. The captains did the same thing as they watch all the viewers with the flag waving on them. She points to a bunch of info in the corner viewer that gave the size of the flag when there singing and, it read 10 feet by 18. After the song is over with the President said.

"That was great I'd like to hear that again that was great … who are you?"

He turns on the speaker to say something but, she sweetly interrupts him on his right shoulder by tapping him with her right hand the speaker still on they talk back and, fourth and, she said he said.

"Captain should we really say anything … well maybe where we're from … oh, and, the dozen galaxy's away too … we should hurry now … you go first … okay Mr. President where from the future."

"Do I hear a young lady in the sky that we can't see?"

They look at each other in the ship and, she said.

"Yes, let me introduce myself and, my husband. We're both Captains of this space ship that you can't see except for just what we want you to."

There all surprised on the ground and, looking at one another and, again he said she said.

"We are from the year 2227 that's when we left this planet to go to earth 2 and, coming back here almost 11 months later … we must go now the ships invisibility time is only 24 hours … yes, and, it's running down and, we've got work to do."

The President has ideas since he's a business man and, he said.

"Won't you stay?"

He said she said.

"You'll see some spectacular events around your world … don't worry we both watch over you and, the United States."

All they see on the ground is the flag speeding away into a giant cloud and, sliced an opening into it and, that's the last they saw of it and, he said.

"Let's go to New York."

She touch's a button or, two and, she moves on his lap like she's dancing at the success. They do the same thing there and, finish up with the states then Europe there on their way to the middle east when he said.

"Hay! You know what I'd like to do?"

She listens with a firm face.

"While were here what are your thoughts on destroying the poppy fields in Afghanistan."

She thinks for a moment about the lives it ruins from her research and, said.

"I'm with you 100% captain."

She turns without hesitation and, moves the lever and, he thought about how fast she came up with the answer and, smiled as he too turned his dial. There at the large fields in an instant with rocking a little and, the ship hovers a ½ mile from the beginning of the fields and, he said.

"Let's use the backup lasers with setting the fields on fire."

They touch a few buttons a piece and, she said.

"I can see a number of armed personnel guarding the fields and, we are ready to commence captain."

"Good captain shall we take them out with a stun from the lasers?"

"Okay I'm set, let's do it."

They set a stun for each one of the guards with one blast it split into hundreds of areas and, they begin with the laser setting the fields on fire and, as they left, he turned to her a little and, smiled and, said.

"I've been wanting to do that... UUMMMPPHH."

Before he could finish what, he wanted to say she grabbed his head with her left hand and, turned him to her and, smashed him with a giant kiss.

Pause … don't they know that time is wasting away.

They finish with the rest just like they talked about earlier. They turn their eyes peak at the controls and, adjust them without releasing their kiss. They stop at the lower part of the Americas work their way up there and, just about to go home as they hover talking back and, fourth and, she said he said.

"You know there must be something we could do for Mexico ... well not really ... and, why is that ... the politicians are corrupt and, the gangs run the country ... WWHHAAA! there must be something that could be done ... well maybe but, not right now ... okay let's talk about it and, research the matter ... I like it."

They finish up with Canada then agree to go home he turns a dial she moves a lever and, the time capsule motions a little with her moving in his lap a little and, they look at the remaining time left for time travel and, it read 22 hours, 47 minutes and, 7 seconds left. The viewers disappear time to exit they reach for the handle she places hers hands on his they laugh smile at each other push and, fall out getting their feet tangled up again in such a confined space. He lands on her she's barely able to hold his weight off he touches her right cheek with his and, there laughing themselves silly. He raises himself up on his hands they look for a while and, he said she said.

"We have to go back to bed and, rest ... okay help me up."

CHAPTER 23

There walking and, talking as they take their uniforms off and, place them on the bedside and, lay down naked on their right sides with him in front.

There sound asleep as they needed that rest when they are awoken by the alarm and, he has his arms around her and, must have turned to her during the night with her arm's tucked inside to stay warm and, her head buried in his upper chest. He draws the smell of her hair into his lungs and, he thought nobody has an aroma like her no wonder animals love her. She looks up at him he looks down at her and, he said she said.

"We got work to do."

"Yes, hurry let's get up."

They jump up from the bed and, they are so, focused cause nothing more is on their mind except what must be done about that dragon. They quickly get their uniforms on have some peppered beef brisket with cauliflower, carrots, peas with berries collect the 2 bags, 2 knifes, and, she puts the 2 Javelin's at the entrance of the cave on the inside where they enter in just for added precaution. Back inside waiting for Samantha to produce the 2 cloaks at the delivery door and, it's 6:06 pm. Time stood still when in the time capsule and, Samantha said.

"The cloaks are ready."

They stand hand in hand watch one coming out like an assembly line as one is dark grey. He grab's the edges of the first one it's about 2 and, a half foot wide because it's folded so, it can come out of the small door. He holds it up and, they look at the asbestos cloak and, there just smiling from ear to ear. The next one comes out and, she grab's that one and, hold's it up above her as well but, not so, high since she's 5 foot 3 inches tall. He can't see her so, he looks over the top of the cloak and, looks at her and, he said.

"Well, what do you think?"

It's heavy knowing not what to say.

He knows what to say because this is how he feels about her and, really wants to show her that he deeply, deeply, deeply loves her. He slowly takes the edges of the cloak and, said.

"Stand still please."

She is wondering what he is going to do she watches his face she knows that something special is going to happen and, relaxes with scratching her nose with a couple fingers and, she's amused.

He goes on and, said.

"There is an Ancient Tradition but, it is very relevant today because I know the ancients did this because it was all that they had to convey with their heart."

He is moving around her she listens keenly watches him and, he said.

"When a man put's a blanket around his bride to be and, has chosen her for his lifelong wife."

He stops behind her start's putting the cloak around her he close's the cloak with his arms around her very tight. He speaks to her in her right ear and, said.

"I choose you for my wife I love you with all my heart."

She closes her eyes and, lets it soak in for a second then turn's a 180 with the biggest smile yet ... that would crack open the ocean floor's her eyes are dancing all over his face choking up breathing erratically with amazement wipe's a few tears away. He's smiling back and, she said.

"Oh, My Dear Baby Maximilian! ... My Boy ... I hope to God I never break the tradition and, keep your arms around me for a while please I want to capture this moment for a lifetime." The music starts [Rachmaninoff-Moment Musicaux No. 4].

She presses her head against his chest a couple of minutes go by he kiss's her head many times as they rock back and, forth she's squeezing him several times with breathing out each time. She's ready and, reaches up with a hungry kiss standing on her toes and, groans. Streams of her happy tears had slowly trailed down turning into shinny gold that were almost to blinding to watch. Its aim was to her swollen lips sealing it. It's a golden thread that aluminates with a [blazing star] that splits in two upon touching her lips then circling very slowly that meet at the bottom of their lips with a [CRACK]. He became fully aware of her tears slowly going around theirs touching the bottom ... like a surrounding force that's very warm and, permanent. When they finally release, he pulls out a handkerchief from his back pocket and, gives it to her and, she gushes out a happy laugh that he always has a handkerchief for her. She looks at his uniform that her tears had made a golden wet spot from the drips off his chin.

"Oh, Max I got your uniform wet ... HHMM, HHMM."

"I hope it never dries my sweet wife."

They talk back and forth and, she said he said.

"I don't think it ever will and, you know what I think? ... what? ... that our kiss just then was a seal by God as a reminder that he still is with us ... I agree because the tears went all around our lips and, he made it binding with the ancient tradition of me wrapping you up with the blanket ... then my tears wrapping around our kiss ... absolutely amazing ... did you feel the heat?"

Then he licked her tears from his lips, and, he said she said.

"MMMmmmm, yours tears taste like real maple syrup and, I must say it would be a tie to tell which is the best in these two worlds ... and, what is that ... either the depth of your lips when I kiss them or, your tears that I taste ... well if you can't decide what are you going to do ... I have a lifetime to test each one ... test them all you want because there yours ... I would die consuming your syrup ... REALLY?!! HA, HA, HA, HA, HA, I will cry on your pancake and, mine ... OKAY! tomorrow morning and, may I have your presence my blessed wife ... YES!!! would you please make us just one a piece and, I'll cry on them. HA, HA, HA, that was funny."

Their joy was interrupted when several feet above them a half invisible hand slowly dropped down. It was cupped and, went between them as they lean back so, the hand could reach for the last drop off his chin. It splashed inside the hand and, the drops that fell on his uniform took a turn upward and, one by one her tear drops went into the cupped hand. When all was collected the hand closed and, went back to the ceiling and, disappeared. They were dumbfounded she dabbed their lips her cheeks and, eyes not saying a word.

Then they realize that they have to collect their thoughts for the work at hand and, she gave the handkerchief back and, he said.

"Let's grab the supplies with some chicken and, veggies with some fruit and, go outside I want to practice the technique of swirling the cloak around each other before we go."

She has a heart of gold after that kiss and, she said.

"Samantha we are going now and, please protect this [Beautiful 27-Trip's] while we are gone, we will keep in touch as the night unfolds."

"AYE, AYE Captain."

He grab's some extra water and, there outside and, practice their swirling technique. They fold the cloak's grab the Javelin's, 4 apiece and, the 2 bags, and, there on their way. They get there heading and, reach their destination. They survey and, locate the dragon's cave on both of their viewer's. They've placed the Javelin's about 15 to 20 paces apart from each other. They plan it so, that he will throw the first Javelin at the dragon as soon as it leaves the cave and, of course the dragon will want to breath fire down upon him as soon as the dragon does that, she will be watching this throw her Javelin into the belly of the dragon. He will cover himself with the cloak. The dragon breath's fire that will come down on him but, with no effect. The second one will strike the dragon she threw. The dragon will direct its attention to breath fire down upon her and, so, on.

They find a resting place and, wait with him close by the entrance of the dragon's cave and, she's about 20 paces away from him they whisper to each other with their inner voice communication and, one of the things that he said.

"I can't stand being away from you."

She grins at his romance even in the face of danger and, she said.

"Yaw ... I know and, that's the way I feel too."

He looks at the time and, it's 1:am then the rustling of the dragon starts and, he gets ready and, said.

"Amyl ion the dragon is moving about in the cave and, I think it's going to come out are you ready?"

"Yes, I'm ready."

The dragon comes out of the cave thrilled to spread misery among the people with carnage throughout the hills and, valleys. [It has burnt scaly skin; Five claws on each of its 4 feet; Large eyes with horns above its nostrils; Spiked skin for eyebrows; A dozen or, so, spikes from one ear to the bottom of the other; Horns on the head that face backwards; Many pointed teeth; Thick spines all along the back; Large bat like wings of light pink and, buckskin color; Arrowhead tail that is hardened for battles].

The dragon takes off Max was ready and, he threw his Javelin at the belly guided it with his tablet and, stuck fast into its belly. The dragon was surprised and, saw where it came from tried to pull it out with one of its claw's or, foot but, it wouldn't come out then headed at him. When it got there above him the dragon breathed down fire he had already covered up with the cloak. She saw this all playing out she timed it to throw her Javelin right after the dragon released its fire. The second one stuck fast and, true a couple feet from his and, the dragon turns its attention towards her and, fly's over to breath fire down upon her but, to no avail and, he said.

"WWOOWW I'm so, glad the cloaks are working are you alright?"

He was already on his way to the next location and, she said.

"I'm Okay the cloak works beautifully."

He reaches the next location releases the Javelin it landed right where he wanted it to right near the heart. The dragon then looks to his area heads there to breath fire on him again the pig's blood is working notice that it can't pull the Javelin's out. That makes 3 they have used as they go from one station to another. She launches another one guides it to the stomach area it lands right on target. There are 4 Javelin's in the dragon its going crazy it can't pull them out. The dragon was heading toward her picking up speed with this and, he said.

"We are getting to far apart from each other and, I'm coming towards you."

Evidently the dragon heard that and, saw him coming closer to her and, she said.

"Okay Max come on over."

He was running over with 2 Javelin's in his hands trips over a tree limb laying on the ground he couldn't see the cloak gets away from him the 2 Javelins roll away on the ground. She sees this throws off her cloak with her arms in the air in shock. She has the most startled look on her face starts to go towards him was watching this all play out with the dragon leaving her now she thinks that he is not going to make it in time to get the cloak back on so, in anticipation she throws her Javelin looking at Draco and, she said.

"[NO, YOU DON'T]."

She threw it to strike the dragon in the mouth to stop the fire coming out. She guided the Javelin at the roof of the dragon's mouth at the back like she planned it. The fire comes out a little the Javelin landed at the back. They saw this with perfect timing they said.

"SAMANTHA BLOW!"

The Javelin's all blew up at the same time the top of the dragon's head exploding brains and, blood spread out the dragon's belly opened up too. That was only a split-second cause she looked over at him took off like nothing else mattered he too was looking at his beloved. She was running over breathing heavy then tripped over a tree limb falls on top of him he catches her they're lying on the ground with her arms around his head and, neck. She couldn't be any happier that he's okay. She was crying a little kissing his cheek talking in his ear he was kissing her and, said.

"Amyl ion you saved my life … and, who said that no man can catch you because you were beyond reach."

She releases some laughter and, she said.

"Only you can catch me and, you did. I was scared to death at what might have happened."

She breathes out a happy gesture that I couldn't make out after she said that. I think maybe it was more of her being happy that it's over and, all is well. Several minutes pass by but, they've got all the time in the world now that the dragon is dead. They keep lying there and, there kind of numb he's thinking having BABY in my arms well I'll stay here till the rooster crows.

The dragon had fallen on the hillside with a big crashing sound landing on the surrounding high chaparral on one of its wing's eventually the weight of the dragon caused the wing to collapse and, slid down the hillside. They heard this turned to watch the dead dragon finally coming to a halt at the bottom and, he said.

"Amyl ion I don't want to leave."

"Neither do I HM, HM, HM."

[Some time passes by after realizing what had just happened] and, he said.

"Say, sweetheart … I hear that there are some stones in that belly over there and, one of them has a Black Rose in it."

Well that finally got them up with enthusiasm and, especially her and, she said.

"Alright let's go get it."

She gets up off of him stands up he reaches his hand up for her to pick him up. She lifts him up with a grunt or, two they brush off each other pick up the Javelin's and, bags head out towards the dragon. They reach it standing for a while looking at it and, have to walk around it they are just amazed that such a thing could exist. They reach the belly blood is coming out they see the 4 stones and, something else but, for now they want to cut just the stones out from under the skin so, they get their knife's out start cutting away. They look at each other their faces showing what a disgusting job this is. She sees that he's cutting the diamond that's supposed to have the Black Rose in it. They get all 4 stones out determine there about 4 by 6 inches in size the thickness at 2 inches. They saw the image of a Black Rose inside of the large diamond. They talk among themselves decide to wait when they get to the Ring of Fire. The other thing they saw bulging out of the belly got their curiosity up. They proceeded to cut that out the dragon and, it was hoarding Gold Nuggets they pulled out 3 large bags of Nuggets behind that was a flat box full of pearls. The dragon's immune system had a seal around them that wouldn't contaminant the insides of the dragon as well as the 4 stones and, Max said.

CHAPTER 24

"This is a wonderful gift from God to ourselves to have a comfortable life together."

He reaches over to his Bride and, gives her a kiss.

They rinse their hands to get the blood off put the stones, Gold Nuggets, box of pearls in the bags pick up the 3 Javelin's with the 2 cloak's and, headed on back to the ship. In about an hour there somewhat exhausted so, they take a rest stop. There're some large rocks around they see that one is rather flat at the top for them to take a nap on because they don't want to be on the ground when they nap. They lay everything on the ground except the 3 Javelins and, the 2 cloaks to cover themselves with and, climb up to the flat spot. They lie down on one cloak cover up with the other they look up at the sky and, remember the full Moon tonight is called the [Honey Moon]. There cuddling and, can't wait to get to the valley. They look at the stars and, see how black it is between the stars. The Moon was bright a little larger than earth 1s moon it had more craters on it and, the more they gazed the more they knew that there were many falling stars you could hear them burn up as they entered the earth's atmosphere. They're having such a good time with their new discoveries. They're pointing their fingers at perhaps new constellation's and, they decide to get a telescope to study them in the years to come and, he said.

"What would you think if we came here every so, often?"

She curled up to him even more and, she said.

"Oh, Maximilian that would be very, very special."

He rubbed her arm that laid across his chest and, he said.

"Okay then at the next full Moon we have a date."

She looks up to him squeezes and, smiles with her contentment just oozing off her pretty face. She rubs her hand on both sides of his face puts it back down to his chest under the blanket.

They pause for a while and, he said.

"[Shine on our Honey Moon]."

She looks up to him as he is looking at her and, smiles and, said.

"[Every Night from a Pocket we renew]."

He spoke.

"[Bring us a Glow at High Noon]."

She spoke.

"[We Whisper I Love You never too soon]."

He spoke.

"What are we going to title it?"

There's a pause and, she said."

"Honey Moon at the Rock."

He spoke.

"We could add more later on."

There gazing a little more with the falling stars their eyelids start to get heavy and, they slowly fall to sleep.

Raven Hades guides his ship about 3000 feet above them on the rock points who he wants for this raid and, said.

"All you Zombie's you 3 Incubus's you 2 Succubus's you 2 Griffin Monster's I want you to go down to the ground there destroy those 2 humans' on top of that rock."

The bottom hatch opens up and, they stream out spiraling down for their attack and, they are screaming and, howling like it was Halloween.

Max opens his eye's see's what's coming without hesitation wakes her up she is shocked they grab their Javelin's both jump up but, instantly they realize the 3 Javelin's are not enough for what's coming down on them. They look at each other and, both said.

"We didn't bring our Laser Gun's."

She's terrified looks to him for anything and, she said.

"What are we going to do?"

He grabs a Javelin and, looks at her and, said.

"Were going to have to use them as clubs."

She does not argue grab's it like a club with the chromium tip out front. The two warriors are ready they wait for the assault but, there

Javelin's as club's changed into Samurai Sword's right before their eyes. They looked at each other and, they both said.

"Thank you, God."

The Sword that he got was a Nodachi Sword and, the one that she got was a Uchigatana Sword. They had no time to think but, only to put their minds on the sword's that they'll guide them to strike. They turn to each other and, they knew what they had to do.

The music starts [Beatles-Helter-Skelter] at The Rock Fight].

She Shout's.

"LOOK OUT MAX A ZOMBIE IS COMING INTO BITE YOU!!!"

Max with his strength was able to turn around with cat like speed with the heavy sword the Nodachi sliced the Zombie's head clean off the body and, head dropped to the ground dissolved then he said.

"Amyl ion turn around quickly you got one coming in."

She turns with a shout swing's her Uchigatana Sword with a precision strike at another Zombie that cuts her head off. They turn to each other she smile's that would split the Moon in half and, she said.

"Max there Perfect."

He smile's back and, said.

"We must face away from each other at all times, I protect you, you protect me."

She excitedly shook her head up and, down and, said.

"I got it."

Then a male Incubus was coming for her to take her to his Abyss she swung as she turned cut the arms off the Incubus came back with a vicious slice that almost took her feet off the rock with that spin move and, its head came off he dropped to the ground and, dissolved. A Female Succubus was coming in on him as a Griffin Monster was bearing down on her. He had his arms straight out and, was pointing his Nodachi at her and, waiting cause his Nodachi was telling him what to do when she got there the Female Succubus didn't see the sword. Max at high-speed move cut her right wing off turned the sword from left to right coming back swiftly cut her head off and, she dissolved to the ground. She's waiting pointing her sword as well at the Griffin Monster that was coming in to fast. She braced herself shoved her Uchigatana right down the Griffin Monster's throat under its beak gave out a yell pushed forward the Uchigatana down to its chest area pulled out the sword as she was slicing down her sword drew back to her left side as she knelt, she held that position with head down, knowing her Uchigatana did its deadly job and, it too fell to the ground and, dissolved. Two Male Incubus's were coming down on her. Max had the other Griffin Monster coming in on him. She put her Uchigatana to her right side at chest level with the handle pointing out her hand's close to her right bicep with the blade at a 4 O'clock position pointing down behind her. He had his Nodachi in front of him pointing at 12 O'clock and, able to see his beloved in his peripheral vision on his left with the handle in his face the sword was waiting for the Griffin Monster to his right. The Griffin Monster got to the point where it thought that it could surprise him but, Max had other plans as the Griffin Monster was just in the right position, he did a 180 that confused it and, then the Nodachi knew what to do. He quickly turned back to his left and, swung his Nodachi hard the Griffin Monster was cut in two just below the wing's it too dissolved and, fell to the ground. He returned to his original position with his Nodachi at his face prepared for another attach. She was ready when the Two Male Incubus's were coming in side by side, she had to act fast but, still be strong not to lose any strength while being swift on the stroke.

She said to the Uchigatana.

"Oh, be swift and, strong My Darling ... [NOW]!!!"

The blade came under the arm of the one on her right and, came out the right shoulder close to the neck of the Male Incubus. She drew her sword up fast and, came down on the second Male Incubus and, split him in two down to the waist which already had his hands on her but, the Uchigatana did it's bidding as she commanded. The Two Male Incubus's fell to the ground and, dissolved but, as the second one was falling it had a slight grip on her just enough to slightly pull her off the rock and, if it wasn't for Max, she would have fallen. He saw this in his Peripheral Vision put the sword in his right hand grabbed her by the back of her uniform pulled her back on top. No time for thank you's it was all do. Or, die now. The Zombies were circling around and, ready to make their attach when the Female Succubus was coming from behind Max as he had his back turned while helping her with his left hand and, looking at her. The Peripheral Vision paid off again as he seen the Female Succubus coming in from his back side, The blind side she thought. He switched his grip on the

Nodachi in his right hand with the point of it facing at the attacker [The point of that particular sword curls up on the tip] waited for the Monster to come in she thought she had him to snatch away take him to her Abyss give him the kiss of death. He allowed the sword to point down in his right hand in front of his thigh and, he said.

"Be true My Sweetheart."

He braced himself gave a thrust backwards with a yell, as she came in at the same time didn't see the sword caught her in the Mid-Section which gave her a surprised look. She had her hands on him as she was falling dissolving, he also was falling off the rock. Amyl ion grabbed his uniform belt pulled him back with a deep throated yell as it was a little harder for her because he was heavier. They regained their positions turned their heads at each other knew that everything was alright they thought glanced around and, he said.

"Baby a lot of Zombies coming in now."

She just smiled and, looked in his eyes she knew he was concerned for her and, she said.

"Yes, let them they come … I'm not afraid Max not with you I'm not"

They both turned around and, got ready. The Zombies came in to them at three apiece for each one. They had their swords to their right at a Semi-Vertical position pointing down a little that would help them thrust to slice the Zombie's whether it was their head's or, body's. Well, they got all Six Zombies because their bodies were soft and, almost hollow.

The Zombies crowded them so, much and, to the point where they slid off the rock it was about a 15 to 20-foot drop they landed on the side of the rock falling on their sides a little to cushion the fall. There laying down on the ground and, he said.

"Amyl ion did any of them bite you?"

"No, they didn't … how about you?"

"No and, how you doing did the fall hurt you?"

She's thinking he is concerned for me as I am of him and, he said.

"We better get up and, put our backs to the rock, cause here comes some more Amyl ion."

They get into position's so; they can't get behind them. Then one by one the new assault comes swinging their sword's as they come in cutting their heads off or, whatever they can cut first then their head. As soon as they would get one well another one was right behind it to take their position and, so, on. Well, I must say that the adrenaline was flowing now and, there seemed to be no end to them but, they weren't giving up. They're screaming and, hollering, the dust was coming up from moving their feet so, fast. The Zombies were dissolving as soon as their heads came off.

Stopping for a moment with swords in the air there was no more attacks and, looking around then relaxing their arms with the swords touching the ground. They stood fast and, waiting positioning their feet catching their breath and, broke out in a pretty good sweat but, nothing was happening. She was thinking I'm glad this is over. He turns to her then she turn's that's when one more comes at her and, Max's hands grabbed the Nodachi it came up instantly he gave out a yell to slice between the legs with the blade coming out the top of its head of the Zombie and, split in two pieces as they watched it dissolve at their feet.

"Max, you saved me … and, we better get back on top of the Rock."

"Let's go I'll climb up then pull you up."

She puts her sword between her belt pants looking around for a few seconds as he climbs up. She looks terrified and, feeling all along it got quite with the crickets coming back. His hand drops down in front of her face she jumps and, he said.

"It's okay grab my hand."

She looked up at him with a sigh of relief and, said.

"OOHHH, MAX! what took you so, long?"

He gave out a little quite giggle and, said.

"Grab my hand."

She already had both hands on his arm and, still looking around. He pulled so, hard she squeaked landed on her feet grabbed her she squeezed her arms around him buried her head and, she said.

"I was out there all by myself Max."

He waited for her emotions to subside.

Raven Hade's is perceiving that his cause to destroy the would be King and, Queen as he sits in his chair prepared for a Devil has ended. There's no one around just an empty ship, he leaves in his ship as it darts across the sky. They see this watch it disappears. They look in each other's eyes then look up to the ship raise their swords in the air and, give a victory yell. Realizing that it is all over, they put their respective swords by their sides still in their right hands. They have to look one more time up in the sky and, around they seem to be satisfied. She looks back at him and, puts her head on his chest and, said.

"Is it safe Maximilian?"

"Yes ... I believe so." [September 16 Sunday]

He kiss's the top of her head puts his chin on the top of her head looking around. They have one arm around each other slowly close their eye's just for a second.

CHAPTER 25

A Coyote begins to yapping and, howling as its signal's the other's that it caught something with the other Coyotes coming over, they all gather start yapping and, howling. That sound wakes them up from their sleep they notice that there lying down start looking around there confused and, thought they were standing and, just closed their eye's for just a second after that battle. She still had her head on his chest and, his chin was on the top of her head. A Javelin in each hand one arm around each other. They hear the Coyotes more clearly and, begins giggling, laughing and, soon they were laughing louder looking at each other with a baffled look and, she said.

"It was a dream but, it seemed so, reel."

"YAA and, that was quite a battle."

She spoke.

"Hey you think maybe Samantha captured that? ... HA, HA, HA"

He spoke.

"YAA ... I want to see that ... WWHHOOO WWEEE."

Well, they're going to have memories for a long time talking back and, forth as they get up playing and, demonstrating how each one was using their swords and, said WOW this and, WOW that how they fell off the rock giving that scene a good belly laugh. I pulled you back up from falling and, YAW I pulled you back up from falling too. [LOL] They were having so, much fun and, finally climbed down with the Javelin's grab the bag's and, head on back to the ship. This time for real they see Raven Hade's ship pass by up into the sky and, disappear as the sun is rising and, she said.

"Samantha, can you come in and, do you locate us?"

"Yes, Captain."

He spoke.

"Raven Hades is he gone or, can you make out the location?"

"Yes, Captain the ship is out of this planet's atmosphere just entering Hypersonic with that speed it won't come back."

"Thank You Samantha you will identify that ship again if it enters at the earliest detection?"

"Yes Captain."

They stop and, rest every so, often. They brought some chicken and, veggies with an apple, peach and, talk about thing's sitting under an Oak Tree and, he said.

"I wanted to tell you something but, I didn't know how well it would sound to you or, how you felt about it."

Her eyes sparkled with anticipation said nothing waited and, he said.

"If anybody said anything offensive to you or, if I hear of something said against you [God Help Them]."

She smiles and, accepted that relaxes even more against the tree with happiness, contentment eating with a smile then she said.

"I was thinking about our love life."

They look at each other with seriousness and, a smile. He waits as she explains herself and, said.

"I want you to make love to me as often as you can."

She leans forward and, is contemplating what she said with her hands on her shins as she looks at her beloved and, she said.

"When we get older let's not think that we didn't give it our all."

He watches her as they finish eating. He thought to himself that because she loved it so, that he would find every opportunity to do just that for her. He surely didn't want another man coming between them and, would fight for the right to have her. They cleaned up a little bit and, he spread the cloaks a little better so, he could make love to his wife right there. She looked at him knew what was going to happen so, she played with her hair to make it right for him. She was thinking Oh, my were going to make love outdoors she could hardly wait. He got everything so, so, for her something to lay her head on picked her up with their hands together he proceeded to take her uniform off as she stood there with a mischievous smile, they looked around to see if anyone was around and, of course there wasn't. She helped him with his uniform they embraced she slowly laid down with his help. He got on his knees between her legs and, climbed on top and, started to kiss her with a tender touch and, release. They're both thinking how different this is being outside. He entered her it took her a couple more seconds to start her delightful anguish for the first-time out-doors. He loves her and, did everything to please her. She has a few soothing rolling occurrences and, wants to get on top so, that her husband can have his. She lays on top for a while as she catch's her breath pushing him in dances when she sits up. They watch each other arrive with distorted figures at the conclusion. In a little bit she rolls off they get cleaned up. They lay side by side reflect on how they can make love after killing that dragon with a well-deserved distance in their minds. They put their uniforms back on and, they're on their way back.

Meanwhile raven has entered his private room with a large chair that's in the center the place is Erie, smokey, sounds of something's sizzling and, dark. People crying with monsters lurking about there all in misery. Two female succubus's were on the sides of his chair that were scantily dressed hair covering their naked breast's that would seduce any man with their large wings slowly waving. They were moving their bodies to bring him closer as they wait for him he stopped he was so, mad when he found out his dragon Draco was killed by Maximilian and, Amyl ion that he concentrated very hard as he placed his right hand on his chin looked into a smoking circle portal and, came to where they were walking back. Oh, how terrible he looked when he found them attacked as the captains were unaware of the large facial appearance 10 feet above them about 5 feet tall and, couldn't see or, hear the loud hitting of the drum within an echo chamber when he appeared. The protective shield that was around them stopped the devil from reaching them. He appeared on a kind of stretching material of clear impenetrable plastic as it smashed his face a little as he tried to break through with moving his face around and, growling but, couldn't. His face looked like the devils [CHUCKY CHUMMER] with black hair his hairline that comes to a point at a normal area on his forehead slicked back with two crooked red horns close to the middle. The color of his face is dark blood maroon with black areas around his eye sockets with crow's feet and, wrinkles and, nasty looking eyebrows that curled up at the end and, a black pointy goatee as he growled. It's like he was burning in hell all his life where he dwelt. His pupils are like cat's eyes that are oval in the vertical position black with the iris of golden yellow moving around like rolling smoke. He snarled at them with his black and, dark blood maroon hands long finger nails rings on each finger trying to break through to them scratching and, scratching. The captains were unaware of this as they hurriedly walked the shield still protecting them. There's a sound of a screaming woman in the background obviously an insane witch with delirious laughter over the thought of killing our beloved [SHE HOPED] as the sounds of tearing paper in the background or, ripping things up but, couldn't be scene while repeating herself and, she said.

"DESTROY THE COUNTRY ... DESTROY THE COUNTRY!"

The devil tried but, in vain he could not break through gave up when he said.

"I'LL COME BACK FOR YOU ... YOU HAVEN'T HEARD THE LAST OF THIS ... YOU KILLED MY DRAGON ... RRRAAAHHHRRRR]."

When the devil started to leave, he turned into a werewolf but, still the teeth couldn't break through. The Halloween scene slowly disappeared as the devil backed off with a werewolf howl. "[AUU, AUU, AAAAUUUUUOOOOOOOooooooo]."

They finally reached the entrance of the cave and, when they're about to enter in, they see a man with sheep with two extra-large German Shepperd's with their heads reaching Max's hips. Beautiful dog's that are black and, tan with the other one that has a little Silver in the black plus tan. There passing by just about 100 Feet to their left between two large boulders on the ground and, he said.

"Amyl ion let's go over and, talk to the man he looks really friendly I'm kind of drawn to ward's the guy."

She stops for a while looks at him with a loving smile but, she wants to be careful at what she wants to say yet not be possessive and, she said.

"I want you by my side at all times and, I feel like this will be very, very important if you go over and, talk for a while for I sense something very powerful and, special."

He agrees by nodding and, he said.

"I do adore you I know how you feel I'm the same way because I think of you always."

She reaches up with her left-hand places it around his neck pulls herself up on tip-toes gives him a well-placed kiss on his lips and, she said.

"I want to do a Captain's log carry these bags on board check out the bee hive with doing some research on the bridge … What do you think Max?"

"Well, let's put these bags and, Javelins down right here I'll take them up later I want to find out a few things from the Shepard over there you go ahead with what you want to do."

She jumps up on him with her arms around him gives him another kiss and, said.

"5 Minutes please … I don't think I can stand anymore being away from you."

He puts his arms under her buttocks picks her up in the air for a minute admires what's in his arms thinks what can I do for her? She's thinking as well of what a beautiful life with this man that I love how God has blessed me with him. There slowly releasing from each other's hold places her on the ground. They depart he reaches the Shepard with the sheep and, said.

"Hello friend … how are you?"

The Shepard turned to him and, said.

"Hello friend … well I'm pretty good thanks for asking."

The two dogs come to Max to smell collect him in to their memory banks. No names were exchanged but, went right into a conversation when Max said.

"I sure love these hills."

The Shepard looked around pondered and, said.

"Yes, it reminds me of Psalm 121." Max already is reading psalms, proverbs, Ecclesiastes, song of Solomon and, said.

"I'll have to look into that."

The Shepard bent over to pet his Shepard's as they came back to him and, he said.

"Enjoy them for Nine Hundred and, Ninety-Nine Year's from the day of your coronation."

His hand had a hole in the back of it Max instantly knew who he was. The Shepard left and, said.

"Well Friend I must tend to my Sheep."

As he was leaving Max said.

"Excuse friend what is the name of your Shepard's? ... if they have one ... there my favorite you know."

"April and, May."

Max was thinking HHMMM how interesting and, how large they were almost twice the size he was familiar with back on earth 1.

Then the Shepard looked at the ground close by Max turned and, walked away. Max stood there for a while thought to himself as he watched him walk away that he looked like any other sort of man for this setting in time.

Then he remembered the hills, that number and, the Psalm as he looked to the ground that the Shepard was glancing at. There was a writing on the ground so, he leaned looked a little closer. It said [Love Her, Cherish Her, Adore Her.] There was a stick laying close by with what he wrote it with. Max was frozen a rush came over him picked up the stick walked back to the entrance of the cave and, picked up the bags of Gold Nuggets plus the stones, Javelins then back on board she was doing a Captain's log as he walked by. He went to the storage area put the stick with the bags of Gold Nuggets everything in one box the Javelins in their box and, told Samantha to seal it. Then came back to sit in the captain's chair next to his wife. She had finished her Captain's log and, was doing a little research she turned to him with an astonishing gladness on her face. He knew that she stumbled upon something and, he said.

"WELL, what puts this look on my pretty wife's face?"

Pause ... She smiled and, leaned forward then placed her hands on his thighs and, said.

"Can you believe it the citizens of the UNITED STATES in the spring of 2022 took a wrecking ball with bull dozers and, destroyed the radical Marxist colleges, universities on earth 1 that were poisoning the students."

He thought how to respond with his face showing how glad he was from the inside and, he said.

"I'm very pleased that you found that ... and, how the people push back."

Her face grew with confidence at the point he made left it at that with a long smile and, wiggled her body because she couldn't decide whether to turn off the bridge or, tell him how fortunate they were to be alive. He thought for a moment that there was more and, said.

"Captain is that it or, is there more to the story?"

She went back to her research for a minute as he waited for her to find it. She drew a breath with another discovery with paraphrasing and, she said.

"Yes! there's more listen to this! The major news outlets were part of or, played the most part of spreading this poison in the UNITED STATES like communism."

He leaned in his chair relaxed with right elbow on the armrest put his right index finger under his ear lobe and, said.

"HHMMM, very good refresh my memory of the news outlets."

"Okay there's more too. SSOOO, the ones are ABC, CBS, NBC, CNN, MSNBC, NPR. Wait there's more! You got to hear this they get the wrecking ball treatment with bulldozers destroying the buildings by the people."

"AAHHH, that's good thanks for refreshing my memory nobody was hurt right?" Let me look? pause … no, not a one thanks to God."

She loves good news of destroying the tyrants, haters of freedom and, she said.

"Well, my dear captain, husband I would like to know how was your friendly visit with that man?"

They looked to each other he's just smiling from ear to ear. After a pause he said.

"I Love You Amyl ion with all my heart."

She smile's that would make the star's look and, he said.

"I'm curious about something?"

She cleared her thought's focused on what he was going to say and, he said.

"On your descent from the heaven's and, your conversation with God … may I ask was there anything about our years or, our lives together that God would have said?"

CHAPTER 26

"Why yes, I would love to tell you anything so, one other thing that God said was that we will live together Nine-Hundred and, Ninety-Nine Year's from the day of our Coronation."

She stopped with a curious face looked at him rose up very alluring with her arms slowly raising up the hands twisting from palms down to palms up took tiny steps over to sit in his chair on his lap. She loved to play it took her a long 30 seconds to finally do it. He reached for her he's so, intoxicated with her he said.

"Could you do that again?"

She busted out laughing while settling down on his lap having a good time at what he said. She slowly put her arms around his head kissed him on the cheek breathed in his smell of manhood relaxed her arms, hands on his shoulder didn't say a word. As a matter of fact, they didn't say anything for the longest time. He made the chair swivel a little watched her as she's deep in thought not worried and, secure in her wonderings he softy said.

"That Shepard tending his sheep told me that you and, I am going to live together for Nine-Hundred and, Ninety-Nine years."

She took a deep breath and, said.

"How did he know and, who was he?"

"He's the second person of the Trinity."

"I believe you Maximilian."

She stayed in her position put her arm's tighter around her husband's neck as he welcomed that squeeze and, he said.

"I want to tell you the other things he said my beautiful wife but, may I tell you later?"

"Oh, Maximilian we have plenty of time."

They started to laugh because they knew now that they have 999 years together.

Both started talking at the same time. One was saying we have to move the ship closer to the valley. The other one was saying we got to find a hiding place close to the valley and, at the edge of the town. They stopped started to laugh again she reached and, pressed the Green Froggy [Squeaky-Squeak] and, he said.

"Samantha, we have to move [27-Trips] to a new location close to the nearest valley on the edge of town where we were earlier."

"AYE, AYE Captain."

They're talking for a while and, she said.

"Samantha, put on the viewer the area close to town were there's a bunch of trees and, if there is a clearing somewhere in the middle put it on the viewer, please."

"Here you are."

They studied the area and, he said.

"Samantha, can you put the ship in that area?"

"Not without scrapping the edges of the ship captain."

He said after talking to her about what he wants to do. She agrees and, he said.

"Samantha when we hover over the clearing around the tree's use the backup lasers on the bottom at about 2% to cut a circle that will be two feet of clearance around [27-Trips] and, then land the ship there please."

"AYE, AYE Captain."

Amyl ion with a faraway look said.

"The tree limbs and, branches on the ground will be a good covering, well maybe a little bit because this is a good size ship hopefully nobody will notice it that comes by."

He raised his eyebrows and, said.

"We hope captain."

She stroked the back of his head and, neck then said.

"But we can't keep the ship hidden for very long we'll have to reveal it sometime."

He covered his mouth with his hand to clear his throat and, said.

"I've got some plans that I've been thinking about perhaps you do too?"

She put a hand on his chest tapped it a few times and, said.

"Yes, I do."

"Amyl ion are you ready to go my sweetheart?"

She smiles that would light up the darkest night gets up to sit in her respective chair and, he said.

"Samantha, take the front seal off the entrance of the cave get the ship out of this cave and, take it to that location at the tree's and, land there please."

"AYE, AYE Captain."

They watch on the viewers as Samantha opens the cave up and, they see the dark clouds windy conditions the rustling of leaves, dust then they leave and, she said.

"Oh, leave the cave open Samantha please."

"AYE, AYE Captain ... Might I add that a tornado has formed approximately ¼ mile from this location and, it's heading in the direction of the valley where we're heading."

Max quickly responded adjusted himself in the chair and, said.

"Stand By at 1/8 mile hold the position of the ship there."

He looks at her thinking I want her to do this one. She's wondering what to do watching the viewers and, he said.

"Would you like to stop the tornado in its tracks my dear?"

He is smiling all the while knowing what to do and, she said.

"Well ... YAW! what can I do?"

He loves her enthusiasm and, said.

"Okay then go to the bridge get a fix on the tornado set lasers at Oh, ... about 5% power. Once you get that you will do it manually just for fun."

She turns has a serious look and, said.

"I got a fix the lasers are set at 5%."

He puts his left hand on his knee with elbow out and, said.

"Okay on the bow of the ship how many lasers are available in your sight?"

She turns to see the information and, said.

"15 main, 13 mediums, and, 11 backups just on the bow."

She is glued at looking to the bridge and, he said.

"Okay the tornado's spin counter clockwise so, you would aim the lasers in vertical fashion from the top to the bottom towards the tornado."

Her brain is clicking with this new challenge and, said.

177

"YAW Okay I get it … a sort of stacking the lasers on top of each other." He pointed his hand at her and, said.

"Right let's use the backup lasers shall we don't need all that fire power nor, do we want the lasers going beyond the tornado. Set the tracking monitor to stay with the waving of the left side of the tornado and, with your information there in front of you … how many of the lasers with the calculations come out to be?"

She turns around and, said.

"It calculates to 8 lasers and, I know now that it stops the spin on the left side and, I hold that for one complete spin."

He had a feeling of satisfaction and, calmly said.

"When your clear in your mind with what you are about to do and, your positive on the outcome then fire when ready … Captain."

She turns back looks at this and, that then she fired they watched on their respective viewers. She held the fire until the tornado stopped spinning shuts down the power with all the water falling to the ground.

He touch's the Green Froggy [Squeeky-Squeek]. She does it too and, is just elated and, jumped in his lap and, grabbed his face with both hands and, gave out a belly laugh while looking at him and, she couldn't believe that something like that could be done. There having such a very good time and, she said.

"Okay Samantha we can go to our original heading please."

He's complementing her throws her arms around his neck there speaking things that are overlapping and, I can't make them out.

The ship is over there quickly the branch's, tree limbs come down the ship lands on its 8 straight legs that come out in a circle from under the ship. They check the viewers and, everything looks good no one's around. She gets up from her chair and, straddles him in his chair and, said.

"Samantha, secure the ship because were not leaving for a while. We will communicate and, let us know of any one that gets close by the ship please."

"AYE, AYE Captain."

She was looking at her husband all the while squirming in his lap with great anticipation scratching her nose a little and, she said.

"Max let's take the bags with the stone's and, the bags of Gold Nugget's into town and wait for the town's people to gather so, we can present these items to them and, of course the Black Rose in the Diamond."

She grabs him by the neck gently squeeze's him tight comes back grabs his face kiss's him passionately with her bouncing just a little that shows how excited she is at the moment with that gorgeous smile they slowly get up grab the bags of stone's and, Gold Nugget's.

They go outside and, have to clear some limbs to get through. A boy and, girl had just arrived close by and, were kissing behind some large boulders and, were interrupted when the captains walked by. They held their kiss turn a little to see them walk by with bulging eyes. Then back at each other while still kissing. The boy surprisingly looked at his girlfriend after releasing their kiss grabbed her by the hand and, said.

"We got to tell the mayor their here."

He took off with his girlfriend she grabbed ahold of her bonnet being in tow she cried with a squeal at being pulled away so, quickly. The captains took a path that had large rocks, boulders on their left or, right which turned to the left then right along with trees of different sizes here and, there. Finally, they reach the building where their first meeting of the town's people took place and, several people had already told the mayor from the young kids that were kissing and, Senior Officials that they had landed the heads of the other valleys were still there in town and, there on their way. Our heroes enter the building and, go to the conference room lay down the bag's as they waited and, he said.

"Won't you please have a seat my Love?"

"Oh, ... after you, my Love."

He takes a seat and, she immediately sits in his lap and, kiss's her cheek they get comfortable with her arms around him and, they think of what is to transpire.

Several minutes go by and, the people start pouring in with the mayors of the other valley's and, Senior Official's. Some are silent but, mostly murmurings. They're whispering to one another watching everything and, all the people are making a fuss over them with smiling gestures. Of course, there looking at the bag's wondering but, some knew what was in the bags. The mayor finally shows up along with Bill, Lavita and, Kenny Ray with his wife. The two lions most of the pride were showing up one by one and, peering through the windows smelling with their keen noses most of the people wave and, greeted them. Everybody gets quiet and, the mayor said.

"Before we get started some people in town came to me and, they were bracing themselves about that tornado that was on its way here to the valley and, now that you're here we were wondering if you had anything to do with stopping that tornado? Because we all saw it fall to the ground."

The captains looked at each other she placed her hand on her husband's hand and, said.

"Yes, Captain Maximilian did that."

The crowd erupted just a little people were talking over one another about this or, that. Things started to quiet down after a few minutes the mayor raised his hands for everyone to simmer down and, he said.

"Well, everyone it looks like we get a bonus with the two Captains we are very thankful."

Everyone agrees some said that saved my house one said that their cattle were right in its path and, Max said.

"Ladies and, Gentlemen ... we both did that and, we're very glad that you are pleased."

She put both her hands-on Max's hand and, squeezed very hard. He was looking at her with that certified smile of hers almost lost track at what he wanted to say and, said.

"Do you want to go First?"

She thinks for a moment and, said.

"No, My Love you go first please."

He looks away from her then to all the people and, said.

"Well Ladies and, Gentlemen we have the 4 Stone's here in the bag's it appears that the Black Rose is inside the diamond stone but, has to be cut out from the back. Oh, a couple of other things, there was 3 bags of Gold Nugget's with a flat box of Pearls that was on the belly of the Dragon."

They all looked at one another. She whispers in his ear ... then she said.

"With these Stone's, Pearls and, Gold Nugget's it will go for the 12 valleys as needed and, my husband and, I want to build a house with the Gold Nuggets."

The mayor comes over and, looks in the bag rummages around picks up a piece of diamond that's as large as his thumb. He held it in his hand looks at it and, said.

"HHMM, it doesn't appear that it came off the large diamond ... so, Maximilian do you know what to do with it?"

He winked at Max. He got the message and, said.

"Do you have a jeweler in town that can cut diamonds?"

CHAPTER 27

He looked at his wife took the diamond put it in his pocket as she watched with curiosity a beautiful smile came forth from this lovely woman as she knew what he had planned the Mayor said.

"Mr. Goldberg or, Mr. Badu on the other side of the valley they'll cut your diamonds for you into many shapes and, sizes. There honest and, will polish the stones in the bag for us. The Gold Nuggets well you can keep them and, that we have no need for that ... its yours to keep and, that we all can agree that this is a gift from our God no doubt. These Pearls in the flat box Maximilian ... well you both keep them too."

Everybody in the room was agreeing ... plus they were all thinking Amyl ion would be wearing some of them some day and, just wanted to wait and, see. She was so, happy about that you could see it on her face it will only take a small portion of the Gold Nuggets to build the house the rest will go on for the rest of their lives with other income that they will accumulate at their business adventures and, he said.

"So, ladies and, Gentlemen shall we go to the Ring of Fire."

They grab the Diamond Stone from one of the bags together Max smiles with pride at her and, said.

"Would you like to carry it my Rose?"

She smiles that would make all rose's twist on their stem's.

She carries it Oh, so carefully sees the outline of the Black Rose or, is it? She studies it thinking now that maybe it's an illusion or, something else. They head out the door towards the rock formation walking hand in hand the mayors of the 12 valley's and, a host of others with the pride of lions having already a spot picked out so, they all could see. They go through the entrance get close to the ring of fire and, all the people that were following came into the area there's plenty of room for everybody.

They all stopped and waited. The inscription on the rock wall was still there but, blurry as they looked at it.

Max took the knife out of his pocket unfolded it and, gave it to her. They looked in each other's eyes she took the knife looked at the back side of the Diamond Stone and, slowly started to cut away the harden skin covering. She looked and, to her surprise it wasn't there. She's in desperation looked up at him with the expression that it wasn't there some started to question well where is the Black Rose? With more murmurs.

God's voice appears to them that only they could hear and, said.

"Tell the people to be silent."

Max remembers that it is the same voice of the Shepard with his German Shepard's April and, May. She knows that it is the same voice as that of the one she talked to in the heavens.

So, they put up their hand's and, said.

"Please may we have everyone be silent for a moment."

They look at each other like WOW what is going to happen now?

God Speaks to them and, all they see is each other's face and, God said.

"Because of your faithfulness draw close my chosen one's. Maximilian repeat the riddle now." Max clears his throat wrinkles his eyebrows a little. Then spoke with confidence and, he said.

"[Seek, Seek the chosen hand], [It's in a descendants land], [Seek, Seek Japheth's hand], [Into her hair facing you she stands], [See the Black Rose in her eye's], [Draw out now and, be wise]."

The Inscription on the rock wall began to clear up and, appear as he was saying the riddle with the same words looking into her eyes as he said the riddle. Her irises turned black with white background a black ring and, a Black Rose in each eye. One of the rose's petals were trimmed in red the other rose was trimmed in green. He reached into the back of her neck with his right hand into her hair for a moment of time. Max finally clenched his fist he had it pulled it out and, there was the Black Rose just as fresh as if just cut. People in the crowd were whispering one person said with confidence she's the Black Rose and, now our Queen. Her eyes went back to hazel. He held it between the two of them the Black Rose petals were mixed on the edges with red and, green. Then a honey bee flew out and, went straight up and, out of sight. A few on the ground that was close by saw that too until it was out of sight and, looked back at them. Max looked at her with a grin and, he said.

"There's one of your workers going back to the honey comb."

She busted out laughing with that smile as big as the ocean and, she said.

"Our God has a sense of humor ... doesn't he Maximilian?"

He laughed back and, they almost bumped noses.

Some people in the crowd were thinking about the seriousness of the moment and, they were having a good time but, they'll understand them more later on.

They looked at each other held that to never look away. The inscription on the rock wall was complete as the crowd watched with amazement as it appeared as Max said the riddle. They both knew that they had to toss the Black Rose into the Ring of Fire so, she slowly raised her left hand grabbed the bottom stem as it was between them and, there was just enough for her hand. They adjusted their grip on the stem of it so, that when they tossed it together there wouldn't be a problem. She turned around faced the same direction as he was. Both facing the Ring of Fire looked at one another approached the Ring of Fire and, he said.

"Are you ready?"

She smiled that would make butterfly's, honey bees come back. No doubt that's precisely what's going to happen in a minute.

"Yes, my husband."

They give it a toss with precision and, right down the middle it goes into the Ring of Fire. The Fire gradually goes down and, out. Then like the wave of God's hand the land is restored you could see it all over those 12 valleys' where the Dragon was doing its best to destroy it. If you were high in the sky, you could witness the wave of his hand and, everything was green again, with bird's, bees of all sorts, flowers, water fall's here and, there clouds were forming to make it rain on the hills to keep the cycle going and, so, on and so, on. The animals on the ground were back too popping up along with squirrels in trees.

Well, the people were just besides themselves with what they just witnessed. The mayor's all gathered around and, the one that was the mayor of that community laughing with joy said.

"Well, I guess I'll go First. The Coronation of the King and, Queen start's tomorrow at the Big Baptist Building a couple of blocks down the street you both will be able to make it there we hope?"

They all start laughing Max, Amil ion look at one another she jumps up to him as he grabs her under the buttock's lifts her up and, smash a kiss. She doesn't waste any time release's their kiss with a breath of air turns to the mayor and, she said.

"What time Mayor is the Coronation tomorrow?"

He raises his arms in triumph and, said.

"High Noon."

Then a White crow flew overhead landed on the ledge above where the inscription is [And, where it will stay]. The big bird is the same size as Oh, White crow was that glided down from the heavens getting her instructions. They all looked another one flew over and, landed next to its mate. One of the White crows said.

"We were just made and, glided down here [Squawk]."

The other one's flapping its big wings and, said.

"We're going to start a Family."

Kenny Ray looked at everyone said.

"There has never been any White crow's here before."

Max is still holding her up in the air turns her around many times.

The town's people of all the valleys came around to say their greeting's and, see you tomorrow. They get to say there good byes even though he is still spinning her. Minutes passed and, all was gone except the future King and, Queen so, they're kind of exhausted after all that had happened. He has her locked in his grip she's got his head locked in her arms she whispered and, said.

"Maximilian … aren't you getting tired of holding me?"

His heads between her breasts, chuckles and, he said.

"Well not at all … because I thought we were in heaven … we're weight less and, I was going to hold you forever as my heavenly wife."

He thought she couldn't be any happier and, she said.

"HA, HA, HA … you say the things that go right into my heart."

She pulls his head back very gently covers his eyes, forehead with her rosy lips and, she was just kissing away. When she was done, he slowly let's her down but, not without a kiss that they're starving for and, he said.

"Amyl ion let's go home my darling."

185

He lets her with a bounce and, they wanted to eat sleep and, think to themselves about the day... especially her. She thought about that bee hive in storage but, along the way back to the ship they met Apple Blossom and, Green Tea, as they relaxed on all fours. They're so, glad to see the lions and, Green Tea said.

"[Hey kid's how you doing]?"

They ran up to the two lion's gave them a real good hug and, Apple Blossom said.

"We are glad to see you two and, we want to Thank You for everything."

The lion's look at one another and, Green Tea said.

"We will have many times to talk and, you two need your rest and, we don't want to be rude but, do you remember our friend we told you all about?"

Amyl ion grabbed his arm with both arms and, both said.

"Yes, we remember, how is she?"

Apple Blossom had a happy face on and, said.

"Well, she's doing wonderful now sense the land was restored it's like night and, day."

Green Tea looked like it was a solid conclusion and, said.

"This land now can protect her as it should."

Amyl ion gave out a serious look and, said.

"We want to meet her and, what's her name?"

Apple blossom was so, happy to respond and, she said.

"Black Jade but, most everyone calls her BJ, she can hunt now that the land has brought about so, many animals back right before our eyes."

"Oh, me and, Max are so, happy for her that she is doing great."

She looks at Max and, he caught on that it was his turn and, said.

"YAA bring her to the Coronation tomorrow you two are coming, aren't you?"

"Oh, YAA me and, the misses well we wouldn't miss this."

Max looks at the big lions and, said.

"Good then see you there at high noon."

They all depart she looks at a tree she noticed before while riding on Green Tea. She got this idea about attaching it to the bee hive but, where she got that idea only God knows. It had this long black fake hair hanging on all the branches that are in bunches at lengths of about 2' to 3' Feet long and, 3" to 4" Inch's wide. She talks to him as there walking over to the tree and, said.

"Could you please cup your hands together in front of you I want to stand up and, cut a lot of those off."

So, she gets her knife out he's got her one foot in his hand's as she cut's quite a number off puts them on his shoulders some get on his head and, eyes to block his view he has to blow air out of his mouth to clear away the hair so, he can see. She wants more than enough. She gets down and, covers her mouth laugh's a little with giggles and, she said.

"Oh, Sweetheart I'm sorry I was so, excited about this because I have it all planned out in my mind."

She takes the fake hair off his head there walking towards the ship joking, and, laughing.

They get inside with a sigh of relief and, he said.

"Samantha close the hatch please."

"AYE, AYE Captain."

She goes right away to the bathroom wash's the strands of look-alike hair dries the hair off with the shower blower. He's thinking where's she getting all this energy and, she said.

"Maximilian, could you get me one of the bee hive's out of storage please?"

He brings it to her with curios look she gets out her knife.

"Maximilian, could you hold the bee hive please? I have an idea."

He has a look like what is it?

"HHMM what kind of idea is that?"

Well, I think I want to cut off about one third off the smaller end of this bee hive and, see if it's possible to put it on my head just a little towards the back and, if it can be mounted to stay on I think I have to put my hair up as a bun or, ball for an anchor."

She's got him as she commands and, he said.

"Oh, okay."

She's grinning about his helping her and, she said.

"Well let's cut it off right about here."

He turns it a little and, he said.

"Okay."

So, they completed it made several adjustments and, it worked out alright.

"I want to put on the fake hair so, that I can place it on and, take it off without too much trouble."

He was thinking to himself HHMMM this could be very interesting. So, they mount the bee hive as she stands in front of the mirror to her existing hair which is also black start wrapping the strands of fake hair on the sides then on top and, they go through several layer's make them intertwined with a couple around the front that connects it to her existing hair from side to side so, you couldn't see the connection. They attached more strands to the back to fill in the curve that went to her neck the strand's hung down very nicely to her lower back. She thinks to try adding some more to drape down her left shoulder and, he really liked it there. She pulls some of her hair down just above her right eyebrow and, they notice a white streak running across her head on top he was going to see if he could remove it but, she said.

CHAPTER 28

"Hey you know what ... I think I like it like that I can change the style now and, then."

"I think that you're the most incredible woman with your permanent markings of wing's that goes past your eyebrow's it's perfect and, I might add is very theatrical now."

"Okay enough of me what are you thinking Maximilian?"

He looked at the total change of her but, still the same. [Or, maybe something else? What do you readers think]?

He grabbed her by the hand she's thinking Oh, I like this as he pulled her to the mess hall and, fixed pork chops with veggies together. While they were doing that he said.

"Samantha, could you reveal the remains of the dead dragon on the viewer please?"

"Here you are."

She's thinking too had a question and, said.

"Samantha, can you produce a few women's scarfs for me please one totally different from another?"

A few minutes later Samantha said.

"Here you go."

They appear out of the exit door at the end of the bridge for small items. They clean up a little bit and, leave the mess hall. She grabs the small items looks them over puts them around her neck then both head for the captain's chairs she grabs the back of her hair puts it to the left side in front as she didn't want to lean back on her hair. They're sitting look at the viewers they notice that people of all sorts of nationality's were popping out of the carcass of the dragon from head to toe as it dissolved and it left a burnt impression on the ground that would stay for centuries.

There were business men and, woman, of all nationality's Japanese warriors with their Samurai swords, and, the Chinese with their sword's. Native American's, Native Africans with Hispanic's. Men, women of all branches of the Military with Russian's, Orthodox Jews and, all kinds of Jewish peoples with Asians of the Pacific along with the Arabs of the middle east the Irish with the Scotts and, Greeks with Armenians from Earth 1. God's plan was the dispersion of all peoples to assimilate into a great society.

[If I missed any one, please fill it in].

"Maximilian you sure picked the right time to look at the dragon … it's like you had a good premonition when to."

He touch's the Green Froggy it goes [Squeaky-Squeak], she does the same thing totally forging about the bee hive they just created for her. She put's one of the extra-long scarf's on to secure it more which gave it a beautiful statement that she tied on her right side that was white and, black and, he said.

"They're all going into the valley and, talking to one another."

She plays with her new found hair. and, she said.

"They'll be in the valley about three hours and, it appears that they all speak one language." He glances at her beehive and, said.

"MMM, that's good I hope they can assimilate in the 12 valleys and, make a living so, lets plan on seeing that they will be okay shall we, my love?"

She nods her head and, said.

"Okay that would be great but, they must make it on their own … say … UM … Max" … "Yes sweetheart"

… We could set up programs that maybe could help the unfortunate because of some misfortune in their lives that was beyond their control they could be provided an opportunity to make it on their own again and, prosper … What are your thoughts?"

"I think that's brilliant to say the least. We could create an office just for that purpose and, we could oversee it. Then after its success, we can assign a manager. I must complement you on your creativity I am the most blessed man alive to be married to you. We will make plans talk about the future of capitalism that will be one of our main focuses."

She gets up as he is talking and, begins to sit on his lap at his left side. He has slowed down at what he was talking about watch's her come over his thoughts are Oh, God Thank You I get to spend the rest of my life with her. She puts her arms around his neck with her right hand in his hair left hand on his right cheek kiss's his left cheek and, start's humming up and, down then put's in and, said.

"[999 years is not enough to Love You]."

She sings with her special creation. He has totally forgotten everything now he's in a euphoric state of mind and, let's add ecstasy, oh, and, one more thing, drunk with passion for her. She rests her head behind his head and, slowly goes to sleep as he follows for 15 to 20 Minutes. She wakes up first slowly moves to his ear and, whispers.

"Relax for a minute my husband and, keep your eyes closed I shall tell you when to open them up please and, I'll be right back."

He puts his arms and, hands on the armrests. She is back in two seconds. He thinks well that was a quick minute. She climbs back on him with her legs straddling him puts her arms and, head behind him where they were before. He takes a deep breath because she has changed into a delicious scent it goes through his mind, censuses throughout his body. She comes back to his ear and, softly said.

"Open your eyes slowly now my beloved."

Then as he does that, she is revealing a change to the bee hive its extra wide at the top like a V shape. Her lips are dark red with large hooped earrings of white with a few markings of red and, yellow. He took a better look as she rose up until she was sitting straight up. There to his gaze she was totally naked with her hands on her thighs smiling with white teeth and, noticed on her biceps were two rings apiece of gold and, red. Her long strands of bee hive hair were in front to her left side but, not covering her breasts. A long scarf was tied around her neck with the knot at the right side that was black, white striped and, it trailed between her breasts with the scarf still in her hair. He notices her hands on her thighs the fingers from the knuckle of the hands were a bright orange, red fingernails with the backdrop of her shinny thighs. She played like an innocent young woman smiling fully then half smile then back to a full smile as she rocked left and, right a little and, she said.

"Hello ... may I have the pleasure of your company?"

She looked at each hand like it was a magic wand started with her left hand and, arm out to wave at the wall it changed to purple only half way to split the bridge. Every time she moved her hands, feet, hair as she dances there was a smoke trail Oh, but, just a little. Then she moved her right hand to wave at the wall as the other half turned to purple then with the snap of her fingers the surroundings turned surreal with waving streams of light reds light blacks or, grey and, a powder blue background then the bridge disappeared. There were palm trees to the left of her palm trees to the right with a white sandy beach right behind this lovely creature with surf rolling pounding its waves of white foam in the blue ocean. She kept her arms up everything was all beautiful fixed her gaze on her husband with her head down.

The music started. [Bernard Herman, the 7th voyage of Sinbad, main theme]. 2 minutes and, 2 minutes again.

She started to twist her arms opening and, shutting her fingers over, over again held her head up high to get his attention. He was being hypnotized. She put her hands on his arms slowly from the shoulder dragged them slowly down to his hands. She looked him in the eyes as if to say your mine and, said.

"Relax my hero... enjoy."

She gets up bent over with arms pointing at him as if to bow she rises up has her arms out parallel to the floor legs out and, bent a little twisting her fingers opening and, closing to show the colors moving with white smoke.

He's thinking how beautiful her skin is shining all over her body I've never noticed it like this before. She turns her head puts her legs together that shows no pubic hair or, under the arms because she wasn't created with that. Her thighs touch from the top stop 2 to 3 inches above her knee caps calves almost touching and, small ankles with small knees. Her toenails are painted blue with golden bands around her ankles that are 3 inches tall with cut outs of various sizes of hearts. Her arms are still straight out and, sometimes they roll. Then she leans on one leg turns starts to dance she twist her arms as they go up spins some more with beautiful black hair flowing out. [The music stays with her as she and, the music slows down when it picks up, she dances, leaps or, spins again]. When she spins with her hair extensions it would have a trail of red smoke along with her hands and, feet. She stopped at one time and, said.

"I want to please God in heaven because he gave you to me...me to you."

She'd squat on one leg the other one straight out as she looked at him with her beautiful eyes that took on a glow of desire. She got up moved her arms in a rolling fashion while on one leg with the other one being straight out parrel on her toes moving her fingers twisting her arms or, rolling them while still having her leg straight out with opening her fingers and, closing them. [Oh, the music was right for her]. He paid close attention to her dimples on her lower back just above her hips and, there, there so, cute with rounded derriere. The surrounding colors must have brought out the dimples more. The music stopped then she stopped and, she said.

"We were rescued from the world my husband."

She turned around flung the black hair and, gracefully ran stopped in front of him and, very slowly got on his lap smiled for him so, seductively throwing her hair from side to side as she turned her head. He put the scarf back between her breasts and, he said.

"Welcome to freedom."

She takes his hands places them on her thighs as she scoots closer reaches his cheek to kiss moves to his ear and, in French she said.

"Amene-noi a Lorgasme. Which meant [bring me to orgasm]."

She puts her arms back around his neck lays her head down behind his head. He caress's her beautiful skin at her back and, her thighs. They wake up slowly he looks at her in his arms as he's still caressing her, she has her uniform on. She moves to his front to look at him they slowly draw their lips together and, kiss for a long time rolling, rolling and, rolling in rapture. They enjoyed their perfect confinement with a touch and, release and, he said.

"I just had a dynamic dream."

They peered into each other's eyes and, she said.

"What was it about?"

"I never knew that you could be dancing in front of me naked with some ornaments and, paint that it could be so, captivating and, the bridge changed to … purple … YAW that's it."

She was silent unable to speak as she searched in his eyes. She was really thinking now and, probably could have guessed why she danced in his mind and, she said.

"What else was there?"

"Oh, well ... the walls changed to purple with the wave of your hands then to a paradise behind you ... your fingers were painted orange with dark red lips and, your fingernails were red."

Her eyes were beginning to open a little wider now she was very captivated he continued and, said.

"Oh, and, the arm bracelets around your biceps of gold and, red with earrings with ankle bands of gold."

Her face is excited and, she said.

"Really, what color were my earrings?" he came back quickly and, said.

"White with red and, yellow."

She starts to take a deep breath grinning from ear-to-ear places her hands on her thighs and, said.

"My toenails Max what color were they?"

She's laughing a little then with her bated breath he said.

"BBBLLLUUU, ... My Dancing Queen you spoke French at the end of it in my ear."

"AAGH! I, I, I can hardly believe it."

Silence for a while ... She's caught in his eyes they can't look away. Eventually she said one thing. He is just loving this attention with her questions he can't forget anything about that dance because it is embedded in his mind. [It's all about her]. After she settles down, she has one more question for her beloved she's ready for the answer as she squirms in anticipation rubbing his forearms, she squeaks in her throat that is so, cute to him because he loves that when she squeaks in the throat with laughter and, she said.

"There's one more item Max what is it?"

He's quietly thinking that she knew it too and, something was going on now he's very caught up into this exchange that will last a lifetime and, he said.

"A Black and, White Scarf tied around your beautiful neck to the right that hung down to your left side and, when you came back to my lap, I placed it back between your breasts."

She opened her mouth exploded with a cry raised her arms because that was the clincher and, she said.

"Max, I had that dream over and, over again as Medusa with God transferring it over to you now and, I don't feel anything bad but, so, so, so, very surprised." He was smiling at this beautiful woman and, didn't doubt her and, he said.

"Did I describe everything?"

She bounced a little and, said.

"Perfect."

She reached for his face with both hands held his cheeks for 15 seconds or, so, smiled that would put a forest fire out then placed them on his chest and, she said.

"I wanted to be free from Medusa and, said to God I will dance for my husband if ever I was to get one in honor of you, my lord."

With a satisfied face he said.

"Amyl ion my dear it's just right because I sensed it too but, now that it has come out I look very much I repeat very much look forward to your dancing and, it will not spoil me."

"I knew you were a good man and, not to take advantage of me. Do you remember the words I said to you?"

CHAPTER 29

He repeated them to her. She fell into his arms he squeezed her tight. She's very happy said to herself I'm going to dance for him as soon as I get the ornaments … thank you God … or, I don't have to get them perhaps I could come up with something of my own. He's thinking should I mention that I wish she'd dance like that sometime. She doesn't need all that paint or, arm bracelets and, he said.

"Let's go looking in town for your ornaments and, paint if it's not here we'll go to the next valley."

She perks up like with a delightful smile and, said.

"Okay."

He was pleased at how well things are going along and, he said.

"Then maybe we'll go on the [27-Trips] find some gypsies that will most likely have everything you need what do you say about that my Dancing Queen?"

She combed his hair with her hands slid them down his face and, came to a conclusion with a deciding face placed her hands on her thighs and, she said.

"I'll tell you what … I don't need all those ornaments I will dance for you without them and, slowly add them as time goes by."

That was just enough for them to realize a big day tomorrow and, with that nap it gave them the energy to carry on and, with that dream … well … they forgot about being tired now. They were charged up and, he said.

"I wrote a song for you."

She was getting excited now and, by her body language that was telling him she wanted to hear it and, she said.

"Alright."

"[I see you sitting in the captain's chair; researching at the bridge hear or, there; curls in your hair; here I stare; I got your black roses; your beautiful dear; as a fact my celestial sphere; music starts Amyl ion's my story]."

There's a pause. She's kicking her feet moving her legs with joy she leans forward grabs his head places her lips on his right ear squeezes tight moves slowly to stick her tongue in his ear as far as she could stick it. If you could be in his mind right now, he's not at home with that sound of her tongue swishing around he loses it for a while. She calms down after a little bit he comes to waking up from that tongue swishing around in his ear and, LOL then she said.

"I wrote one for you too I remember it."

He focused after her tongue lashing and, said.

"Oh, Darling I've got to hear this."

She squeezed her forehead a little dropped her hand and, said

"[Sleep on my boy; I touch you and, go hoy; Wake up at your leisure; I'll wait turn to me; Amyl ion's your treasure; Lay me your Gold of Pleasure; Love me Oh, so, slowly; I'm gone in my black seizures]."

That was very private for her and, only for her beloved to hear and, he said.

"Sounds like a duet and, what do you think about that? … Or, just leave it like it is?"

She looked him in the eyes and, said.

"How about adding to it a little later today or, some other time because I know you have other writings?"

His face was happy at that statement and, said.

"Let's do it."

They whisper to each other I love you I adore you and, he said.

"Baby let's have a nice meal together and, find a resting place for your beehive?"

She's spoiled by his pampering acts like a young girl and, she said.

"Oh, please my dear husband after that would you take me to the shower?"

She adjusts her position straddles him closer smiles that would make lava stop flowing from an erupting volcano. He raises himself from the back of the chair has a thought go through his mind. Can I love her more than I already do? He's already at full erection puts his arms around her at the same time lift's her up rise's out of the chair and, carries her but, doesn't want to get in any hurry. She has her arms around his neck her legs have wrapped tight around him. He slowly gives her a 360 Degree turn but, oh, so, slowly as she puts her head back breath's out in excitement, laughing sounds coming deeply from her throat her eyes looking at the ceiling he ask's her as he sing's it and, said.

"[Will you be my Queen]?"

He slowly stop's she comes up she aims to kiss him, with those gorgeous lips pressing on his she released with a [SMACK] and, she said.

"Yes, AH, HA."

They crush another one. They're still in their uniforms on she starts rubbing her clitoris on his erect manhood she starts blooming into an overwhelming Orgasm has to release the kiss they go cheek to cheek as she starts to grind a little harder breathing like she's running then a little harder to get the full effect she convulses many, many time's with her back rolling at peaking with a mouthwatering finish combined with a UH, OHH, UH, MMAAH he's holding her like she is light as a feather cause he feels her whole body as it's at her full blossom in her garden she's enjoying he just watches her moment of escape. Her breathing was heavy with screaming a little she starts to come to the end as he smiles, she begins to giggle and, laugh with joys of relief.

He takes her to the bedroom has her pick up a thick blanket and, pillow while still in his arms she's wondering what he's going to do? She smiles with curiosity scratches the side of her nose a little with her right index finger. Then he takes her to the mess hall swishes the items that were left on the table with her dangling feet they make a crashing sound with tin cups banging on the floor sets her down on her feet by the long ledge of the table with the blanket and, pillow in her hand. He takes it spreads the blanket and, puts the pillow in the middle of the table. She's still standing there watching him and, she thinks YAW I know what's going to happen now. He faces her puts his arms around her kiss's her without saying a word and, she responds back. He releases their kiss to take her top off she raises her arms breasts bouncing. Bends down to take her shoes off then comes up undoes her pants pulls them down to her knees. She's willing smiling he looks at her as she put her hands on the edge of the table sat on the edge lifted her legs so, he could pull the pants off. He takes his pants off as she's watching with her mouth half open, they kiss one more time. He reaches down to pick up her legs she leans back on her elbows and, watches her with head almost on the pillow with her legs raised in the air. He gets closer searching to enter her doesn't take his time because she just had an Orgasm a couple of minutes ago thrusted himself in. She thought Oh, YAW this is fantastic go faster Max. He watches her knows when she's going to explode. Then in 30 seconds or, less she is right there he slows down to watch her groan take a deep breath hold it with her hands grabbing the edges of the table above her she's in the ultra-pain of blasting off driving the back of her head into the pillow her shinny abdomen shacks, her breasts moving up and, down. After she has her earthly plunge, they talk about having his dad and, mom taking that long journey of almost 11-months between her three more full blossoms. He pulls her up and, off the table set's her down. She's a little wabbly he carries her to the bedroom they manage to get the bee hive off place it on the special stand that they made for it. They take his top uniform off he takes her by the hand head to the shower and, she's loving it. Cleaning each other now becomes easier the air dryer has finished its job. However, they come out more focused at their love making approach the bed turn towards each other she's thinking I want my husband to use my clitoris any way he wants to then she gave him a big kiss laid on the bed she fluffed her hair laid her head on the pillow because she wanted to look beautiful for him then pointed towards the middle of her legs puts her arm's back and, opened her leg's wide. They were looking at each other like they're drunk. He walks to the front side of the bed starts crawling towards his beloved wife stops to kiss her legs lifts one leg at a time starts at her ankles on up to her inner thigh's.

The music starts [The Dell's-Oh, what a night].

She is just beside herself she's thinks Oh, this is wonderful I can't move. He's thinking of starting at her lips before he goes completely to her clitoris stops just before her clitoris opens his mouth gives her thigh a sucking and, tongue lashing for each one. Her stomach shutter's a little bit she breathing irregularly her body can hardly wait to surrender of non-resistance. He releases with a big kiss goes to crawling over her body starts to kiss her lip's over and, over again because he loves his wife with all his heart. Then he starts to go for her cheek she turns for him to present her cheek then slowly starts for her neck she moves her lovely hair aside for him to kiss offers her neck up he stays there kissing her feminine neck at the middle moves up to her ear and, whispers.

"Love You, Love You, Love You."

He's having a feast she's making sounds that words can't be invented to relay to you. He then moves to her chest rests on her bullet breast's grab's a breast for each hand squeezes while sucking her nipples from one to the other she takes a deep breath holds it while she shakes and, her vein's show on her neck from the pressure inside she needs a variety. She continues for about 30 Second's then slowly subsides. She licks her lips adjusts her eyes rub's her upper chest in a euphoric state of mind with no worry's, she's plays with her hair to make it nice for her husband again adjust the pillow to lay her head on. He slowly release's her breasts gives them one more kiss apiece. She's watching as her beloved moves down and, he said.

"My wife when we are Crowned King and, Queen, we must have a just weight and, balance for the people."

When she answers like the way she does that's only her style ... it means she has the highest respect for him and, said.

"Yes, My Husband."

He knows her learning abilities and, said.

"The words we say must be final."

She's like a sponge with righteous teaching and, she said.

"Yes, My Husband."

He continues knowing her mind and, he said.

"My beloved we must not err in Judgement."

Totally at his commands and, she said.

"Okay, My Husband."

He kissed her 7 more time's as he trailed towards her clitoris. She is anticipating all of this thinks to herself he knew what I wanted at this time. He finally reaches her inner thigh's kisses her left one first then her right thigh humming with delicious sounds of sucking wet kiss's. She puts her fingers in his hair as he finds her clitoris starts to move it around with his tongue, she applies the right pressure that she wants. He reaches around with his hands finds her breasts starts to squeeze them pinches her puffy areoles and, messages them. She puts her hands on his hands and, squeeze's the hands to apply the right pressure she wanted. She puts her hand's arms on her pillow totally relaxes she drifts to the connection of her breasts and, clitoris. He pays attention to her and, her body signal's to where she is about to have an escape from jail. It doesn't take a minute she starts to grab the sheet's next to her squeeze's it in her fist's, she takes a deep breath of ecstasy holds that while she has some deep groans with her back arching convulsing with leg's coming up and, bending at the knee with her vein's popping out of her neck when she holds her breath. He is thinking I'm going to wait until she comes down and, I'll enter her. Her thoughts are this that is its so, natural I'm so, glad that I was made this way. He realizes she has just finished what was a long-lasting run down the hallway as she runs from her captive. Then pops the exit door open falls into his arms. He stop's what he was doing. They giggle she's laughing out loud breathing with excitement at what had just happened giving sounds of relief and, the most wonderful feelings in the world just happens when she has her jail breaks. oOHs, and, oOHs as she is calming down. He gets up on his knees and, shins with an erection as she looks at him raises her arms welcoming him as she beckons him with her fingers. He starts to go forward crawls to her before he enters her. He stop's they look at one another he searches to enter her with the slowness of a snail. She's fussing with his hair, and, she pet's his hair. He finally enters her as he lays on top puts his head next to her ear on the edge of the pillow kiss's her ear whispering. She's laughing a little whispering back and, kissing his cheek. I picked up one thing and, she said.

"Our plans for us and, the 12 Valley's we can discuss them right after the Coronation My Love."

"Yes, the sooner the better My Wife."

She gave him a big hug her thoughts were he will be calling me his Queen tomorrow night and, I will be calling him My King.

He talks to her with her handcuffs off but, knew she'll be tied up again in between one. They talk about starting a secret investigative service [S. I. S] that will protect the people from radicals that would try to kill or, injure innocent people as they go on about their daily lives and, wanted to know what she thought about that plan?

She comes back after a good long minute … thinks for a while … likes the idea and, wants to work together with him on protecting the people. They'll probably be groups getting together to plan an attack against a religious people or, Christians. They finally have their jail break together after planning with the intensity that it always is.

They're both pretty tired after what they both went through the last couple of days and, told Samantha to wake them up at 6: AM.

[Note I'm exhausted after writing their love making].

The Coronation Day arrived they're up he looked at some of the writings he wrote down during the night. He has an inspiration almost every night. [A note pad on the corner of the bed]. Which only took a couple of minutes in his journal laid it on the counter next to the bed he'll work on it later.

They had breakfast, showered putting their uniforms on did some research on how a Coronation was to proceed. They finished their research and, decided that because of the times that they are now living in that they would just wait and, see. They sit in their captain's chairs face each other and, he said.

"It looks like we'll be sharing a birthday together."

She's pleased catching on to statement and, she said.

"That's right."

Both look at the date it's [September 17th, 2228 Wednesday] Jewish history month and, she said.

CHAPTER 30

"It's going to be a most special day for us My Love."

He was thinking smiling, moving his chair from side to side looking around. She was reading him and, said.

"What are you thinking about Maximilian?"

"Our wedding day."

She jumped back in her chair a little and, said.

"Yes, the most important."

They let that soak in for a while and, she said.

"Earlier at my research I discovered some tiny chips with markings on the package that said, U. S. of A. Space Force and, one of them said A. I. for [27-Trip's] what exactly is that my darling?"

He thinks for a moment and, said.

"Well, that's Artificial Intelligence that will upgrade the ship to a thinking and, reasoning ship."

She's somewhat intrigued by the idea he break's the silence and, he said.

"I needed time to reason this A. I. out."

She tilted her head in response and, she said.

"I think I know why."

He gestured with giving his hand out to let her answer and, he said.

"Please go on."

She put her hands together placed them between her thighs and, she said.

"Well with that A. I. upgrade the ship could disagree with our command's or, questions the decisions we make or, have made for the future or, present day."

He reaches to the Green Froggy gives it a couple of [Squeaky-Squeaks].

She's so, happy she was right leaning forward in her chair with her hands together in her lap and, is just smiling about half way. But I must confess she would stop me in my tracks and, he said.

"I'd like to talk to the President more about this A. I. and, you were very, very bright about picking that up."

He thought how excellent my wife is and, said.

"Thank You very, very much."

She smile's that melt's his heart she sees it knows he loves her and, he said.

"Something I wanted to do and, I need your help."

She fluffs her hair and, she said.

"Anything and, always what is it Maximilian?"

He loves her black hair watches her magic on him and, he said.

"We need also to send a message to the President and, tell him how well the E. G. C. Javelin's worked."

She's anxious to do everything she can and, she said.

"I want to do that right now Max."

She thinks to move the chair towards the center of the bridge turns it around and, proceeds by sending those messages out while he looks at his writings and, she said.

"Maximilian I'm just fascinated at all this information that's right here at our fingertips."

He's writing a poem in the captain's chair several feet away. He looks up at her at the bridge she's looking down at the flat information counter. He stares at her beautiful curly black hair as she sits there. He smiles goes back to looking at his poem and, he said.

"Overwhelming to a point that will make one wise."

She nods her head and, said.

"You are so, right."

Then he whimsically said.

"A thirst for knowledge; a sponge to absorb; darling BEE a good judge; receive your just reward."

Her body twists a little and, she said.

"HA, HA, Max you just thought of that sitting, there didn't you?"

She gives the Green Froggy a couple of taps [Squeaky-Squeak]. They laugh she turns around to look at him and, said.

"What are you writing?"

"A poem and, I just finished it."

Her face got excited and, is very curious and, she said.

"Oh, good may I read it Max!?"

"Of course."

Her thoughts to get close to him moves the chair alongside of him. She reaches for it as he hands it to her. She puts it in her lap like it was something very precious to her and, reads it silently. A minute later she gets up to sit in his lap with a big smile and, she said.

"Please Baby read it to me."

"[Long does your lips taste; take it slow it won't BEE a waist; turn our heads same kiss retraced; I love you that's why we faced; can't forget my arms are fully embraced; Captivated by the stream of your lips; Each of us sow in tears; She receives my precious seeds; Children come forth wife and, I rekiss; Bags full of money; Hook line morning honey; Bridge line to valleys; Side by side chorus and, verse; Melismatic ending bandages and, nurse; Captivated by the stream of your lips]." She plays with her hair pulls it to the left side and, she said.

"I'm speechless Baby what are you going to title it?"

"Well first of all I got to explain the title because kissing you is of such pleasure for me … I got to have you because you're my candy."

She lowers her head still looking at him with a humble gratitude squeezes her shoulders together and, relaxes. Oh, she's happy that he wrote of her about something or, anything under an inspiration and, she said.

"Baby take my lips anytime."

It dawned on him and, said.

"[THAT'S IT I JUST CHANGED IT]!"

She starts to laugh at his excitement with an open mouth laugh and, said.

"HA, HA Changed it to what?"

"HA, HA What you just said."

"Baby take my lips anytime?"

"YES, that's it!"

He puts it on the counter they sort of laugh a little more she lays on his shoulder they hug for a while he's whispering to her about the instruments in storage they could rehearse and, record a demo. She whispers back it will be a total focus.

Before they could have said anything, else Samantha comes on the speaker and, said.

"Four individuals are approaching but, stopped calling for you both by your name's."

Amyl ion looked up and, said.

"Put them on the viewer please Samantha."

"Here you go."

She gets off his lap he rises to see on the viewer and, he said.

"Sweetheart it looks like Bill, Kenny Ray with two women, I wonder what they want? there about 50 Yards away at a location we went by yesterday."

She puts her arm around him and, said.

"They must be looking for us or, need us we better go meet them."

He looked at her and, said.

"I was thinking the same thing."

He kiss's her cheek and, said.

"Maybe we better cover a few things up if they come inside."

She looked around scratched her chin and, said.

"Maybe it's a good time to show them were the ship's at."

They cover just a couple of things and, he said.

"Samantha were going outside so, lower the hatch please we will be bringing some guest's inside then scan them."

"AYE, AYE Captain."

There outside clear away the branches decide just to leave it open they hear them calling their name's and, he said.

"Hay over here."

They all meet and, greet ask them to come aboard the ship the group of 4 thought in separate ways about her beautiful black hair and, wings on the sides of her eyes. There all on board Amyl ion grab's four extra chairs from storage and, they all sit at the bridge area. Then what appeared to be an earthquake shake's the ship a little they look at one another and, Max said.

"Samantha, report what that was."

They look at the viewers.

Their guests are wondering holding their breath and, Samantha said.

"A 4.5 Earthquake no damage to the ship Captain."

Kenny Ray cleared his throat and, said.

"That is quite common around these valleys."

His wife looking around at things she didn't understand and, said.

"This is an amazing ship oh by the way my name is Bernadette, Kenny Ray's wife my husband told me a lot so, I'm very glad to meet you all."

They all shake hands.

While they're socializing back at the cave that the [27-Trip's] dug out to hide from Raven Hade's to preserve the ship. The earthquake opened up a crack at the back of the wall a rattle snake had noticed that crack. The snake was there just to look around go back later to the heat outside but, decided to go in the crack it was surely wide enough and, went in all the way. Little did that rattle snake realize that it was about to meet its death. The snake kept crawling with its tongue darting in and, out. The crack had started at a point where a small vein ended from the inside. The vein opened up to a larger vein which came to the opening of a large cavern. The snake was thinking this would be a nice home. That cavern turned out to be the home of a monster that Raven Hade's left behind because he couldn't find the would be King and, Queen to destroy. He planted the monster at the other end of the cavern sealed up the opening in his hope's it would kill the would be King and, Queen after all he wanted this planet for himself.

The monster would roam from one end of the cavern to the other. That little crack brought in a little light which came upon the crystal's that were scattered everywhere to aluminate the cavern at that end.

Meanwhile back on the Ship, they're having a good time Bernadette and, Lavita were asking questions and, Bernadette said.

"What are you going to wear at your Coronation?"

They were wondering ... looked at each other and, Amyl ion said.

"Well, uummm we really hadn't thought about it but, we're glad you brought that up."

Max pulled his ear lobe and, he said.

"I guess our space suits would be inappropriate maybe Samantha can come up with something."

Lavita would love to have the future queen at her house and, she said.

"Maybe you could come to my house we could come up with something good for your Coronation?"

She glanced at Max with a devoted face, and, said.

"I'm afraid I don't want to leave my husband's side.

Max looked at Bill, and, Kenny Ray and, said.

"I got the two asbestos blanket's that saved us from the dragons fiery breath I know you want to see them."

They're thrilled at the thought and, bill said.

"Why YAA, that would be Great."

He went to go get them gave each of them one. All 4 were surprised that the fire from the dragon didn't affect the blankets at all.

Lavita fussed with her dress and, said.

"Well, it's absolutely amazing what you two did."

Bill was quick to respond and, he said.

"Especially me now that I can see. I can see that I'm actually touching the blanket."

They all Laughed and, Amyl ion said.

"You know I think that Samantha can make up something for me to wear."

Max thought he was rude not to ask about refreshments and, he said.

"Would you care for some drink's and, what can we expect at the Coronation?"

They said on at a time.

"Yes, we would like some drinks and, that would be fine."

Amyl ion said.

"Samantha, could we have 6 Ice Tea's please?"

Lavita came to a good point and, said.

"The pew's and, balcony's will be full."

Bernadette wanted to join in leaned forward and, said.

"Just come in the entrance of the building walk down the aisle together the Pastor will be sitting in the front pew, he'll see you then stand-up walk to the podium you'll go there too. The Bible will be on the podium when he's ready after a prayer then he'll ask you Amyl ion to place your right hand on it then Maximilian you put your right hand on top of your wife's hand because the King always cover's the Queen and, repeat after the Pastor."

Kenny Ray briefly raised his hands and, said.

"Don't worry you two about a thing."

CHAPTER 31

The drink's slowly drop down from the ceiling in a row Amyl ion gets up give's one to all and, sits down.

Meanwhile back at the cave the snake had wandered to far or, its curiosity got the best of it. The monster was restless and, was at that part of the cavern stopped heard the hissing of the snake and, knew exactly what it was the monster hid and, waited for it to come by. A grizzly looking hand appeared from behind the snake as it crawled and, stopped. The snake knew something was up. The hand was rather large coming out from behind a large Stalagmite the colors of the hand were blue with black streaks looking like fire and, long nails. Probably a poisonous monster. The fingers were moving just a little bit as if they were dancing to get its prey. The hand swopped down on the snake right behind's it's head and, neck and, grabbed it. The snake wrapped its long body around the monster's left arm but, couldn't do anything. The monster was slowly drawing it up but, turned the snake away from its face gave out a blood-curdling sound of female laughter that echoed throughout the cavern. The next thing that happened was the monster put the other hand around its neck ripped off its head but, all you could see of the monster was the backside with long black snakes that made up the hair on its head. Those snakes were making hissing sounds when the rattle snake was caught. They're moving in all directions with two dark red one's on the top of the monster's head. The shoulder's, arm's and, hand's you could see the black steaks looking like fire on the blue skin. The monster drew the snake's body to its self-disappeared behind the Stalagmite threw the head down all you could hear was ripping the flesh off the skeleton and, eating it.

"Chomp, Chomp, Chomp ... mmMMMmm."

The monster dropped the skeleton with the rattler attached next to the ripped off head and, gave another blood-curdling sound of female laughter that echoed in the cavern. Insanity is what I would call it. Then it slipped away very fast with cries like a Lunatic or, was it the laughter of a witch. I wasn't able to make out clearly of what or, who it was but, I did see the lower body of a large snake with rings of black and, blue section's, with jagged edge's separating the two colors.

Meanwhile back on the ship they finished their drink's and, getting ready to leave.

Bill was going to be cute and, said.

"Well folks we'll see YA there."

They all laugh that bill can joke about his new gift of sight and, Lavita said.

"Well let's all go and, I'm sure you two will call upon us at any time."

Max got up first and, said.

"That we will and, we'll escort you all out and, a little way's down."

They get back on the ship and, look at the time. They sit in the captain's chairs they give the froggy a [Squeaky-Squeaky] with her happy cry she loves it so, and, they never know when to do that. They look at their uniforms they crack a smile and, she said.

"Samantha, could you make up some men's and, woman's clothing for us?"

"Can do captain."

Happy with that said. She continued and, said.

"Okay then, captain Maximilian need's a new dark suit, maroon tie with little dark grey diamonds on it or, whatever your taste is for it a matching handkerchief for the top pocket a XL white dress shirt with size 12.5 brown dress shoes, brown belt and, captain Amyl ion need's a burgundy mermaid long gown, matching long gloves shoulders showing and, gold hooped earing's please."

He nodded his head at her selection and, said.

"Samantha when will the items be ready?"

"57 Minutes with the measurements of both captains registered. Your clothing should fit precisely."

He thought I hope she wears that dress shirt around here I believe that's one reason why she ordered it. She tap's the Green Froggy [Squeaky-Squeak] it goes.

He smiles hoping, hoping and, said.

"Are you going to wear your bee hive which I really like by the way ...?"

She gets up from her chair goes to get it comes back straddle's his lap sits with her knees and, shins on the sides of his thigh's and, said.

"I love it so, and, Max I didn't want to be presumptuous."

She puts it on they adjust it just right with the long strands of hair on her left side to her waist with extensions going down the back to her waist with a long burgundy, olive-green scarf a small knot on her right and, he said.

"Okay then... whatever you want."

Samantha put on the viewers and, said.

"Bernadette and, Lavita are on their way back to the ship."

Max put his hands on her thighs and, said.

"Amyl ion I wonder what they want?"

She played with her extensions with a spirit of inquiry and, said.

"Samantha, could you open the starboard speaker please?"

"Hear you go."

Max tapped her thighs which meant for her to answer and, she said.

"You're welcome to come aboard Lavita, Bernadette."

They're thinking I wonder what's going looking at each other moving in their positions. The two-woman come up the step's walk inside and, with overlapping conversations. The woman sees them her on his lap and, her bee hive on and, Lavita said.

"I Left my purse here somewhere."

They all turn their heads then Lavita sees it then Bernadette said.

"Wear on earth did you get that beautiful piece of headwear?"

Amyl ion looked at Max he nudged her thigh as a sign of approval gave her a wink Lavita clutch her heart and, said.

"Oh, my dear that really is just for you and, with your wing's ... well that is so, natural."

Lavita, Bernadette gushed out a little breath and, said.

"May we approach?" Amyl ion raised her arms parallel pointed at them and, said.

"Come."

The Royalty is beginning to present itself Max thought with her pure blood that God gave her flowing through her body.

That said we have got a long time to observe her coming of age or, maybe she's there already.

Lavita and, Bernadette has their mouths open looking at one another then back at her. He's thinking I know what they're thoughts are and, the women got that right. He think's on … even though it's not official, Amyl ion is a Queen. Bernadette has an index finger on her chin and, finally comes to grips at what she wants to say.

"You must wear it my dear … and, you will, won't you?"

She looks at him he smiles with a look that say's, need we say anymore? She humbly said.

"Okay I will."

Lavita grab's her purse and, said.

"Bernadette let's go."

The woman hustles out the ship he pull's her towards him she scoot's closer he gives her a kiss on her right cheek she rests on his left shoulder he puts his arms around her she has her arms and, hands around his neck and, head she adjusts her sitting to get more comfortable lays her head between the chair and, the back of his head with her face down. They fall asleep until the time came that the clothes were ready and, Samantha said.

"Captain's your clothes are complete out the chute dispenser waiting for you."

They get up from their nap walk over to the clothes unfold them both agreeing and, he said she said.

"HHMMM not bad."

"Thank you, Samantha."

"Well, we've got an hour."

"Let's try everything on and, go."

"Samantha we are going to our Coronation and, would you secure the ship when we leave because we don't know when we'll be back perhaps later today."

"AYE, AYE Captain."

She's has got her dark red lipstick on gold earring's she pierced through her lobes. Bee hive with the hair to her left side draping down the back to her waist and, her naturally gifted black wings past her eyebrows burgundy mermaid long gown showing her shoulders with long burgundy gloves.

He's got a dark suit on white shirt, maroon tie, matching handkerchief, brown shoes and, brown belt.

They exit come around to where the building would be people from all over were there and, stop to survey all the people. She went from holding hand's to putting her arms, hand around his left arm, with a squeeze crushes her breasts on his arm they looked into each other's eye' they're a little nervous he reached over with his right hand held her left cheek and, he said she said.

"Can I kiss your lip's?"

"I wish you would the lipstick won't come off."

"Remind me that we I must send a message to my dad and, mom on how well the Javelin's worked."

"Oh! Max don't forget to tell them about the coronation."

The crowd turned to see the pride of lions coming around their way about 1 to 2 hundred yards when Max, Amyl ion were talking and, hadn't noticed the crowd of people were watching then released their kiss. The crowd opened up towards the door it could have been 50 Feet just to get to the door that must have seemed like a mile. He took the first step they slowly walked together still having her arms, hands wrapped around his left arm. They were very humbled smiling all the while walking through the crowd their thinking how incredible all this is for us she turned up to his ear and, she said he said.

"I see what you mean about a Just Weight and, Balance towards the People."

"They ask for us and, here we are."

"God put us here and, [no matter where we are, there we shall be]."

"You took the words right out of my mouth."

They reach to kiss the crowd cheer's and, someone said.

"It's as if they don't know anyone is around them."

Max out the corner of his eye looked and, he said.

"There's about a dozen or, more lions to the right ... can you see them our friends are there too. I wonder which one is BJ?"

They wave to the lions they respond by making their unique sounding roar and, what a sound they all made. You readers should have been there!

They're making their way through the crowd, a man and, woman approaches and, she said.

"This is my husband, he's a master carpenter, and, he'll build your house."

Max thought AAHHH this is great and, he said.

"We'll talk first thing right after the Coronation."

Oh, Amyl ion was so, pleased with that she just squeezed his arm crushing her breasts and, smiled as she looked up to him. He knew how important that was for his wife, and, of course there first born is coming in 21 months from today and, he said.

"I was dreaming a little bit a go that we could have a building encircling the [27-Trip's] with a lot of glass so, people could walk by see the ship that brought us here a retractable top that Samantha can control when we leave for a trip."

She's unrestrained smiling big for him and, she said.

"Oh, my darling what an incredible plan."

She raises her left hand to caress his right cheek brings it back to his arm. Making it to the door they stop for a moment to take it all in. The people were silently talking stopped while they proceeded on down the aisle. The congregation rose from the pew's and, one by one they went to the aisle where they could be closer and, rub shoulder's you might say. She's deep in thought and, she said.

"I also thought along your line of thinking that by keeping the trees around the ship putting down a floor inclosing the ship with glass just like you said so, people can see through with a restaurant inside and, that the money could go back to the people somehow ... what are your thoughts?"

He looked at her for a moment as he can't get enough and, said.

"I like it!"

There walking down the aisle with Sasha and, Dominic on the right-side edge of the middle pews and, Dominic said.

"Sasha do you ever wonder what they talk about?"

She puts her arm around him and, she said.

"I guess if we want to know we'll just have to ask them."

People were welcoming them to the valley it was getting crowded hard to get to the podium but, she wouldn't give way nor, leave the position next to her beloved husband. A couple of times they had to stop wait for it to clear before they could proceed down the aisle cause some people wanted to shake hands or, say a few words. A couple of boys in the balcony were a little rowdy they were having quite a discussion [I think] looking at this gorgeous woman talking back and, fourth then one of the boys shouted with conviction and, said.

"[QUEEN BEE]."

Of course, everyone heard the boy that concluded that discussion between the two. Max turned to her with a smile then looked into the balcony to remember the boys and, he said.

"That boy just announced to everyone what God had promised you. I would like to nurture him along in his life."

She looked at him put her left hand on his right cheek gives him a kiss on his cheek and, said.

"Oh, Maximilian I'm at a loss of words but, I want to turn to the boy, wave and, smile. What do you think?"

"That would be the start of something most excellent and, I must emphasize the word BEE, My Beautiful wife."

CHAPTER 32

"Maximilian would you put your hands on my shoulders like you do right after I turn around and, I'll wave and, smile at the boys."

She turns around smiles first then waves with her right hand puts her hands together in front of her looks at the boys that are with their girlfriends next to them gives the boys a special eye message for several moments telling the boys that it was alright and, blew them a kiss. Well, the two boys stood up and, smiled back and, they shook hands and, the other boy said. Maroon blouse nice butt cheeks could you come back and, sit down with me?

"Anything for you, My Queen!"

The crowd heard that and, they kind of perked up.

She acknowledges that too and, turns back around and, has his handkerchief out. She sees it instantly and, said.

"Oh, Maximilian I am so, happy with the way that things are turning out. It seems like a fairy tale, doesn't it? There's your handkerchief MMMM, always ready for me."

Her tears are just about to fall and, catches them regains her composure glances at his eyes resumes her arms around his arm clutching the handkerchief. They make it to the front the Pastor gets up and, gets along side of them to go to the Podium and, said.

"How you both doing I knew you could make it. If you would please stand right here and, it will be over within a couple of minutes and, if I may say that our God sure picked out the best-looking pair this side of the Galaxy or, maybe some other one."

That broke the ice for the three of them and, laughing at what the Pastor just said. The Pastor holds up his Bible it was all but, wore out you could probably ask him anything and, he would just turn right to it and, he said.

"Let's begin, shall we? Amyl ion place your right hand on the Bible here on top and, Maximilian place your right hand on top of hers so, now let's get through the formalities please and, repeat after me and, just say yes to the question's."

Meanwhile back at the cavern the Monster is roaming about its surrounding's screaming.

"I GOT TO GET OUT OF HERE!!!"

A newspaper reporter was there and, gave an eyewitness explanation and, he said.

The music starts ["Ain't Talking About Love" Van Halen [cover w/ backing track]. Kramer Guitar.

"There's a chance we might get to see this Monster up close but, some of you should cover your eye's or, better yet leave your seat go out into the lobby or, go outside so, that you can't hear her vicious screams that's like a Psychopath. Okay now ... you that are left in your seats get ready but, I don't know when I can catch up with this Monster. It appears that its searches at different locations slams against the walls of the cavern to find a weak spot to get out and, be free. Wait just a minute I think our paths are going to meet. I see the side of it but, not the face there's these wild snakes on the head with two red ones on top as it concentrates and, can't sense me there and, we get a chance to witness this Monster. The long body is a snake round as a sycamore tree weaves and, turns that's quite interesting to see. Then it poised as it stopped with the tail rattler making that distinct sound. I can see closer now that the body is what I thought it was. Black and, blue with rings but, with more rings than what I first saw. I was able to count and, there were 19 to 20 rings with jagged edges separating the 2 colors. It dawned on me that it's an evil woman and, the transition from her snake body was distinct from her upper human body and, it appeared that her buttocks were as clear as it could be like she was placed inside the snake's body and, you could pull her out. She looks around and, notices that she is in the narrow part of the cavern slams to her right on the wall but, nothing happens. She is shaken a little but, turns around and, I get a clear view of her as she faces me. She couldn't see me because I was looking through a tiny hole in the Stalagmite. She must be

25' feet from me and, the fangs must be 2" inches long as she opens her mouth. She has a snake's tongue that darts in and, out that's pinkish red with black snakes for hair that are darting all over her head and, the lower ones are longer. There're 2 red ones at the top front and, there hissing like the black one's but, a royal kind of look about them with perhaps a crown. Her body is muscle toned thin with her abdomen small ribs showing a little. Her skin is dark blue with black streaks like small flames her breasts are cupped underneath with a bronze-colored silver maple shaped leaves and, the tip of it covers her areoles. Her upper arms have 3 rings of bronze snakes that wrap around and, two heads on the rings with one at the top and, bottom. Oh, I see better now that she's facing me and, I see the snake skin that blends just above her hips and, the irises are bright lime green that glowed when she turned my way. I also notice a few words that were faint on her skin and, able to make them out and, they read [HATE, KILL, DESTROY]. Something is wrong she is starting to turn Psychotic clenches her teeth then opening her mouth as her tongue is darting in and, out then picks out an object in my direction. She breaths in and, hollers out several times she's trying to make out what it is. Her arms are out to her sides a little her palms are facing out in my direction. Her snake body is twisting pushing her closer and, closer what can I do I can't run she'll bite me with her poisonous fangs. There's one thing I could do is squat down and, cover my face hoping it's a bad dream and, this will pass away. It's been a minute sense I did just that and, I think I heard her body brush against the floor of the cavern and, maybe she's gone away so, I looked up saw her rattler a little way down the narrow passage. I saw the snake body trailed to my right which her body came up behind me I turned around and, there she was starring right at me at the same time her eyes turned a bright blinding white and, a cold bolt of shock waves went right through me. She started laughing and, screaming that she got me and, those snakes on her head were hissing, darting at me like they knew I was had. I looked at my hands that were cold already and, my fingers were turning to stone traveling up my arms faster, faster it's going … and … I … can't … Breee … th …!"

Meanwhile the crowd at the Coronation starts clapping because it's all over. The photographer has his equipment set up with his flash pan and, said.

"Smile for the camera."

PPOOPHH.

The pastor had already dashed away the new royals had gotten their picture taken for posterity and, the Pastors wife comes over to welcome them with their 9 kids and, she's pregnant with her 10th child. A line formed some gifts were presented to the royals. One was when a Japanese couple offered Amyl ion a Uchigatana Samurai Sword. She was most gracious to receive such a gift then they look at one another and, bowed to the gift givers. Then more people came by and, shook hands. The King leaned over to her and, said.

"Those cute dimples on your lower back were really noticeable when you danced in my dream."

She got excited to tell him and, turned at him and, said.

"Well guess what? Those dimples you call them is when our God took his index fingers and, pushed me towards you after I was transformed … and, you know I felt them HA, HA, HA isn't that something?"

They grinned, smiled, bumped shoulders and, hips and, play a little. A minute goes by and, another Japanese couple came up to offer a Nodachi Samurai Sword to Max they bowed and, thanked them for the gift and, he said.

"Amyl ion can you believe this with the two swords that they were in our dreams and, I'll never forget that great battle we had."

"Oh, Max, I wish it would have been captured for history's sake of two people fighting back-to-back protecting one another with these Magnificent Samurai's."

There came another couple nothing was unusual except the gift. It was an instruction book on how to operate an [Alien Space Ship] and, the King said.

"Where on earth did you get this!?"

The couple just looked in the sky smiled then walked away. They were shocked and, holding back their laughter. They thumbed through it a little bit and, the Queen said.

"Why couldn't we have found this manual aboard the alien ship in our dream?"

The king nodded his head and, said.

"YAA that would have saved us a lot of trouble."

They look at each other he bends down to give her a kiss she reaches up to meet him it was a delicious kiss touching and, releasing a couple times and, the pastor in the crowd said.

"Hey everybody lunch is served."

"Go on in Wang Wei and, his wife Li na will place you at your seat's."

There weren't enough chairs for everyone and, were directed to sit in a couple of the arm rest chair's they set down their gifts at the table and, wanted to sit next to each other. A couple of kid's were playing under the table tied a string around the King and, Queen's ankle's they finally noticed it she slipped it off without untying it and, laid it on the table. The Royal couple were amused at this. Then someone banged a large spoon on an iron skillet and, said.

"Come and, get the food on the table's take what you want and, now is the time to rub shoulders with the King and, the Lovely Queen but, … [They all laugh] … I must warn you that the King is most jealous of his wife and, now the Queen."

The man that finished that for the King look at one another and, gives a thank you gesture. The Kings thoughts are that that was a very good beginning the people will know that it's true and, she leaned into him with a couple of giggles and, said.

"Oh, that was perfect and, you didn't say a word… he, he, he, he."

She kept smiling with a cute squeak that would make a Buffalo stampede stop and, look.

Pastor said a prayer they picked their food from the long table and, sat back down with her on his right. They starting to eat and, then the people started to eat. He was tapping her foot and, she placed her foot on his and, 10 seconds later she had her leg on his legs then eventually had both her legs on his legs. Finally, she scooted herself onto his lap with her left arm around his shoulders now she's so, very happy smiling and, giving him some food once in a while. The People were watching this and, really liked what they saw. She whispers in his ear and, he'd smile while chewing his food.

The owner of the Local Newspaper came by and, wanted an interview. They turned to each other … he gave her a concerned face shrugged his shoulders that meant I don't care and, she said.

"The King and, I am very flattered we will do it next week please."

The owner was pleased with that and, said.

"How about in 9 days from now on a Friday at 9: AM?"

The king was having none of that and, said.

"UM pardon me but, I have made plans with my wife, the Queen could we make it the following Monday at 9: AM please?"

The owner said.

"That would be perfect, see you then and, would you come to the conference table once you walk in if you don't mind?"

The King looks at the Queen, and, winks with a smile. She has to think fast because she was not aware that he had made plans or, even discussed them with her she turned to the reporter and, said.

"Could you please have Coffee and, Tea for us?"

The owner pauses and, said.

"Why of course your Majesty's."

He talks to his wife later on about reviewing what the editor may say about them and, if they don't like it or, is negative about them then they can decide not to have it printed.

The owner goes back to sit with his wife. She looks at the King and, said nothing but, her facial expressions with her eye's a little wide she's thinking while giving him some salmon on her fork. He chewed it up and, he said.

"Sweetheart if you're not busy with your Royal Duties, next Thursday evening to the following week on Monday morning could I have the pleasure of your company?"

She puts down her fork looks around and, everyone is looking smiling at what their witnessing. She decides just to be herself goes to put her arms around his neck and, head whispers in his ear and, kiss's his cheek. She turns to everyone and, said.

"I guess you all know by now that we are crazy for our love and, about each other."

He reaches in his back pocket pulls out the same handkerchief for her cause he knew her tears were forming. She sees it then gushes grabs it just in time to catch the tears. Inside of this woman she is realizing that this Coronation has finally come to fruition she can hardly believe it and, the King spoke to the crowd and, he said.

"Everyone here as time goes on, you'll know more about us and, our beginning's."

One person said.

"I think it's wonderful the children need an example of love and, how its play's out."

Another person said.

"Your Majesties could you come to our schools and, interact with the students in the classroom's we would love to have you."

The King and, Queen look at each other she reaches for the string on the table that the [Two Kid's Tied Their Ankle's] with places it in the King's hand squeeze's his hand with her hand's and, he said.

"[Sqweaky-Sqweak]."

Well, she just loved that kissed his cheek with her hand on his right cheek and, smiling so, beautifully for him. The King thought about the message the Queen is sending him and, said.

"How's about tomorrow morning."

She agrees by kissing him on the lips turned to the crowd and, she said.

"Where is the school?"

The mayor wiped his mouth and, said.

"In the middle of town someone will pick you up at 10: AM."

He wants to say something in the Queen's ear she turns, listens and, he said.

"I adore you."

He kiss's her on the ear she giggles raising her shoulder's a little. Samantha intervenes and, said.

CHAPTER 33

"Captain's."

The King and, Queen seem to leave their happy state of mind the King said to the Queen.

"Since you're Facing me a little could you turn to my ear, please respond to Samantha."

The Queen understood did as the King asked, she was thinking as well as the King we don't want to alarm or, cause a disturbance at the table and, she said.

"Yes Samantha."

The people thought they were sharing an intimate moment went to talking amongst themselves and, Samantha said.

"I picked up a thumping sound from the mountain behind the cave where the [27-Trip's] was stationed. Also, Captain's a blocked detection device has weakened when a thump has occurred and, that I can pick up movement but, only 34%."

There Majesties wipe their mouths talk ear to ear and, he said.

"Samantha we will be over as soon, as we can open the hatch when we approach put on the viewers for us. Anything that you can find out like size, living or, machine and, if the blocking device has weakened again?"

"AYE, AYE Captain."

The King and, Queen slowly summon the mayor and, Pastor over. The Queen rises to her feet stand's next to the King waits for the mayor and, Pastor to arrive so, that they can tell them they have an urgent need to attend to at the ship and, the Pastor said.

"Come on our study hour on Sunday if you can make it?"

"What time?"

"10: AM."

The King acknowledges that gave him a nod gets up the Queen picks up the manual he takes the two Swords in his right hand. She quickly takes the King by his left arm they walk away and, some of the kid's come over grab their leg's give them a hug they hug them back and, stroke their hair talk awhile and, the kids said.

"See you at School tomorrow?" she loved their attention gave their cheeks a touch with her hands and, said.

"Yes, the King and, I will be there."

Then they ran away and, one said to the other one.

"Oh, boy I got to talk to a King and, Queen."

The King and, Queen notice the master carpenter swing by him with his wife 3 kids and, said.

"Come on over tomorrow night at the ship after supper and, bring some plans."

They get to the ship set the Swords and, the manual on the counter sit in their Captain's chairs look at the viewer's ... pause ... and, he said.

"Samantha, can you detect any movement in or, around the mountain."

"Sketchy at best and, what I can pick up is blurry but, here you go."

The viewer show's a long curly object and, that its cutting in and, out.

"Amyl ion what do you think of it?"

"Well after what has happened in the last couple of day's I got a gut feeling that something alive is in that mountain."

They keep watching for a long time go to the bedroom and, change into their uniforms then he decides to lay down watches the viewers in the bedroom and, ask her to come with him to the bed and, rest. She stands for a minute by the bedside her patience runs out takes his hand and, lay down while watching the viewers and, she said.

"There's nothing in the mountain."

He turns to her while still having her hand kiss's it and, said.

"My Queen we can't risk it and, I'm disappointed that we won't be able to finish our song tonight."

She turns to him and, said.

"I knew you would call me your Queen tonight and, we'll reach in that pocket together and, finish it later on Oh, King of mine MMM."

Then the object moves quickly to its right and, turn their focus on it as it stops abruptly.

"Captains with that thumping sound the detection device is weakened again and, I can pick up 39% of the object."

That's good he thought and, he said.

"Samantha we will have a direct dialog now and, you've recorded the sound could you replay all movement's that you can detect with that sound and, put it on the viewer's please."

She tapped him on his chest with her fingers and, said.

"HHMMM a direct dialog that would make communication easier."

They watch as there are 4 detections at 12% and, 25% then 34% and, 39% all with the quick movement from a limited space inside the mountain with that thumping sound then the object makes an abrupt stop. Amyl ion now has her suspension's and, he said.

"That's good and, maybe we can see how this all shapes up."

Samantha plays them over and, over again and, she said.

"That static is getting in the way of seeing what it is."

They're intrigued by this and, almost hypnotized. She's got her head on her hand elbow on the bed the other hand on his chest.

"Max well we know our Coronation birthday and, my birthday."

They look at each other he smiles then climbs on top of her starts kissing her neck and, cheek's then to her lips and, he said.

"Happy Birthday."

Over and, over again as he kissed her. She was loving it all with her giggle's, laughter and, cries of happiness. She gently rolled him on his back and, mount's him on his stomach but, just for a few minutes start's kissing his lips, cheek, neck wrap's her arms around his head with happy breathing, whispering sighs and, she said.

"We are so, Blessed. It doesn't get any better than this ... Oh, I know what I wanted to ask you?"

Max perks up cause her questions are very important from his now queen and, he said.

"YES, my Love and, what is that?"

She stuck her tongue in his ear canal swished it around. He left earth for about a minute or, two until she was done and, said.

"When is your Birthday?"

He gets off the bed shakes the chills off from her tongue in his ear. She lays on her back fluffs her hair and, watches. He does some play acting for her walking around with hand on hip putting on a little debonair and, said.

"Well, well… if this is such a pressing question from my Queen, I have no choice but, to tell you because I do not want to go to your gallows for refusing to answer nor, do I want to remain in the dungeon's the rest of my life for contemplating such a question."

She's laughing hands over her mouth in her unique way a low squeaky deep throated sound and, very womanly. She is having such a good time that she gets up from the bed very casually and, struts around with his handkerchief waves it in the air with her nose in the air like she doesn't care. She faces away from him then turns around sexy like looks at him with face down and, looking very serious waving the handkerchief very arrogantly and, she said.

"My Dear servant it is imperative that I know all my subject's and, I can decide to do whatever pleases the Queen because I must preserve and, protect my beloved King."

"Well, well, well if that's the case your Majesty and, [without further ado]."

She is cracking up with laughter but, tries to keep it under control and, thinks I'm going to pounce on him and, he said.

"My Birthday is August 10$^{th.}$"

"Then you are free to love me as you please your Highness [Squeaky-Squeak]."

She just cries out with a happy voice as she loved that throws her arms forward makes a mad dash at him to jump on him, he caught on waiting to catch her. He braced himself with just over 100 pounds coming at him opening her arms and, legs she landed and, he said.

"Whoa … I got you HA, HA, HA."

He spins her around several times with her legs hanging out from the centrifugal force. Their laughter is quieting down he lays her gently on the bed holding each other tight for a few more minutes.

Then another thump sounds off they look at the viewers and, Samantha said.

"47% detection is available."

Their playfulness has ended and, he said.

"Run them together Samantha."

She gets up for a closer look he comes to her side and, she said.

"Maximilian your thought's?"

They put their arms from their sides around each other while he examines it all and, she said.

"Maybe something or, somebody is trying to get out of this here mountain."

She has gotten much more interested and, said.

"Samantha, can you scan the cave from where the ship was stationed?" … pause.

"Yes, there is a small crack in the back of the cave from the 4.5 earthquake which wasn't there before."

They turned to each other folding their legs put his hands on her shoulders and, she loves it then placing her hands-on top of his and, he said.

"I think we'll have to take the ship at the entrance of the cave put the All-seeing Fly in the cave through that crack and, we can learn more."

She's relaxed as they look in their eyes and, she start's laughing and, said.

"What's that? the All-seeing Fly?" he thought she's going to learn something new and, he said.

"There's this Mechanical fly we release it buzzes around that cavern that appears to have no exit or, entry and, it attaches itself where ever we want through our thought's that's connected to it from the ship and, we watch on the viewer."

She tilted her head left and, right and, thought how interesting this is and, said.

"Then we'll know for sure. I like it."

Samantha said.

"Captain's! the object in the cavern is not mechanical."

They confer with one another then she said.

"Samantha if not, Mechanical what then is it?"

Samantha said.

"[A Live Breathing, Lunatic]."

He put his head back a little looked at her with his gut turning and, said.

"We've got to get over there."

He holds his beloved and, they look at one another realizing that it is going to be dangerous. Must have been about a minute as they move around from side to side he strokes her face with his right hand. There humming and, lost in themselves and, he said.

"Wweell … aa … we better go huh?"

She so, loves his attention and, can hardly break away and, lovingly, softly she said.

"Yyaaww, I guess so, and, release the All-seeing Fly."

He takes her by the hand goes to the bridge and, he said.

"Amyl ion please sit in your Captain's chair and, I'll sit in mine so, that we can have Samantha connect our thoughts to the fly and, while that is being done, we can leave from here and, go to the entrance of that beautiful cave that Samantha made for us."

She watches him as he takes command of things.

"Samantha, would you connect myself and, Captain Amyl ion to the all-seeing fly. After you've done that direct the ship back to the cave at the entrance about 50 Feet away with the bow facing the entrance, please? Amyl ion the metal object's will come out again but, only on our Temple's and, Prefrontal Cortex and, connect us to the fly, are you ready?"

Rubbing her palms together between her thighs with a smile that would remove the very mountain she said.

"Yes, I'm set captain."

"Samantha we are ready."

The metal object's come out to do their connection the ship slowly goes to the entrance of the cave. The metal object's release they land and, he said.

"Now we go out in front of the ship or, stay in our chair's release the fly from the front of the ship and, direct it with our thought's."

She likes the outdoors much better and, said.

"I would like to go in front."

"Let's go."

He grabs her hand there off she just loved it with a little squeak … then there out in front of the ship and, she said.

"Wait I can't see the back of the cave."

He looked and, said.

"Samantha put on the search light on the back of the cave please."

"Here you go."

The light comes on they walk closer reach the back of the cave they see the crack and, she said he said.

"Just enough room for a rodent or, a snake to get through."

"Do you think that has anything to do with what's going on inside … what are your thoughts?"

"Well let's release that fly in there and, find out."

She caress's his neck with her hand and, gives it a squeeze.

"Let's go back to the ship."

They stand in front face each other and, he said she said.

"Okay now since where both connected, we don't want to get our thoughts crossed because one must release control of the fly mentally while the other one control's it."

"I got it."

She's taps the side of her thighs with her palms thinking to herself I get to do this and, he said.

CHAPTER 34

"I'll release it from the ship take control for a minute and, then it's your turn. Samantha, would you display the viewer in front of us and, release the All-seeing Fly."

"Here you go."

The fly from a small hole comes out from the front he's controlling it mentally it's in front of them and, he [think's stop]. The viewer picks it up they see it look at each other he makes the fly go up and, down as she watches this and, is very amused. He's still looking at her makes the fly go left then right come back and, stays in front of them. Max points to his head then deliver's her the fly with the other hand gesturing like [here you go] without saying a word. She looks to the fly puts it in her mind thinks left, right and, it goes where she wants it to. She thinks up, down and, that's what it does. She's like somebody has tickled her funny bone a little. He's clapping gave her a bow raised his fist as a sign to hold the fly right there in front of them and, he said.

"Okay, we go into the cavern My Talented Wife and, find out what's going on in there."

Amyl ion ... well she just loved that that her husband called her his Talented Wife and, thought I don't want to disappoint him and, she said.

"Captain any suggestions?"

"You can do the honors of directing the fly into the crack but, go slow so, we can look around oh, by the way it has a light that you can also control by your thought's. Whenever your ready captain we can watch on the viewer."

She guide's the fly into the crack they see a smooth circular tube that's damp and, as it creep's along it opens up to a larger space he motion's with his finger to go up she takes it to the ceiling and, it too is getting larger.

He motions with his hand like a cup with his fingers on the ceiling, she understands and, puts the fly on the ceiling. She thinks to hold it there while they wait and, talk. Her face is filled with excitement that she can do such a thing. They look at the viewer they can see from the All-seeing Fly the layout of the cavern with its Stalactite's and, Stalagmite's and, she said.

"I want to go inside the ship and, watch."

"Okay captain but, hold that thought on the ceiling."

As he smiles and, is well pleased and, she said.

"Samantha were coming inside close the viewer outside here please."

She's thinking stay on the ceiling fly. They sit in their Captain's chairs look at the viewer's they see from above thanks to the fly notice a few snake skeletons with their heads separated from their body's and, talk back and, fourth and, he said she said.

"Something is eating snake's but, first tear's the head's off."

"That is some kind of thing I'd like to know what we are dealing with?"

He was thinking ... well my wife isn't squeamish and, she said.

"That direct dialog with Samantha is like another person."

He combs his hair back with fingers and, he said.

"YAA I thought I would try it out and, it's working fine without adding the Artificial Intelligence Upgrade. Samantha layout a grid with dimensions from the fly please."

"Here you go but, there's more to the cavern from where the fly is it is only a portion of the cavern."

They look study the area he mentions to her and, said.

"Can we find a spot a little further down the cavern? There might be a Stalagmite to land the fly on that is dry, I don't want any drip's landing on the it we want it high enough so, we can see down."

She takes the fly off the ceiling and he said.

"Don't use the light yet the crystal's give just a little light we don't want that thing to see the fly."

She's slowly looking, looking ... and, spot's a figure and, she said.

"Captain look at this!"

He leans forward and, he said.

"Oh, WOW ... get a little closer."

The fly buss's down and, around to see the frozen body in a squatting position. She gives it a little light from the fly and, there shocked at what they see. The stoned face of a man that was startled at what he saw and, turned to stone. Then they noticed an old-style writing tablet, pencil that was designed in that era and, they're lying close by. They get close to see perhaps the writing on the tablet but, it was too risky. Maybe later they could try to retrieve it because it might have some valuable information on it. She took the fly to the nearest dry Stalagmite and, turned the light off and, said.

"How did he get in the cavern?"

He was silent about that writing tablet kept studying the viewers then she too turned her attention along with him.

Well folks ... we draw in close to the monster as she is facing away and, hears something turns her upper body to the sound of the mechanical fly before it settles on a stalagmite that made just enough noise for her sensitive ears to pick up and, we get a better view of the monster. Her full lips are together she listens with her eye's looking up and, down. The tail start's rattling and, her body turns towards the sound. She looks left, right and, she moves that snake's body so, smoothly and, appalling. She stops rattle's her tail but, nothing is happening so, her mouth open's up her poisonous fang's present's themselves and, that tongue darting in and, out feeling her way trying to sense something and, Amyl ion points her finger and, said.

"Hey look there at the edge of the viewer something is coming into the picture."

They see it and, whatever it is, it's being very cautious. He gets up close to the viewer she follows and, grab's him by the arm with the monster coming into sight. There mouth's drop open and, see 20 to 25 snakes with 2 deep red ones on top of her head. There eyes open wide and, glance at one another.

Amyl ion wraps her arms around his waist buries her head between his arm and, chest and, in disgust goes [UGH]! She knows now that it is [Medusa]. She's thinking why God? Why God? is [Medusa] here? He thought yep ... that's [Medusa] all right but, what is that democrat doing here I thought that was all over with? He holds her until she wants to look at the viewer again and, thought I would hold her for the 999 Year's we get to spend together and, hold her in my grave. She's thinking well I've got to face the music lift's her head stands on tippy-toes kiss's him on the lip's with meaning release's her beautiful lips looked up to him and, she said.

"Satan has created another one of those beasts."

He focused on her while he examined her hazel eyes thinking I must be careful with what I say to her and, I'll be quite until. [BOOM]. That's when another thumping sound occurred that interrupted his plans to be quite and, both turning to the viewers and, she said.

"Samantha was that picked up by the fly and, if so, could you replay it please?"

"Here you go and, with that thumping sound the creature weakened the non-detection device attached to its body to 59%."

He didn't want to say medusa in front of her hesitated and, he said she said.

"Now we can see enough of that … object as it slams into the walls at random to find a weak spot to get out. I think."

"I wonder if Raven Hade's that devil knew if we were in that cave planted her there or, if it was the only location, he could find to put her at?"

He thinks for a moment with his index finger and, thumb on his chin and, said.

"UMM … probably just a coincidence, I really don't think that he knew we were there."

Samantha said.

"The grid revealed a crawl space on top of the mountain that wasn't detected before."

He snaps his fingers and, said.

"That's were that man got in there and, it was from the top and, who is he?"

"I think I know what happened."

As she looks back and, forth from him to the screen. He's waiting as she thinks to herself … She goes on starts to pace a little back and, fourth flips her hair and, said.

"Raven Hade's put Medusa in the cavern hoping she would escape at a later date but, the 4.5 earthquake closed the crawl space on top so, this man lost his life with his curiosity that got the best of him and, was already in side but, couldn't dig himself out."

"How interesting."

"There's more! Medusa tried to get out after the quake but, the crawl space wasn't big enough that's why she bang's the cavern wall at random."

"HHMMM, that makes sense."

"Oh, there's more … now if she try's that crawl space again there is a possibility she can escape and, roam the country side."

He grab's her face gives her a big smack on those beautiful red full lip's she's thrilled that she thought this all out plus he rewarded her with a loving kiss. She throws her arms around his neck and, gives him a hug then puts them under his arms on his upper back squeezes some more her hands go down his back slips them to his side looks up to him arms around him again with a big hug that will go down in the annuals of time as one of the greatest hug's. She tilts him left then right a couple of times release's him then grabbing his biceps and, she said he said.

"Captain we cannot let her leave that cave we've got to seal it up and, figure out how to destroy her."

"Let's get ready and, go to the top of the mountain okay … I've got an idea."

"Okay captain let's go the quicker the better."

"Have a seat."

She quickly sits in her Captain's chair with anticipation with her hands on the armrests she leans forward and, said.

"Samantha, close the hatch take us to the opening on the grid on top of the mountain please and, when you get there, stop and, hold that position then we can decide on what to do."

The ship leaves and, hovers at the center of the entrance there still looking inside of the cavern as they transferred their vision to the veiwers inside thanks to the All-seeing Fly and, Medusa has curled up for a nap between some Stalagmite's and, he said.

"Samantha set only 3 backup lasers on the hulls outer edge at 5% then seal that entrance with a steady burst so, as to pile dirt on the opening."

Samantha blast's that area the earth is piling up the entrance and, he said.

"Make it 10 feet high please."

A few moments go by they witness this to the completion then notice's it woke up Medusa. Amyl ion is focused and, forgotten the dreadful monster that caused her an emotional stress and, she said.

"Let's see what Medusa will do now?"

Medusa hears, looks in the direction of the dust coming down growl's grit's her teeth then growl's some more she uncurls her body then heads in that direction. They watch her as she goes to the location where she will try and, get out. She stretch's that snake body as it pushes her up to the hole of the ceiling. They look at the snake's body and, they're amazed that something like that can exist. Medusa gets in just a little bit of the ceiling hole try's digging with her hands trying to go further but, can't so, she gives up and, slinks to the floor puts her head down a little slips her fingers into the snake pit on her head the snakes have sounds of sympathy for their master and, she [SCREAMS]. The snakes on her head go to coughing from the dust but, quickly get back to being scary the echo's last a long time and, medusa threw her hands down looked to the ceiling closes her eyes and, said.

"[HOW DO I GET OUT OF HERE]?"

More screams are emanating from the creature and, those echoes are terrifying. I got chills and, people are leaving the theatre.

They're relieved breath out a sigh along with their body motions reacting they look at each other after that display of insanity ... there not smiling and, he said.

"Okay Samantha let's go back to the original station at the entrance of the cave please."

The ship turns 180 tilts in front then gets to the front of the cave turns another 180 lands and, Samantha said.

"The Two Lions are heading in this direction, E. T. A. 3. 5 Minute's."

He smiled with his head back a little because the relief it gave and, he said.

"Let's go outside and, welcome our friend's."

She had a concerned face scratched her noise as she rose and, she said.

"Samantha let Max and, myself know of any changes about Medusa. Document the lunatic as Medusa please."

"Very well then captain documented as Medusa."

They get up from their chairs as he grabs her hand quickly and, there off as she gives out a happy squeal. She didn't have time to think much of her decision on just calling the monster medusa. I would call it a maturity on her part and, not to dwell on the past and, she said.

"Samantha, lower the hatch please."

They hold hand's he thinks how good she is at everything. He thought again that when a person is put in charge of a high position it comes naturally and, loves being with her. They get outside look around notice that the man with which Max had a conversation with was not too far away either. The Lion's get there first and, he said.

"Well, captain we certainly have quite a number of friend's now."

She just puts her arms around him and, lays her head on his chest … closed her eyes and, whispered a prayer that said.

CHAPTER 35

"Thank you, God, for our friends watch over us protect our friends … yes, we do captain … HHMMM."

Apple Blossom and, Green Tea come into view and, Max said.

"Let's walk and, meet them, shall we?"

She touch's his lips with her right two fingers and, said.

"I was thinking it while you said it."

They meet one another and, Green Tea said.

"Hey kid's how you doing?"

Apple Blossom nodded her head up and, down and, she said.

"We watched your Coronation we're very happy for you both."

Green Tea thought I'm going to skip a little forward and, he said.

"Me and, the Miss's we're talking one day we decided to take you on a tour of the land every so, often and, it would be our treat, now what do you say about that?"

He nudge's her as to say … YAW. Well, she's overwhelmed breaks into a bigger smile gushing out just a little and, she said.

"AAHHH, WHEN DO WE START?"

The lions and, Max are look at her laughing that she was so, anxious. She looks at them smiling, anticipating, acting like she's getting a new space ship on her 14th Birthday. She takes him by the hand takes him over to give Green Tea a few feet away and, then to Apple Blossom for a big hug the captains say there thank you's and, Apple Blossom said.

"What day would you like?"

They look at each other they know that it would be Wednesday of next week and, he said.

"This coming Wednesday and, what are your thoughts captain."

She agreed quickly moving her head up and, down with that certified smile put her right hand in her pocket wiggled a little and, Green Tea said.

"Okay then 6: AM?"

He looks at her as she gave a resounding.

"YYEESSS."

He whispered to her but, they all heard and, he said.

"[Honey Moon]."

She smiled again that would make the surrounding rocks go.

"OOOOHHHH."

She had a quick thought and, she said.

"We would like to come over and, visit if that's alright?"

Green tea was surprised at her joy with them and, treated them as any other people and, he said.

"Sure, thing we live at 25 Prowse place half way to the valley from here you'll see the trail to the right cause it's the only one that leads to our place."

They say there good byes the captains walk back to the ship side by side and, he said.

"Anything new from Medusa, Samantha?"

There both thinking at the big problem now at hand.

"Nothing to Report captain."

Then they turn notice the Shephard with a sea of sheep out on the flat land and, two German Shephard's all three acknowledge one another and, she said.

"HAY I want to talk to this man."

Max laughs gives her a squeeze around her waist and, he said.

"Well, I thought you would ask me along?"

She's laughing along grabbing his right arm with her hands and, she said.

"Wherever I go you go My Darling ... come on."

The Shephard that sat on the rock at their first meeting was there waiting for them still on the rock and, they take turns and, all said.

"Hello."

The two Shephard dog's approach sniff them over there logged into their memory base and, the Shepard said.

"Don't be alarmed they do that to everyone."

She's amused at the Shepherd's and, she said.

"There beautiful do they have names?"

"Yes, these two are called June and, July."

Max remembered their previous meeting and, he said.

"Oh, you have two more called April and, May, don't you?"

"Yes and, there over to my right."

They come trotting into Max, Amyl ion give them a sniffing over as well. Their having a therapy session as there petting the Shephard's they respond in kind and, there all happy and, Max said.

"I guess you have to have them to manage such a large flock of sheep."

She came right into another question and, she said.

"Well, if there all here how does the flock stay together?"

"Oh, there are 8 more that are tending to the flock now."

They look at one another and, back at the Shephard and, he said.

"Well … they check in once in a while with me by twos with June, July departing having just checked in."

Max was thinking I wonder if my wife and, I could get a couple of these Shephard's for our boy I would love to have them I'm sure she would too and, the Shephard said.

"Well, I've got to go … got a busy calendar."

[He laughs with no concerns and, he said.]

Before I do here's a gift, I'd like to give it to both of you I think it would be beneficial."

The Shepherds right hand reaches behind him brings forth an old rolled-up piece of Parchment with jagged edges an old red band tied around it in a knot the Shepard blew on it to get some of the dust off shakes it then hand's it to them and, he said.

"Sorry about the dust I thought I'd lost it."

[He laughs]

"Both of you can have a look at it when your back in the ship."

[Just in case you readers missed that. The Shephard pulled it out of thin air.]

The two of them realize that it's no secret that he knows about the ship being in the cave. She thought with a puzzled look for a moment then it dawned on her that the Shephard's voice is the same as God that she talked to in the heavens along with her descent to her beloved and, at the ring of fire.

The Shepherd knew her thoughts as he glanced at her. They shake hands with the Shepherd as he leaves Max knew not to look at the holes in his hand because he knew who he is. She saw his hand when shaking hands with a hole through it and, felt it with her thumb. They stood there watching him leave the Shephard turned around, made her look at him just for a split second drew her eyes to a spot on the ground. She grabbed Max by the arm and, with other hand on his chest she said.

"I've got to look at something for a few seconds wait here captain please."

He waited as she looked at the place where the Shephard drew her eyes to it and, saw on the ground the words which said. [Love him, love him, Love him]. She saw the stick there right beside the writings picked it up stood for several seconds a cool breeze came across her face blew her hair around she closed her eyes and, could have sworn that the breeze said.

"Don't forget he knows too."

She turned rather abruptly with self-confidence oozing off her face as she walked back to him. She had a walk that was totally woman with a wiggle and, that smile was as big as ever took hold of his right arm. He was already turned around with his elbow out for her to grab and, walked back to the ship, with arms together. There looking at each other she has the stick in her other hand as she waves it forward and, backwards acting like she has a new found love. He already knows now that her thoughts are the same as his with this meeting they just had and, she said.

"Max, I felt the hole in his hand when I shook it and, how can that be?"

He told her on the way back to the ship everything he knew in the short period of time that they had. He put it all together for her. There back on board she takes him by the hand to the storage area and, she puts the stick next to the one that he brought on board earlier and, stops with putting her hands on his chest ... then stands on her toes with an enlightening look and, said.

"Oh, Maximilian ... I believe with all my heart."

He puts his right hand on her cheek and, said.

"That's good ... very good."

They stand together for several seconds then puts her arms around him and, he has one arm around her with his right hand still on her cheek she presses her left cheek on his chest he presses a little on his chest.

There's silence for a while he still has the parchment in his left hand. Then she looked up at him she wanted to see the inside of the rolled-up piece of parchment and, with excitement she said.

"HEY let's go to the mess hall table and, unroll this."

She mentions to him about his voice being the same when she was O' white crow and, he believes her 100% and, talk about the father and, the son being one. There was silence for a while and, he said.

"Let's go."

He grabs her by the hand she squeaks with her feet trying to keep up with the rest of her body.

He places it on the table and, starts to pull on the string and, she said.

"Stop before you go any further."

She wants to sit on his lap he's eager for her to join him now as they sit together with her on his lap and, she said.

"Baby you pull the string and, we'll both un-roll it."

So, he pulls the string then it disintegrated with small stars, streams of smoke and, sparkling sounds then disappeared. They grin pull their head back a little at this phenomenal thing look at each other and, chuckled. They un-roll it look for about 10 second's look at each other and, back at the Parchment and, she said.

"Look how old this is with these letters and, there so, faded."

They look at it intently notice that there are some markings on all four corners but, decide to look at that at a later date they wanted to study the words that were already legible and, he said.

"Well let's read it, together, shall we?"

"[Drip-Drip-Drip from the Black Rose], [A little blood brings to a close], [Separate now from the abuse], [Skin and, flesh, take one not to confuse], [Heaven knows skin will decompose]. They look at each other with a Quizzical look and, she said he said.

"Let's read it again."

"It's a riddle."

They read it the 3rd time. Just when they were reading it Medusa made another attempt to find a weak spot on the wall of the cavern which made her appear at 77% this time and, much more visible now. They stop reading the Parchment look up at the viewer in the mess hall and, Samantha said.

"Medusa at 77% here you go."

She maneuvers on his lap with her left arm around his neck look at the viewer and, he said she said.

"She's out of the picture."

"I wonder where she's at? Max, could you take over handling the All-seeing Fly please?"

"I'll be glad to."

She points to her head then with that hand she motions to give the fly over to him he takes control they both smile and, laugh a little. They look back at the viewer with the fly in slow motion as it makes its way to find Medusa slowly she comes into view it stops to hover at the ceiling and, she points her finger and, she said he said.

"Wait a minute right there do you see what I see?"

"What's that."

"That snake body where its tail end is and, the part where the bottom of the dark blue body of Medusa takes over from the snake line … captain do you see it?"

"YAA looks like the hips of a woman and, the buttocks of a woman."

Medusa is turning at different location's now to find a spot that she hasn't slammed into which gives them a better view to examine the separation of Medusa's flesh and, her snake skin and, he said she said.

[Readers please follow the dialog].

"Good Lord God All Mighty look at this Amyl ion."

She look's surprised at him for his slight outburst and, said.

"What is it, Max?"

As he looks at the parchment and, Medusa.

"Flesh and, skin right there."

As he points to it so, she can see it.

"I got a Hunch."

"Go on Maximilian."

"Take a look at the reference of the Black Rose."

"Okay I see more clearer now."

"Someone mentioned you as the Black Rose when we tossed the Black Rose into the ring of fire, do you remember?"

"Yes."

"With all the indication that … that means you're the Black Rose."

"I'm very flattered Max."

"God is giving us a message and, it's right here in this riddle."

"Now let's look at the first two lines that it mention's. Drip, drip, drip and, the blood with you as the Black Rose."

CHAPTER 36

She's glued to what he has to say and, said.

"Go on Max."

"It's asking for your blood how much I don't know … then its saying with your blood something will come to a close."

"HHMMM … Max go on."

"Flesh and, skin separates."

He points to Medusa on the viewer.

"Do you see the separation there My Love?"

"Clear as a kiss coming from you."

He stops gives her kiss … she puts her fingers through his hair and, he said.

"Now the next reference is, heaven knows skin will decompose and, the skin is the snake part of Medusa."

She puts her hand on his head combs some more as she looks at him after a pause … he didn't mind her attention because he loved her so, so, so very much then she said.

"I want to read it to you maybe that will help you and, I can read the Riddle better."

She reads it to him as he thinks with his hand on her thigh. He thinks on the [Little Blood] and, said to her.

"Okay 3 drops of blood."

"I'd gladly give 3 Drops of blood to separate the flesh and, the skin."

He got excited and, said.

"That's right you said it."

She looks surprised and, said.

"Go on Max you're doing great."

"Okay look at Medusa the hip's the buttock's it looks like she can be separated from the skin of the snake."

"Maybe there's a woman trapped in that snake body?"

He gives her another Kiss.

"Let me put this in a nutshell."

There's a pause … and, he said.

"3 drops of your blood, comes to a close, the abuse, pull her apart, the skin will decompose."

She wrap's her arms around him and, said.

"Baby you did it."

They're all excited looking at each other very closely talking back and, fourth I can't understand them with their overlapping sentences and, she said.

"How do we get the 3 drops of blood in that beast without looking at her?"

"Now there is a Question and, it is either by intravenous or, in her mouth."

She moves around on his lap looking at the floor for a few seconds and, said.

"Well through her mouth would be easy enough."

"That's right because she eats raw snake's, rodent's so, why not do it that way, unless we are missing something?"

He's thinking as he taps her thigh rolling his four fingers rolling, rolling them while he looks at her and, thinks … Amyl ion sure is pretty and, she said.

"What's on your mind Maximilian?"

"The intravenous way with plasma would take too long it has to be 3 drops of your blood through Medusa's mouth."

"Why not the plasma and, my blood intravenously?"

"Well because it would take too long and, to dangerous."

He was thinking to himself that he did not want to risk her life and, he would just rather destroy Medusa and, she said.

"Now we are in a dilemma, if you would call it one?"

"What's that?"

"Do we go into the cavern with the laser guns on stun put her under drop the 3 drops of my blood in her mouth wait for that right moment to pull her out of the snake's body?"

"Sounds pretty incredible, doesn't it?"

"YAA but, that's what the words on the parchment said we have to believe it cause look who it came from."

"Enough said here's where it gets scary Amyl ion, we have Samantha blast a hole at the back of the cave with Samantha telling us where Medusa's location is at all times, we're standing by with a stretcher waiting to enter in we put on some blinder's that Samantha can direct our lasers to point shoot Medusa to stun her. We need more than enough of your blood in a vial just to be sure with a dropper."

Then he lifts her quickly from the table on his lap as she squeals loving it. They get to the storage area gives her one spin and, sets her down. They grab the holsters with the laser guns and, find the blinders. Then they get a needle, syringe from the nurse's station with the vial to hold her blood in. There back at the mess hall and, she said.

"Wait let's change into our uniform's and, take my bee hive off."

He grabs her hand again takes off she squeal's and, laughing. They get her blood in the vial she puts it in her pocket get their holsters on with two laser's a piece grab the stretcher they're on their way out but, have to coordinate with Samantha first.

He has one thought now and, that's to preserve the Queen and, stops she stops and, he said.

"Amyl ion my sweet darling if you would please stay at the control's and, guide me for I trust only you?"

She slightly grins lays her part of the stretcher down walks over looks up to him puts her arms on his shoulders with her hands hanging behind him looks around his face smiles, strokes his hair brings her hands down to his neck caress's it squeeze's a little she has a look like you can't fool me and, I appreciate this protection and, with a tee-hee she said.

"HM, HM, HM, HM, Oh, Maximilian I adore you."

She takes so, long to say some thing's to him turns her head eyes looking like I know what you're thinking and, she said.

"Now who's going to help you with the stretcher … HHMMM?"

He knows he's busted smiles at her she reaches up on her toes kiss's him with her luscious lips she lays it on him like she has never kissed him before there a little wet moving from side to side its one after another. I finally heard her speak between their kisses.

"We live together … we die together."

Well, I don't know about any of you readers but, I feel like I'm under the fire escape steps at webster junior high with Helen after those kisses.

He's reflecting on all they've been through never to forget the kiss he just got there all so, much the same but, yet different. HHMMM, he thought I'll have to write a poem about that [Same but, different]. They're still rolling with that kiss she released just enough whispered and, said.

"Max, you need me to pull that woman that's trapped in the snake's body out just like the words on the parchment said to do."

They release he looks into her eyes as she wiggles back down from her tip-toes and, he said.

"Our kids are going to Love their mother."

She smiles that would stop Medusa and, drop dead. [like you know the opposites] and, he said.

"We need blankets and, sheets."

He said that to solidify they're going together on this monster hunt. She goes gets them then rejoins him and, he said.

"Let's go and, get this thing over with."

They kiss with a deep half open mouth there so, ready now and, she said.

"Samantha you ready for this?"

Let's do this."

They crack up because they really can dialog with Samantha like never before and, he said.

"Okay as soon as we get her on the stretcher, we put her on the ship find a doctor in town."

They get to the back of the cave set the stretcher down and, he said.

"Samantha, can you make us out clearly?"

"Affirmative."

He glances at her while he said.

"Let's check our Laser Gun's for stun. One at 75% and, if that doesn't work, we can always increase the effect and, we have all 4 with us so, our backup is set for 100% stun and, well draw that one just in case. What do you think of that?"

"Just fine and, I like the backup at 100%."

He decided that he didn't like the 75% because she made it clear and, said.

"Let's go to 100% stun for both I like that better since we are dealing with a deranged lunatic."

They got everything set and, put on their blinder's and, he said.

"Samantha, okay we got the blinder's on can we see the inside of the cave please?"

"Here you go."

"Okay can we see the outside now as we face the ship?"

They look around see everything look at each other and, they see one another. He gives her a wink she smiled and, wink's back.

He wanted to be coolheaded for her and, he said.

"Samantha, I hope I can explain this to you but, the purpose of these blinder's is so, that we don't look into Medusa's eye's because that's how she kill's people."

"Understood."

She was thinking along that line too and, added something else and, she said.

"Samantha even with these blinders on we can't risk looking into Medusa's eye's so, could you block Medusa's eye's when they shine bright?"

"Yes, I will block the head out."

"Good thank you is the fly still operational and, where's Medusa now?"

"The fly is operational Medusa is approximately 27' Feet away going in the opposite direction."

They both look at each other and, smile then he said.

"YAA I'd like to send her on a trip."

She gave a little bit of a smile at him with a look that said I know what you mean and, he said.

"Okay now as soon as the rock's stop fallen, we rush in find the nearest backing of the entrance cavern wall."

"Okay captain I won't be afraid to fire."

"I know you won't."

They contemplate about what is going to happen taking looks at each other knowing that this is dangerous and, could get killed and, left in stone. That someday the Marxist/Anarchists can tear down and, he said.

"Samantha how long is that vane that you will be opening up for us to get into?"

"11' feet long."

He leaned his head back to think looks at his beautiful bride and, he said.

"Samantha, use one medium laser at 25% for the 11' foot thick rock and, we'll be able to stand once we get to the 11' feet range that's where we need to be at?"

"Yes, captain you we'll be able to stand."

Amyl ion was listening, watching, leaning on one leg and, she said.

"Are we forgetting anything? Yes, wait! it must be wide for us to enter side-by-side."

"Will do captain."

They stop think for a while he shakes his head, I guess that's it. Grabs the stretcher with the blankets and, sheets they stand aside about 40' feet because there will be flying rock when the ship blasts a hole for them to enter and, he said.

"Oh, yes, hand signal's no talking unless absolutely necessary once we get a position inside the cavern entrance we go forward looking left and, right keeping each other in sight."

She nods her head yes with a serious look on her face. He takes a couple of deep breaths she does too. They stand back put on the blinders and, he said.

"Here we go ... okay Samantha open up a hole for us to walk in."

The ship blasts at the crack area from the 4.5 Earthquake about 15 seconds go by they wait the laser from the ship stops and, she said.

"LET'S GO!"

Those hard chargers went in side-by-side stumbling on small rocks with laser gun's out-front reach the standing area stop and, look for Medusa scanning the layout of the cavern. It had all the looks of a rolling floor with Stalactites and, Stalagmites with some together and, some still forming. Medusa hears this crash of falling rock turns around and, the light comes on her from the daylight coming in and, we see how gruesome Medusa is with fangs of blood dark blue skin with some little black flames flowing up on her body and, dreary words that were twisted and, smeared that faintly read [Hate, Kill, Destroy]. Then we see her black snakes on her head with

249

two red ones on top in the middle and, there all hissing one after another. She's got bronze arm amulets on bronze leaves under breasts with the tip of the leaves curled up to cover her areoles. Then that rattler comes into view behind her as it raises itself up and, makes that distinct sound ... [BOY]! it's a frightful appearance.

Now she sees her chance to escape the cavern she goes towards the light. Her forked tongue dart's in and, out along with that snake body turning on the ground making a scratching sound. Medusa's looking around stops and, yells [YYAAAA] to see what would happen. The captains hear this and, they hand motion in the direction it came from. Medusa slowly inch's forward and, her mouth is opening and, closing as she stops quickly peaks around the corner of a Stalagmite. Amyl ion shoot's as she came into her view hit's Medusas right shoulder, she fall's back against a Stalagmite grabbing the shoulder the Stalagmite breaks with a crashing sound Amyl ion glances at Max motions that she hit her in the shoulder. He gives her an old thumb's up signal and, another signal that we should guard the entrance. She quickly looks back and, fourth nods yes Medusa hollers out and, said.

CHAPTER 37

"EEAAUUGGHH ... WHAT DO YOU WANT?"

Medusa's crafty eyes are shifting gritting her teeth holding her right shoulder thinking what to do? She turns to her left wants to maneuver to their right to get outside. Amyl ion motion's she hears her moving to their right. Medusa wants to try to turn that person who shot her into stone so, she looks out around a Stalagmite thinking she'll surprise that someone. Medusa's face turns ugly as she prepares herself and, shows her bloody fangs and, teeth then comes out with her eye's a blazing white with a yell [YYAAHHHH] but, no one is there. He motions to her right that that is where Medusa is. They both turn a little but, keep an eye on the left of them. Unexpectedly Medusa appears at Amyl ion's right quickly she turns fire's her laser the same time that Medusa's eyes are a blazing white. Samantha blocked the head of Medusa her aim hit's Medusa in the other shoulder which made her fall backwards but, her snake body braced her up she rose back up with more adrenalin running through her she was more determined attacks again sense's that she can't turn her into stone but, she'll try and, bite her to poison her. That's when Max jumped to her side and, said fire both fired at her mid-section. They see that she has been pushed back a couple of feet her eye's stop from that blazing white she had seconds ago. She slowly fall's forward with eyes shut and, drops unconscious. They walk towards her with gun's pointing at her he moves her with his foot Medusa is out cold and, she said.

"I can see she's still breathing."

He acknowledges that too and, said.

"We've got to turn her over and, don't take your blinders off captain you turn her upper body and, I'll grab her lower body twist it just enough at the same time and, if she so, much as makes one tiny little move shoot her again."

She grasps the seriousness of his comment as she connects to him with many more to come and, she said.

"Okay Captain."

He takes a deep breath that it's over and, his bride is safe and, he said.

"Samantha, I know you can see what's going on and, we are going to raise our blinders and, set them on our forehead just in case she's faking it or, comes too and, if so, we'll have to shoot her again."

"AYE, AYE Captain."

They lay there gun's down close to them to grab if needed and, he said.

"Okay turn her over now."

They turn her over without any trouble she's really out and, grab their laser's just for an instant to be sure. They talk back and, forth about her fangs, the snakes are limp her skin color and, the black flames and, so, thin but somewhat larger woman and, they guess maybe she could be 6' foot 5"inches tall if she wasn't in the snake skin and, he said.

"Okay … captain take your vial out drop 3 drops into her mouth and, I'll stand watch."

She puts her laser guns in the holsters while keeping an eye on her and, gets the vial out opens it up drops 3 drops into her opened mouth she puts it back in her pocket pulls out just one laser gun steps back to see what happens. They waited and, it seemed like waiting for water to boil. Then Medusa started to move her tongue as she was tasting the blood swallowed and, they waited again. She started to change from a dark blue to a human color. Her fangs with-drew into her gums as eye teeth then the snakes disappeared shrinking to lovely long black curly hair to her elbows. The bronze arm amulets and, bronze leaves under her breasts dissolved in smoke the breasts moving a little. Her physical size was shrinking down to about Amyl ion's size with the progressive words to destruction disappearing … a complete metamorphosis. They could hardly believe it right before them a scene they'll never forget and, she said.

"Amazing isn't it Maximilian?"

"It sure is transforming right before our eyes."

They waited to see if anything else was going to happen in a span of 15 seconds they saw the snake's skin loosen wrinkle a little her body seemed now that it was able to be pulled away from the snake skin. He puts his guns in their holsters took his blinders off looked at Amyl ion. She turned her head looked at him took hers off and, put away her gun away. The two of them just relaxed cause it was all over now. They laid there blinders down and, walked behind her head. Together they reached under her arms and, pulled her away from the snake skin laid her down gently and, she said.

"That poor baby ... she looks at peace now that the devil has left her."

He put his head down in sadness and, he said.

"YAA no more battle's, no more eating snake's and, rodents."

He was watching Amyl ion's face and, she just looks at what was now a new woman. He turns to walk away squeeze's her arm and, said.

"I'll get the stretcher and, blankets with sheets."

She looks at him with a feeling of gladness that this is all over with her hand touching his hand they look at her what was once medusa for about a minute. He leaves comes back to see Amyl ion on her knees bending over a little talking to her he stops and, listen's. Her right hand is on her right cheek and, said.

"Maybe, just maybe I hope you can hear this ... we wish you and, hope you're going to have a peaceful life with a very, very good man coming into your life that will take of you and, you'll have kid's a nice house. Don't be a stranger we'll be around for a long time."

She looks up at him she's wiping away the tear's pouring down her cheeks and, said.

"I'm ready now Max have you got anything that I can wipe these tears with? It seems God gave me a lot of emotions along with many tears."

He pulls out her scarf. She stands up and, said.

"When did you put that in your pocket?"

"When you took your bee hive off [Every night from a pocket we re-new]."

She takes a breath and, thinks for a moment then remembers and, said.

"[We whisper I Love you never to soon]."

She jumps in his arms kiss's him he holds her tight. She releases with a sigh of relief and, said.

"Max let's get her to the doctor in town."

They help each other with the stretcher set it on the side of her and, he said.

"What shall we call her now until we find out who she is."

"I don't know of anything right now but, a nick name would be good."

They take the edge of the sheet spread it out on the stretcher pick her up with him at her head she's at her knees and, she said.

"Please be careful with her neck and, head Max."

"Okay … YAW she seems pretty limp."

She pick's her lower leg's up the detection devise falls off her hips she sees it steps on it twist her shoe on it to destroy it smolders with sparks of white and, red. Max was nodding his head as if to say good job.

"Max have you noticed that her legs haven't been in use for some time."

"Maybe some rehab will get her walking again."

They get her on the stretcher he spread's the other sheet on top with a warm blanket as she tuck's it in on the side of her body she looks at her face. They put the blinders on the side of the stretcher. She was thinking of [Ruby] as it flashed through her mind looks at him as they pick up the stretcher.

"Max, what do you think of Ruby for her nick name?" He got a blank face and, he said.

"I'll walk backwards as we take her to the ship HHMMM … I like it, how did you come up with that nick name?"

The snake skin dissolves as they walk away and, stop to watch it makes a hissing sound some smoke appears that disappears quickly and, a burnt impression was left that would last for centuries.

They will use that for the tourist attraction along with the Griffin Monster's impression next to the cave with the man that turned to stone by medusa.

Also the King and, Queen or, captains with saving the woman trapped inside of a monster that's one of many victory's over Satan that attempted to destroy them and, how the ship opened up the cave so, it could hide for a while because the two Captain's wanted to preserve the ship against an enemy, they didn't know how much fire power it had. Then there's Sabrina the [Female Succubus] and, the Griffin Monster with the burnt impressions of their body parts where they fell to the ground and, dissolved. Draco the Dragon had to be killed that's where one of the Captain's almost lost their life and, there too is a burnt impression on the ground. The [27-Trips] will be on display at all times for the public with a restaurant and, a little later a mall but, still operational when called upon. That's their plans for now any way. The upgrades of the ship will be delivered by the President at E. 1 on the cargo ships. The technology will improve by that time and, it will take less than half the time that it took the captains to get there. Maximilian's dad and, mom will come along with the President and, 1st lady on that visit as a surprise but, nobody is supposed to know. They will fall in love with his bride never to fall out of love. OH, okay back to our beloved and, she said.

"Well one of the Stone's from the dragon was a Ruby Stone and, we just pulled another [Ruby] out." Max is in love with how they're connected and, he said.

"Samantha, we have someone coming on board on a stretcher and, I like Ruby."

He was thinking about Stone because there's people with a last name like that and, mention's it to her and, said.

"Hey, Amyl ion how do you like [Ruby Stone] as a complete name for her?"

With-out hesitation and, a convincing face she said.

"Oh, Max that is perfect [Ruby Stone] it is."

Samantha said.

"How shall I log this person in?"

They look at each other both said at the same time [Ruby Stone] they smile that would make an ice age quickly disappear the water would wash out making the Grand Canyon and, Samantha said.

"Captain's Congratulation's on a Successful Operation."

Amyl ion thought about how well the ship communicates and, she said.

"Thank You and, could you lower the hatch please."

There laughing a little at Samantha with her Congratulatory statement he winks at her she blows a kiss he turns his head to receive it. They put Ruby next to the captain's chairs he sits down she set her part of the stretcher down she sits on his lap he taps the green froggy [Squeaky-Squeaky] it goes. They look at Ruby he draws her near kissing on her cheek. She's loving it kicking her feet a little there just elated at what had just happened and, he said.

"Do you want to put your bee hive on?"

She Jump's up to get it sit's back down on him they secure it with a wet scarf that he pulled out of his pocket there giggling about the tear's she puts the waist length hair to her left side in front and, he said.

"Well, I wonder where the hospital is in the valley?"

She fusses with her bee-hive looks t him and, she said.

"Max, do you want to risk some people seeing the space ship?"

"Well, I guess we are going to have to unless you can think of something else we have to get her there fast so, anyway … you know the secret is out."

Ruby starts to come around breathing a little more turning her head to the other side to ward's them and, Amyl ion said.

"Max, you know I really liked that when you said get Ruby to the hospital fast I delayed and, I shouldn't have."

She gives him a Big Kiss and, said.

"Samantha [Lift off] can you find the hospital in the valley around where we were stationed at the circle of trees?"

"Yes, here we go."

They look at Ruby lying there and, in less than a minute they're there at the back of the hospital the ship lands 8 legs coming out with people rushing out many people already knew about the space ship and, he said.

"Samantha, lower the hatch please we're taking Ruby out to the hospital we don't know when we'll be back secure the ship when we leave please."

"Understood captain."

A couple of nurses come out that were at the Coronation and, Doctor Carson right behind the nurses. They pick up the stretcher take Ruby outside they meet the hospital staff they're all bug eyed at what they're seeing with this big flying saucer and, Amyl ion raises her voice to them and, said.

"She need's immediate private care."

Max saw the man with a stethoscope as he too is anxious about Ruby and, said.

"Doctor take her vitals' please."

There're carrying the stretcher the Doctor is thinking that this is unusual starts to do what Max wanted. They have never taken vital signs before outside like this. People were saying it's the King and, Queen and, Max said.

"Amyl ion the Emergency Trauma Center's at the back of the hospital's haven't been created yet."

Her face got very serious and, she said.

CHAPTER 38

"That's going to change because we'll have to start one right now."

They get Ruby in a private room put the stretcher on a hospital bed the Doctor examines her said what's her name they tell her and, the doctor said.

"Nurse give her some water … she's in bad shape but, with some of my wife's cooking she'll be coming around slowly really good and, her legs will need messaging to get the blood circulating better then get her walking in these hills around here then she'll be Okay."

They take her off the stretcher place her on the hospital bed and, the doctor said.

"We'll wash her you're in luck or, I should say Ruby is. She's going to get some of my wife's cooking any minute now, my wife brings me dinner at this time of day."

Max knows they can pay for her complete recovery and, said.

"Get her anything she needs."

One nurse came in as she was writing on a piece of paper and, said.

"What's her name?"

The Queen looks at her King knowing their thoughts smiled she started then him and, she said he said.

"[Ruby]"

"[Stone] and, have we got some water? to give to Ruby she's probably dehydrated."

One of the nurse's runs into the room with the water. The Royal couple are standing at her bed side with Amyl ion up close he's just behind her. She's drawn close to ruby put's her hands on her right arm and, said.

"Ruby my name is Amyl ion this is my husband behind me his name is Maximilian … Max grab her hand, speak to her please?"

The other nurse comes in with more water pour's some into Ruby's mouth she gulp's it down and, he said.

"Ruby Stone when you wake up, Amyl ion is my wife my name is Maximilian we want to be the first people you see there are many things that are here in this land that are available."

The nurses are listening and, looking at one another and, one nurse said.

"That's a very good pep talk."

The royals look at her smile and, he thought that was an inspiration and, Max said.

"With what you learn here you could be a nurse or, a doctor. Then later on the administrator of a hospital."

The other nurse was a smart aleck and, said.

"Ruby you could even become a space pilot too."

The nurse cover's her mouth with a deep breath but, everyone just started laughing and, Amyl ion said."

"Hey that was very witty."

They all noticed that Ruby was a bit amused breathed out a sigh with a tiny smile moved her head from one side and, back and, Max said.

"Doctor when do you think she will come to and, open her eyes?"

The Doctor think's out loud so, everyone can hear and, said.

"Well, with the lack of water, malnutrition, plus knocked out by your laser's probably two hours."

Amyl ion had an idea with a sudden rush on her face and, she said.

"The King and, I want to spend the night here in this room with Ruby and, we want to be here when she wakes up."

The Doctors wife came into the room and, said I hear that a young lady need's some of my cooking?"

Max looks at her with raising his hand and, said.

"Yes, right here just give her some small pieces of that chicken with a little bit of peas and, sweet potato."

He gently took the plate Amyl ion moves aside with gladness he start's putting the food in Ruby's mouth. I guess there's nothing like doing it yourself he thought. She put her hand on his back as he fed her and, she said.

"Doctor can we get a bed in here please?"

A nurse was already pushing through the doorway with the bed before she was even done with the question. Ruby is slowly tasting moving her tongue around starts to chew but, ever so, slowly they all watch for a few minutes then she can't get enough of her own juice's to swallow so, the Queen took some water in a cup poured it in her mouth and, she was able to swallow. She took a couple small bites of peas, sweet potatoes swallowed and, slowly went to sleep and, the King said.

"Doctor what do you think her age would be?"

The doctor looked at her studied her face and, he said.

"About 18 to 25 Years."

The Queen thinks that this is enough and, tells everybody and, she said.

"Thank You for all that you did on such a short notice."

All the people in the room were saying something altogether but, I think the one thing that put's it all together is we're so, happy to do it they start leaving the room and, Max said.

"Well, the Queen and, I have to go and, take the ship back to the circle of tree's get a good meal in us clean up doing a Captains log and, I hope we'll be back before Ruby wakes up, we know she's in excellent hands."

They're all gone the door closes then turn to look at Ruby he stands behind her and, wrap's his arms around the Queen above her breasts and, whispered in her ear and, said.

"I Love You and, Ruby is going to be okay."

She does a 180 and, just melt's as he's holding her tight puts her head back smiles for a good minute while humming a little she's so, very happy he's very content to hold her for as long as she wanted and, she said.

"My husband, my husband we did very good … Let's go to the circle of tree's eat what the Doctors wife brought in because we have it frozen on the ship. Then take a shower I got something to tell you that I've never told anybody … then we can walk back."

She turns around they look at her and, she said.

"Sleep, sleep Ruby my husband and, I will be right back in two hours but, you sleep as long as you like. Ruby Oh, the nurses are going to wash you. Okay Max I'm ready to go now."

They walk out the door holding hands he asks the nurses could someone sit at the door until we get back and, check on Ruby give her a drink of water every 5 minutes until we get back.

One of the nurse's jumps to the call as to beat everyone out to watch over Rudy. The nurse grab's a chair goes to the door sits down with her journal and, just smiles and, he said.

"WOW, that was fast my wife and, I thank You."

She looks submissive to the call and, she said.

"Your most welcome your Majesty."

They leave out the back of the hospital he stops slowly puts his left arm behind her back she catches on raises her arms puts his right arm back behind her knees picks her up she loves it.

The music starts [The Platters, Twilight Time].

There're several shooting stars as they talk, watch and, hear them burn up in the atmosphere.

Sitting on a bench behind the hospital an older couple see's their romance the husband turns to his wife and, he said.

"Yeah, you know Cocoa they probably heard about us when we were younger, they finally picked up on it."

His wife crossed her leg towards him put her arm around his neck laughed and, she said.

"I think you made a funny thing of it [PICKED UP ON IT]."

The couple just laughed watched as they got on their ship and, the King said.

"Samantha escalate the steps when I'm on the first step."

"AYE, AYE Captain."

Back on the ship arriving at the circle of trees they start preparing a meal sit down talk back and, fourth and, she said.

"I can't wait to get in the classrooms with the kids."

He wipes his mouth takes a drink of water and, he said.

"Yeah, and, have I got a story to tell them."

"I'd like to hear about that now but, that would take away my interest when you tell the story."

He smiles thinking I hope she likes it.

"Max, you went to school no doubt?"

"Yes, I did."

Silence for a while as their eating.

With an appealing expression on her face, she said."

"Oh, where was that?"

"At the University of Moscow was my last school of learning."

He was thinking about his education there and, how it's going to pay off now. It's so, incredible that God has done all this in preparation along with my wife ... WOW and, she said.

"What did you do there?"

"Well, my beautiful wife first of all I've been blessed with you. I studied economics graduated from the University of Moscow and, came out a Capitalist."

They finished their food and, cleaned up. He took her by the hand she was just smiling as he took her to the bedroom and, proceeded to take her bee hive off. She enjoyed it very much working together then looking at his beautiful Queen he said.

"Shower My Love?" Her cuteness came out as she pulled her shoulders forward squatted a little with legs together in her joy hands on knees and, that smile of happiness [WOW] then rose up with arms straight up so, enthusiastic then slapped her thighs on the sides and, said.

"Why yes, My Love and if I may clean you myself first then it's your turn."

He grabbed her by the hand and, took off. She was enthused squealed and, in a matter of minutes they had their uniforms off and, into the shower washing themselves rinsing off, air dried, stepped out. He grabbed her by the hand went to the bedside and, said. "[I Love You] [I Love You]."

She was all smiles while feeling good inside and, thinking Oh, I just love this.

She rose on her toes and, that kissing that would melt a snowcapped mountain. She stuck her tongue in his mouth and, he chased it then she started sucking his tongue then released and, he said.

"Keep your arms around me."

He lifted her up she wrapped her legs around him he barely laid her on the bed as she was under him, she was just loving it with giggling and, laughing. They know what to do look at each other as she hangs not touching the bed and, she said.

"Are we going to start a business?"

Her legs and, arms still wrapped around him like they were in their ocean dream and, he said.

"[Squeaky, Squeak]"

She's loving it all the more almost loses her grip and, he said.

"I want to start a Toy Manufacturing Company."

In her cheerfulness she said.

"[Squeaky, Squeak] may I help?"

"Yes, the first toy will be a [Green Froggy]."

She breath's out seductively… [Sqweaky-Sqweak] he searches to enter her she helps by moving her hips. They join adjust as she is almost starting to shutter and, whispers in his ear and, said.

"Let me do this for a minute or, two then I'm all yours."

She breaths out a little then takes that deep breath to start her mysterious trip with groans of pleasure pain then a higher voice. She's squeezing him tighter and, tighter with her arms and, leg's locked convulsing with her blissful breathing and, it's as if she's in a mad dash to the finish line. She's jerking many times releasing the tension that's been building up with the riddle of her blood and, medusa. She comes to the finish line waiting for the most pleasurable pain that's starting to set in. She's slowing down cover's his cheek with kiss's she's catching her breath and, licking her lips with sighs of relief as her head goes back, he begins kissing that beautiful neck. She's beginning to laugh release's him from the hold she had on him he stays with her as he lay's his head on the pillow next to her face. She's coming down from passing through a lost time he whispers in her ear and, said.

"Baby I was thinking about wearing clothes of the day like all the people do. What are your thoughts?"

He rises on his hands with arms straight as they talk slowly stroking her.

She clears her throat concentrates in her state of ecstasy puts her hands-on his hair and, curls it with her fingers as she smiled and, said.

"Baby that would fine and, do you know why?"

"WWHHYyy?"

"The way people look at us with some woman lusting after you and, I don't want that ever … cause I'm very jealous of you."

He adores her watching for another trip she prepares for and, he said.

"Okay, let's talk later on about formal and, informal clothes."

She raises her hips up and, down stroking her husband and, she said. "I would like that too."

She's getting a closed eye look and, looking deep into his eyes. The next minute passed by ever so, slow as he waited, she's there drops her hands to her temples shakes her head while looking at him intoxicated as the pain comes. She slips into her lost time to regain what was lost with a deep breath her veins in her neck popping out under pressure driving her head into the pillow. Her fingers in her hair she as her body rolls up and, down. She had several more trips then his passing of time arrives with her last one. They went wild and, it's a wonder they don't have a heart attack.

They hurry to the bathroom to clean up and, resume their love making.

CHAPTER 39

They also talk about having a tourist attraction's and, it was an incredible opportunity because of the locations of where the monsters had died and, left their impression's. He didn't talk too much between the next 3 or 4 more of her passing's she wanted to say some things. He just enjoyed this beautiful wife of his and, was very thankful. She was entering the last one and, he picked up speed she molded into anticipation at his hard pace that will match their plunging into their abyss. More and, more seconds of eternity pass they're wild and, crazy oh the sounds that they're making it's just the purest of satisfaction and, enjoyment.

Sometime later after catching their breath they must get up and, go back to the hospital and, he said.

"Well, I wonder how Ruby is doing?" her body is little limp she placed her hands on his shoulders while he has to help her get the uniform on and, she said.

"Yaw I wonder too?"

Uniforms on her bee hive on and, interchange with Samantha that there leaving and, don't know when they'll be back and, staying at the hospital all night with Ruby and, let us know if anything goes on around the ship and, he said.

"Oh, and, I forgot the All Seeing-Eye at the cavern and, we'll get it later."

"AYE, AYE Captain's."

They leave the ship the hatch close's as they start walking down the weaving path with trees on both sides a variety of rocks boulders with some brush and, finally exit out the path. The sound of a horse and, buggy appears coming by and, the man said.

"WHOA Annabella, hello there you fine looking people do you need a lift?"

"Yes, were going to the hospital."

The man with the horse and, buggy was glued to her beauty as Max helped her on the seat and, the man said.

"Climb on in I'm going right past there."

They were thinking that these people are very hospitable as all three are making a deal then arrive at the hospital out front and, Max said.

"We will come by tomorrow pick up the horse and, buggy that we agreed upon."

That man was the local horse and, buggy salesman in the valley. They all shook hands said their good buys she wraps her arms around his left arm and, on their way to enter the hospital and, he smiles looking at her and, said.

"When we get the horse and, buggy let's go to town look for your arm bracelets with the earrings oh and, that paint if we can't find it in this valley. If not, we'll go to another and, the next one maybe taking the ship looking for some gypsies that will have your bracelets, Oh, we can't forget that beautiful scarf."

She agreed with everything and, was going to ask anyway if they could do just that but, didn't know about the gypsies and, she said.

"In the ship we could wear our uniforms then in town wear our formal clothes at functions and, social gatherings. The informal clothing, we could wear around town when we walk and, I show you off."

He looks at her and, thought well who's showing who off and, said.

"I got to get some boots, how about you?"

"Boots and, a Bee-Hive that's for me Maximilian and, Samantha can make that black and, white scarf."

The music starts [Blanco Brown-The get up]. There just laughing at all this with their overlapping conversations and, he said.

"Oh, we will have to make a barn for the horse and, buggy close to the ship so, when we are doing [a roundabout in the valley] I can show you off."

She squeezes her breasts again on his upper arm and, she said.

"Yes, and, I guess we'll start living like all these wonderful folks do."

She's mostly dancing a little down the hall a natural twist in her hips as they get to the hospital room door the nurse is still there, they walk up to her and, Amyl ion said.

"Good afternoon, how did it go and, is she alright?"

"Just fine and, if I may say you two have a glow about you … your Majesties … and, I was so, glad to watch over Ruby I heard of everything that had happened. If I may introduce myself, I'm Mr.'s General George Armstrong Custer and, I'm a writer I'd very much like to write about your life story up to this point."

They look at each other put their arms around one another and, smile then look at Mr.'s Custer and, the Queen said.

"When do you want to start Elizabeth?"

A surprise look came over her face with the ease that they accepted so, fast and, she said.

"Oh, call me Libbie please."

The three make the arrangements cause the royals have such a busy schedule now. They walk into the room go to Ruby's bed side and, he turns to Amyl ion with a happy face and, he said.

"I know her from the history books and, she's right here at this time in the hospital … WOW!"

She knew that this must have been very important turned to him when he mentioned the history books because she's taking in history like a sponge reaches with her left hand and, places it on his right bicep [Their conversation goes back and, fourth]. And, she said.

"What does history say about her?"

"She wrote some books about her husband and, tried to clear his name."

"Really! from what?"

"Well, General Custer … that's her husband helped hastened the end of the civil war with his gallantry unwavering bravery and, it's a fascinating story with two lower rank officers later on about a decade or, so, being put on trial betraying the General. Those two got him killed along with over 200 of his soldiers."

"Officers!!!? … Maximilian how can that be I thought that officers were among one of the highest callings for anyone to achieve or, acquire?"

"Yes, my dear sweetheart your right that's why when someone that is in authority like you and, I we must be blameless in our life."

"What happened to the officers that betrayed the General?"

"They were acquitted because the Army didn't want to tarnish itself."

"I want to do some research at the ship on that one."

"There's a library at your fingertips my dear Amyl ion waiting for you to explore."

Ruby sort of hears this conversation at her bedside she moves her head a little which got their attention and, turned their heads towards her and, he said.

"She looks much better now with pajama top and, bottoms wow she's cleaned up."

She grab's his forearms as they front and, she said.

"She sure does and, look at her hair how pretty it is. The bed for us is here and, we can sleep and, wait for her to wake up."

They quickly notice the two white crow's landing on a large pine tree limb outside the window they smiled point their fingers and, he said.

"Hey look 2 white crows."

The two white crows squawked several time's apiece as they looked at them. He grabbed her by the hand went to the window opened it and, he said.

"Hello you two gorgeous beauties."

She thought to herself rather quickly about when Max said hello gorgeous to her when she landed from the heavens next to the ship as a white crow to join him and, one crow said.

"How are you two love birds doing?"

She throws her arms around his neck and, gives him a big kiss on his right cheek and, moves it around his cheek [SMACK]. Then he gently took her jaw and, cheeks with his left hand turned her head he reached down gave her a great big couple of kisses on her luscious lips [SMACK, SMACK]. She's loving those kisses with moans her knees buckled with his passion released to look at the crows and, smiled really big with a WWHHUUOOO!

The other crow shook its head and, said.

"Oh, we see and, keep that up for us ... WOW ... for we feel the same way about each other."

They all have a belly laugh and, he said.

"Don't make yourselves stranger's come on over and, peck on the ship and, say hi."

Ruby is giggling a little too … and, they stopped their meeting and, he said.

"Well, the Queen and, I got to go now Ruby is waking up we think." The crows said.

"Oh, YAW we heard … we'll be pecking soon."

They watched as they flew away thinking to themselves how beautiful those large white crows were. They quickly went over to Ruby noticed her eye's opening and, shutting she's starting to come around he reaches for some water and, gives it to her. Amyl ion thought of saying something to Samantha about the crow's and, said.

"Samantha there'll be two white crows coming over sometime and, they will peck on the ship to let us know that they are there to visit and, there our friends."

"AYE, AYE Captain."

He looks at her holding Ruby's arm he's right behind her his hands on her shoulder's and, peeking around her head. They watch as she looks at them with her dark blue eyes, dark eyebrows, black hair that's been cleaned up full lip's, and, musters up a question and, ruby said.

"Was that you two talking to me all this time?"

They're beaming over her coming around and, Amyl ion said.

"Yes, this is Maximilian my husband and, my name is Amyl ion just in case you forgot."

Ruby smile's and, looks around and, said.

"Please don't leave me can I have some food please?"

The nurse [Libbie] is at the door listening lays her journal on the chair writing everything down and, said.

"I'll be Right Back."

Amyl ion give's her some cool water as ruby watched Libbie leave the room and, the Queen said.

"That's Libbie she went to get food for you."

She swirls her tongue around her lips looks at Max, Amyl ion and, said.

"Oh, that's good, water could I have some more."

The nurse brings some food in he takes it. There he goes again as if nobody can feed her like he does. The Queen looks on with her hand on his back Ruby chew's and, swallow's. She moves her arms and, body with that tasty food and, she said.

"MMMM that's good."

The Queen is delighted with her coming alive and, she said.

"We'll be in that bed tonight if you need us for anything."

Ruby looks to her right then in that direction gives a sigh of relief looks at them standing there reaches to touch someone's hand they grab her hand hold on until she lets her hand slowly drops and, she drift's back to sleep. The queen takes the plate from him sets it on a nearby table they pull the bed spread up to ruby's neck and, she said.

"Baby you wouldn't happen to have an extra scarf on you?"

"Yes, I do darling it's right here in my back pocket."

He hands it to her she' crying happy tear's laughing at herself wiping them away and, she said.

"Where did you get this one?"

He thought deep and, couldn't recall where and, remembered then he said.

"Right next to the rolled-up parchment when I set it down it was right there."

She wipes the happy tears away her thoughts were quickly swept aside about the matter.

Ruby opened her eyes for just a second as they were talking smiled and, went back to sleep she's thinking about how they get along that it made her feel at peace.

She asks herself.

[1] "Is it because I'm warm all over or, [2] their voices almost seem like there heavenly HHMMM ... heavenly I'd like to know more about that? [3] maybe they're sent to rescue me?"

They stand there looking at each other wiping her tears. She took ahold of his hand went over to their bed she spread the handkerchief out to dry. They glanced at each other noticed that there's German shepherds on the handkerchief which must have been the Shepard's sheep dogs and, they're all in different positions whether it was laying down, standing at a rock formation or, on a boulder. They noticed the background at the hill side where the ship was in the cave. They were intently looking and, started to count the Shephard's with their fingers taking turns and, he said.

"How would you like to count by starting with January?"

"Baby I would love it because there are 12 Shephard's and, you go first please."

He starts and, take turns with the dog's barking a couple of times after each count and, laugh. They do realize that any one of the dogs could be any month of the year.

"Oh, Max what a gift this is, it's just indescribable."

He wonders about the Shephard and, that it must have been him that set it there and, said.

"I'm totally amazed at this."

She puts it on the other side of the bed to dry out better they climb in the bed with their uniforms on and, face each other lying down pulling the sheet up over their heads and, laugh and, giggle for a while then put it down to their shoulders and, look over to ruby and, she said.

"We're right here Ruby."

They're in the same direction as Ruby to keep an eye on her. They get close she's between his left arm and, chest they talk a little and, one thing I did catch was that she said.

"I really want to start a tourist attraction at the cavern and, I don't know how well it would turn out?"

"Sweetheart well you never know and, it depends on the advertising the reputation it has. I will say this that with the permanent burnt diagram of Medusa and, all the rest of the monsters there and, what happened it shouldn't be a problem." She combed his hair with her fingers with a serious look and, she said.

CHAPTER 40

"Hey Maximilian I just thought of something ... that the unknown man that's frozen in time in the cavern that it's going to make it one of the best attractions if not the biggest attraction."

"YEAH... I get it with Medusa turning the man into stone ... I feel bad about that and, I wonder who he is? What about his family?"

"Maybe the Sherriff might know. We can bring him down there sometime soon." He yawned she followed and, they laughed that she did the same and, he said.

"Good night ... My ... Sweet ... Queen,"

"Good night my King ... HHMMM."

She puts her finger on his noise and, back under the blanket. They slowly close their eyes as they watch each other and, went sound asleep.

[MARISA TOMEI NARRATES THE FOLLING].

They wake up there eye's slowly open only about half way they can't make out the sound but, it sounds as if something heavy is brushing up against the wall and, the floor. Their eye lids are heavy and, can barely keep them half open they think about that sound and, a shadowy darkness with snakes on a head and, arms that came over them then they hear the rattling sound of a rattle snakes tail and, hissing sounds of snakes then more and, more hissing sounds. They have to open their eye's wide now they look up to their surprise that it's Medusa right above them just 2 feet away and, her snakes on her head numbered about 20 to 25 with 2 dark red one's on top in front and, the rest were black and, they're all hissing. The snakes on her head were lunging towards them with their mouths opening and, shutting with their tongues darting in and, out just 2 inches away [FRIGHTENING]. There scared out of their wit's and, frozen and, can't move. Medusa has her mouth open and, those fangs [How awful] are showing and, she's screaming with laughter with her tail wagging behind her that you can see and, her snake body is wrapped around their bed moving it around the room to keep them dizzy unable to focus and, with her still above them. Her body is a dark blue with small black flames here and, there. Those words of [Hate, Kill, destroy] were able to be seen on her body. They were crisscrossed all over in a dripping manner Oh, so, scary [Trick or, treat] Medusa screams and, said.

"AAAHHHHAA ... GOTCHA!!! NNNAAAHAHA ... I GOT YOU!!!" I GOT YOU!!!" She Screams again with the laughter of a raving lunatic.

Those killer glowing eyes started her tongue dart's out. They looked right at her then Unexpectantly that Cold Bolt goes through them. Their bodies are shocked and, jilted. They look at each other with their eyes all bugged out as their finger's turn to stone move up their arms and, they draw closer cause they know that this is the end. They throw their arms around each other with desperation oh so, sad and, [Kiss One Last Time]. They crushed it as if they were going into eternity that way. They feel the Cold Bolt of Stone move in their chest called each other's name out but, couldn't finish it and, said.

"MMMAAAxss."

"AAAMMMyyl."

The Stone-Cold Bolt cover's their face and, they are no more and, all that's left is their love for each other that can [Never, Never, ever] be duplicated. Medusa falls slowly having done her evil deed retreats to the floor and, all is quiet.

Well, this is certainly a surprise because Ruby wakes up calling for [Max, Amyl ion] very quietly and, said it again louder [MAX, AMYL ION] they wake up with Ruby calling their names that second time very slowly open their eyes and, look at each other and, come to realize that it was all a dream he starts to chuckle a little with a surprise look on his face now she join's in with her giggles of laughter and, they said.

[END OF MARISA TOMEI'S NARRATION].

"Oh, WOW ... it was a dream!!!"

There laughing has increased very hard and, glad it was all over with and, he said.

"HAY! ... are you for real my Precious Baby Doll?"

"YES, YES, and, YES cause it's all for you!!! Pick me up and, take me away anytime my dearly beloved."

Kissing is in order he covers her face kissed every part of her luscious lips and, around her face again and, they remembered Ruby. Looking over they see she's sitting up in bed and, watching their love play out. She was smiling with a little surprise but, glad to see it happen. That will make a lasting impression on her throughout her whole life. The royals throw the blanket off and, go to her left bedside with Amyl ion on his right-side ruby wants some water and, starving and, she said.

"Can I have something to eat please? Pause... Oh, Max, Amyl ion could you take me for a walk outdoors ... Oh, and, tell me the ways of love ... I couldn't help but, notice how you love each other and, I want that so, bad!!!"

Max begins with a collection of thoughts and, said.

"Well, what a question ... Ruby ... let me try to explain ... as I look at my beloved wife here beside me ... you see I love her with a passion that can't be compared ... except for that one ultimate sacrifice ..."

Amyl ion jumped in with fervor and, said.

"That's right Ruby ... no man can love me like he can ... so, I return that love ... because it comes from him."

Ruby's face grew to a questionable look and, said.

"How did you know my name was ruby?"

The royals look and, leaned their faces into each other and, started to laugh. They knew it was given from above and, ruby giggled a little and, said.

"What's so, funny?"

Pause ... Amyl ion put her left arm around his neck and, look at her she tapped Max's chest with her right hand as if to say well you answer and, Max said.

"We just happened to guess."

The local photographer comes in and, sets up his equipment as they talk about it.

The Music starts. [Expose-Point of no return]. [Pretty Poison-Catch Me [I'm Falling]].

The nurses and, doctor in the hallway they're so, happy at what they see and, join in their good times.

The photographer is ready and, holds up the flashlamp and, said.
"Smile for the camera."
PPOOPHH.
Could this be the end of Medusa?

Printed in the United States
by Baker & Taylor Publisher Services